River of Light and Shadow

Allen Kent

AllenPearce Publishers ©  ©

Library of Congress Cataloging-in-Publication Data
Allen Kent
River of Light and Shadow
Kent, Allen
ISBN 978-0-9898400-2-6

Allen Kent © 2013

To my Whitlock and Shattuck ancestors whose
courage and strength inspired
future generations.

Acknowledgements

The first draft of this novel was written in the late 1980s and during that period I spent a number of days in the State Historical Society of Missouri in Columbia where the Reference Specialist at the time, Elizabeth Bailey, was particularly helpful. I would also like to express special thanks to my "editorial staff," my wife Holly, Richard and Anne Clement, sons Jim and Paul, Jim's wife Erica, and Diane Andris. When publishing directly online, editing becomes the author's responsibility and this committed group read the initial manuscript and helped me develop a clean copy to place online. Paul's wife Jillian also serves as my technical advisor on map and cover design and I am deeply indebted to all of them for their assistance.

NORTH MISSOURI TRAILS
1840

Iowa Territory

Illinois

Indian Territory

WITH SETTLEMENTS
OF INTEREST

Allen Kent

1

FIRST ENCOUNTER

Four horsemen broke from the autumn-burnished wood with a fury that startled the dozing meadow into frenzied panic. Cottontails darted in directionless flight, bouncing through yellow grass and foxtail that spread from the forest edge to the nearby bank of the Chariton River. A covey of bobwhite burst from among the red birch, slapping the air with mottled wings and glided in formation into the brush beyond the clearing. Near the center of the meadow, a clump of sumac exploded in a shower of reds and oranges as a white-tailed doe and her fawn, necks and ears erect, bolted from the path of the riders in arching leaps toward the screen of oak and shag-barked hickory.

Beside a heavy wagon that lumbered awkwardly along the near bank of the river, David Whitlock's sorrel mare reared and whirled, dancing backward with pawing hooves. Her rider had been slumped loosely over the mare's neck as she plodded beside the wagon and as she rose, he grasped wildly for the saddle and the butt of an old rifle that hung beside it. He missed both and slid helplessly down the animal's quivering rump, his right boot snagging in the narrow stirrup, twisting him onto his face as he smacked into the brick-hard clay of the wagon track. Jarring pain flashed from David's forehead into his neck, followed by dull swelling throbs and the warm salty taste of blood as teeth cut into his thrusting tongue.

His mind reeled dizzily, fighting to remain conscious but mixing the sounds that had shattered the quiet of the late November afternoon with the horrors of the week before. He was again lying among the dried thistle and burdock that backed the blacksmith's shop at Haun's Mill. He had heard the first shot as he rounded the corner of the log building with an armload of kindling, and leapt backward against the wall of the building as shrieking riders whipped the shallow ford of Shoal Creek into foamy spray, firing at random at the scattering villagers.

From his hiding place behind the smithy, his face pressed tightly against the base of the rough log wall, David's dazed eyes stared through the wide chinks of the building as mobsters thrust blazing barrels through gaps in the opposite wall, discharging volley after volley into the huddle of men and boys who cowered beside the forge. One by one their victims dropped into a crimson pool that spread with each shot across the packed earthen floor. Aroused by the pungent mingling of blood and black powder smoke, the marauders shattered the dry plank door and burst into the room to finish their slaughter.

The scene that followed came now more sharply to David's swooning memory than it had as he had watched in mute horror from his screen of thistle. Thomas McBride, a withered but agile veteran of the War of Independence, lay helpless with a ball-shattered thigh, the musket that had dropped a dozen Red Coats resting across his quivering leg.

"There's one for you, Rogers," one of the mob laughed, pointing at the old soldier. A towering man with a tangled scar slashed from forehead to chin across the left side of his face snatched the weapon from McBride's leg, checked it for load and pressed it against the old man's breast.

"Time to meet your Mormon god, old man," Rogers sneered.

McBride's eyes, still conscious, flashed angry then widened as the ball ripped open his chest. Rogers laughed hoarsely, the empty black socket of his ravaged left eye disappearing into the thick scar.

"Another one gone to glory," he said, and drawing a long corn knife from a sheath on his belt, hacked at the lifeless body until lured away by more enticing sport.

Sardius Smith, small and wiry for his ten years, had struggled from the tangle of bodies beside the hearth and crawled beneath the wide horsehide pleats of the forge bellows. As the mob entered the shop, one of its members spotted the boy's trembling foot and beckoned the others to his hiding place. Pressed tightly against the chinks in the log wall, David could see only the legs of the men surrounding the terrified boy. He strained to cry out, to warn the child who trembled on his knees beneath the leather bag, head buried under his arms and chest heaving with soundless sobs. But instead of sound, vomit rose in David's throat and he choked it back, realizing that his cry would not halt the murder and would lead to his own.

"Does anyone feel a nit?" one of the mob shouted, thrusting his rifle down toward the shaking child. The circle of legs tightened around the bellows.

"And nits, if they live, become lice!" another laughed. A ring of black barrels appeared among the legs, pressed against the leather bag, and fired as one into the small body. The boy's breath released in a whimpering sigh, he shuddered for a brief moment as his bloodied arms dropped to the sides of his head, and he was still.

David screamed now through the blood in his mouth as he had not been able to on that Tuesday afternoon at Haun's Mill. He felt strong hands grip his shoulders and struggled to break free, only to be thrust back against the packed earth by other pairs of hands. Forcing his heavy lids apart, David gazed dizzily at the circle of faces that looked down at him. They were the faces of strangers.

"Lie still. You've taken a bad fall." The man who spoke was older than David's father, with a short cropped white beard and brown, leather-tough face. The others were younger, clean shaven and curious.

"Sorry we spooked your horse," the older man said. "Me and my boys here were after a pair of wolves that's been killing off our stock. Got a calf last night at our place and two others the night before over by the Hill Spring. We chased them this way and ran onto you in a real heat. Your head all right?"

David reached up and carefully fingered the swelling knot above his right eye, noticing for the first time his mother standing above the crouching strangers, her dark eyes and thin face worried but alert. He pushed up onto his elbows, shook and blinked away the remaining fuzziness, and spit a red stream onto the wheel-packed clay. Gently he touched the punctured tongue against the inside of his cheek. The flow of blood was beginning to stop, his head clearing. He was not a good horseman but his face flushed as he remembered the fall and his surge of fear as the shouting riders burst from the trees.

"I'm all right." He spoke firmly, scrambling to his feet with the circle of men rising with him. He stood half a head taller than the strangers and they stepped away as men do when uncomfortably close to a taller man. David's father leaned against the wagon box, his face sour.

"The boy never could stay on a horse," he said. The man's burly shoulders and neck dwarfed David's when they sat but when standing, he too came only to his son's shoulder.

"The accident couldn't be helped," his mother said calmly, turning to the strangers. "The mare's spirited – and you took us all a bit by surprise. Thank you for your concern." She was also unusually tall for her sex, meeting the older rider's gaze evenly.

The man studied her with open curiosity. "You're eastern folk, sounds like to me."

"Philadelphia," she said. "We're resettling here in Missouri."

The man smiled broadly. "Not much of a place for a Philadelphia lady. Specially up in this part of the state. There's nothing at all up this river."

"We're taking over the Parrish place. Homesteading."

"Ain't no Parrish place," the oldest of the younger men said casually. "Just some timber that he was claimin'."

"Yes, we're sadly aware of that." She spoke softly but her voice was full and strong. "We'll have to build...but forgive me. I'm Lydia Whitlock. My husband John and our son David." She nodded to each of the men. "I hope we didn't spoil your hunt."

The older man returned her nod with an awkwardness that showed he was unaccustomed to gentility.

"We lost them just before we ran into you," he flushed. "Clever devils. The big gray one's been killing our stock and getting away untouched for years. We don't ever seem to be able to get to him. Shattuck's my name. Thomas. My sons...Samuel, Lyman and Benjamin." The sons nodded and shuffled uncomfortably, also unaccustomed to introductions and to Philadelphia ladies who spoke so directly. David guessed Benjamin to be a year or two older than himself. Nineteen or twenty. And Lyman a few years older than that. Samuel was already graying at the temples and seemed much older than his brothers.

The oldest son stepped to the side of the open wagon and surveyed the meager collection of wooden trunks, tools, household goods and rough-cut lumber.

"Wasn't expecting to find anyone this far upriver," he said. David heard cautious suspicion in his voice.

John Whitlock lifted a protective arm along the edge of the wagon box. "We didn't bring much. Lost most of what we had in a fire and had to sell some of the rest as we traveled."

David watched his parents and the Shattucks as though he were not part of the scene, measuring each movement and expression with the detachment of a spectator watching a play. Lyman and Benjamin were barely part of the performance, standing silently with furtive, curious eyes beside their horses. Their father had not moved since David arose from the wagon rut and now watched his eldest son attentively, his weathered face guarded.

The friendliness of introduction had cooled to uneasy suspicion. David's arms and stomach tensed as his father stepped closer to Samuel, green eyes darting beneath black bushy brows. Lydia moved slowly between them with apparent ease, the bodice of her long cotton dress stained beneath the arms from the heat of travel but her face and tightly knotted brown hair showing surprising freshness. She turned smiling to the man who continued to inventory the contents of the Whitlock wagon. Around them the meadow was again still, the brown grass unruffled by afternoon breezes and the surface of the river below, flat and opaque as poured glass.

"John is a builder," she said. "We've lost so much he will have to build most of what we use in the new house."

"Have to build a house first," Samuel muttered.

"That too," Lydia said in the same even voice.

"Kinda late in the year to be starting a cabin. And it looks like your provisions are low," the oldest son said, easing his way around the wagon bed.

"We'll manage. We are very resourceful and the weather has favored us so far."

Samuel Shattuck fingered the handle of an iron-bladed plow, strapped to the rear of the wagon bed. "Hope you ain't planning to farm. That land's not even brush – just stands of timber. Bigger than these." He waved with a wide gesture toward the thick tress that bordered the meadow.

"That will suit us nicely," she said. "In truth, John is a cooper and we came up to the Chariton from Independence because of the white oak. Mr. Parrish said there was a good stand of it up here."

"Well, he was right about that." Samuel looked again at the wagon bottom. "Not many tools here. And there's no mill within fifty miles. You might have been better to settle nearer a town."

John Whitlock's voice, though controlled and steady, rolled like an oak keg across the open meadow.

"We plan to build a sod house to begin with. As soon as the cabin's built, we'll turn the sod place into a workshop. We like the quiet of the woods and don't need a mill. I choose to cut and split my own staves."

"Sod house? Can't say as I've heard of such a thing."

With a twist of his head, John Whitlock gestured back over his shoulder at the meadow. "You cut blocks of sod out of the ground and stack them like bricks. Folks settling over west of the Missouri on the prairie are building them where there's no timber. When our house in Independence burned, a settler who'd been living over there showed us how to put one up."

Samuel Shattuck sniffled skeptically. "Don't sound like much of an idea for up here. There's no prairie 'till you get up to the Iowa Territory."

"Parrish said there's a good-sized meadow and this river bottom land is good soil. The sod will work just fine."

"A cooper buildin' a house out of dirt? If that's to your likin'...."

David stepped back into the scene, anxious to keep his father from losing his temper.

"These wolves. I hadn't thought there were many left this far south. They sound like trouble."

Thomas Shattuck turned toward him, tugging at his short beard.

"There's fewer than a year ago. This gray one's taken over these woods. Him and a black bitch. You'll hear from them and their pack before the winter's out."

"You said they got your calf. You live near here?" David asked.

The older man pointed back down river. "Ya just passed us. Three cabins there together with a dozen acres cleared along the river." He turned to his younger sons and beckoned for the horses.

"Time for us to be getting back. Once it's dark, the wolves will be moving again. They know we got hogs and we don't want Suzanna havin' to worry about them. Come on Sam."

Samuel looked for a long moment into Lydia's thin, smiling face, at her fierce-eyed block of a husband, then glanced quickly at David and walked to the horses, mounting with his brothers.

"Hope you get that cabin up before the snow," Thomas Shattuck said, wheeling his horse toward the south edge of the clearing where the narrow wagon track was all that separated the darkening forest from the Chariton. "I wouldn't give you more than a couple a weeks." The men prodded their mounts into a slow trot, riding four abreast along the meadow side of the trail, then spurred to a canter without looking back.

John Whitlock glared at his son. "Can't you stay on that damned horse? Your scream set them to wondering. They wouldn't have thought a thing about us without that."

"Please John. I've asked you about your language." Lydia's voice was quiet and tired. "They would have wondered about us, fall or no fall. People don't move up into a place like this with an empty wagon." She climbed wearily back to the wagon seat, tucked long folds of dress beneath her to cushion the bare plank, and looked resolutely up the wagon trail.

"They were suspicious," her husband growled. "We left your Mormons at Far West after the attack on the Mill, knowing that wherever they went in numbers, there'd be trouble. Now we're out on our own and there's already trouble following us here."

"There won't be trouble," Lydia said firmly. "That Mr. Shattuck looked like a man of sense and reason. We have been hounded by senseless and unreasonable men. Besides, if they ask if we are Mormons, you can say no. And that will certainly be the truth."

David mounted the mare, glanced over his shoulder at the disappearing riders, then sidelong at the hunched back of his father. He had seen only one person speak back so boldly to the rumbling barrel maker – the tall quiet woman whom the cooper had somehow lured, for reasons known only to herself, from a very respectable schoolroom in Philadelphia. Her smooth, pale face belied the years of strain and fear that had followed. After fifteen years of marriage she had stopped in a park one Sunday afternoon to listen to the preaching of two wandering ministers. Their message had kindled a curiosity in the teachings of the young Mormon religion, a curiosity that had turned to interest and had led her to join the Colesville branch of the Latter-day Saints and follow them from Thompson, Ohio to Jackson County in Missouri. The cooper, for reasons only he understood, had accepted the moves but not the strange new faith.

David loved his mother with more than filial affection. She was his spiritual and intellectual guide, understanding the greatest philosophies of the mind and the simplest yearnings of the heart and soul.

"You don't come to know truth with your mind," she told him. "I have always been a serious student of the great minds of our time, but much of what I learned with certainty as a girl has since been found to be completely in error. I fear that we can never know whether anything about the world is really true, but only that it seems to be true within our abilities to observe it."

When she accepted the tenets of Mormonism, viewed by her friends and family as strange and heretical, she was thought to have lost both sense and reason. She laughed at her detractors without bitterness.

"Religion is religion because we can't understand it totally with our minds," she said. "Otherwise it would be science. We understand religion with our hearts and spirits."

"You said," David reminded her, "that we can't know anything with certainty. That would include religion too, I suppose."

"Only to the degree that our hearts and spirits can misguide us," she answered. "And I've found both to be much more dependable than my mind." She had not elaborated on the thought and David had often wanted to ask her about it. He knew now, as she spoke of Thomas Shattuck, that she was viewing him with her heart and spirit and that she was right. He wouldn't bother them or bring them trouble.

"He isn't the one that concerns me," John Whitlock said, climbing up beside her behind the mules. "It's that son Samuel. He poked about too much for my liking."

Lydia looked straight ahead over the backs of the harnessed team. "If Thomas Shattuck is the man I think he is, his sons bide their tongues even if they don't like it. They will be fair people."

John Whitlock grunted, flicked the reins over the mules and started the wagon slowly northward along the river. David nudged the mare with his heels and fell in behind. Long shadows now stretched across the small meadow to the darkening water of the Chariton. He guessed they had traveled about five miles since leaving the Hill Spring Trail at the crossing and must be close to the Parrish timber. With a cloudless sky, the night would be cold. On a grassy spot beneath the trees they would hang the small tarpaulin from one side of the wagon to ward off the night wind, line their few trunks between the heavy-spoked wheels to discourage curious skunks, possums and raccoons, and sleep beneath the wagon bed. Coons would come anyway, rattling about in the wagon box above them and sniffing at their bed rolls. Wary of the human scent, the animals stayed away from their faces and David had learned to sleep among them without worry. Tomorrow they would start on the sod house.

.   .   .

The four Shattucks rode in silence, slowing their mounts to an easy trot as the wagon disappeared behind them beyond an arm of the forest. Thomas was thoughtful, aware of his brooding eldest beside him and the silence of the two younger men who had fallen into double file behind.

"Mormons," Samuel said with a surety that assumed the word explained much.

"Might be," Thomas said, "and might not."

"Mormons for sure. I heard in Gallatin when I was there last week that they'd been burned out of a place south of there called Haun's Mill. Folks over there have petitioned the Governor to force them out of the state. They're Mormons all right."

"They said they was up from Independence," Lyman said behind them.

Samuel half turned in the saddle. "Probably are. That's where that man Smith wanted to set up their new Zion. But come up to Ray County when they got chased out of Jackson, then got their own county set up and started taking over things. Caldwell, they call it."

"People lose their houses to fire without being Mormons," Lyman observed, urging his horse forward between his father and older brother whose agitation had quickened the pace. "Grahams and Abbotts both had fires this year and lost most everything."

"And had most of it back within the week," Samuel said. "People step in and help when a family gets burned out... 'les they don't want them around. Those people back there got no more than two pieces of furniture, that cooper's bench, and half a sack of flour. Nobody would have left them in that state unless they wanted them gone."

Lyman looked to his left at his father who rode in thoughtful silence.

"What we gonna do?" he said.

Thomas reined in his horse and the others instinctively pulled their mounts to a halt. The older man leaned slowly onto his saddle and surveyed his sons who had turned their horses to form a nervous, shuffling line in front of him.

"Nothin'," he said. "We're gonna to do nothin'."

"There's a decree been signed," Samuel snapped. "The Governor's ordered them exterminated from Missouri."

"You exterminate rats and vermin. Not people," Thomas said coldly.

"It won't matter what we do," Samuel mumbled. "They'll be found out and chased or killed. We'd do well to move them on before they get worse from someone else."

"Whatever they get, it won't be from us." Thomas straightened in his saddle to end the discussion. Samuel was unmoved.

"They got strange ideas about things. Think God chose 'em above everyone else – and they's abolitionists."

Thomas scoffed with surprise and irritation. "If strange ideas was a crime, we'd a all been hanged. And what do you care about abolition? We got no slaves and no interest in them. Don't think much of it ourselves."

"The Mormons is land grabbers...takin' over whole towns. There'll be more of them comin', you can count on that."

Thomas snorted into his beard. "They're going to build an empire in the Parrish timber, I 'magine. If they's Mormons at all – and I'm not so sure o' that -- they're hidin' out." Samuel began again to speak but his father raised a silencing hand, leaning again across the saddle.

"We don't cause 'em trouble. You hear me?" He pointed a tough, twisted finger at Samuel. "And we don't provoke others to cause them trouble. We forget about them bein' there at all. And don't let me hear otherwise." The two men glared at each other as the younger sons steadied their restless horses and watched the exchange. In the west the sun dropped below the edge of the forest and cool dusk wiped the last shining glint from the surface of the Chariton. From the northwest rose the chilling hunting cry of a timber wolf, sharp barking that swelled into a sustained howl, pulling the men's heads about as if jerked by a common string.

"That's the gray," Thomas said coldly. "If he comes after the hogs, Suzanna will try to stop him by herself. We'd best be movin'." They whirled their horses and fell into line again, pushing their mounts into a brisk cantor. Behind them the lone wagon creaked to a halt beneath the brown-leafed branches of a broad oak as night moved silently across the north Missouri hills. On a rock-crusted ridge to the west, a gray wolf and his dark mate, black as the night forest, thrust pointed noses skyward, tested the gently rising breeze, then trotted silently into the trees toward the river.

2

SUZANNA

Suzanna Shattuck did not hear the wolves and her thoughts were far from her father's hogs. She stood in front of the cabin with her own face lifted to the evening breeze, her hair released from its workday roll and lying in loose brown waves about her shoulders. With slender fingers she combed it back from both temples, spreading her elbows wide to pull the damp material of her dress away from her sides. It continued to cling and she unfastened the top few buttons of the cotton bodice and tugged it free from her skin. She did not remember a November being this warm and thought fleetingly that it signaled a hard winter.

Suzanna had seen the wagon pass earlier in the afternoon, hearing first the squeal of dry axles and shod hooves clipping against the baked clay. She had been sewing – loathing every minute of it as much as she disliked the spinning and weaving that produced the coarse cloth with which she worked. At the sound of the approaching wagon she willingly dropped the shirt over a spindled chair back and stepped toward the window, praying for the sight of new faces. She needed something to liven thoughts that had found little new to wonder about over the past few weeks. The approach of winter had slowed visits among the Chariton's scattered settlers.

The wagon presented three new faces. On the high board seat a thick, dark haired man hunched wearily over a team of gray mules. The woman beside him was taller when sitting, or at least her straight back and slender frame gave her that appearance. Her head was bare and she wore a plain but expertly made dress. She was not a woman of the woods.

The face that interested Suzanna most was that of the third traveler – a young man who rode beside the wagon on a chestnut mare. As she stood now in the deepening afternoon, tugging absently at her dress top, her thoughts were on this rider. He had looked toward the house as they passed. Not a long, curious look, but a furtive, cautious glance that kept her from stepping into the lighted doorway. His face was long with deep-set eyes, a straight high-bridged nose and wide mouth. A serious face, she thought. Attractive, but not handsome. And a good sight more interesting than the broad-faced, thickly-thatched frontiersmen who occasionally stopped at the Shattuck farm to swap lies with her brothers and stare at her as she reached to hang the skillet above the fireplace.

The travelers hadn't stopped, adding to both the mystery and the excitement of their passing. The Shattucks were the only cabins north of the Chariton ford and surely anyone who passed would stop to take refreshment or at least be sociable. Yet the strangers had passed almost as if the clearing didn't exist, and though nothing lay upriver but thick forest, they had not returned.

She walked the hundred yards that separated her father's cabin from the river and stood beside the motionless water, feeling the air begin to cool against her face. Evening was her favorite time...less hurried than the mornings that drove her from bed before providing light enough to strike a fire and prepare breakfast. By the time the men were fed and the table cleared, she was expected in the garden or beside a quilting frame in one of the other cabins. Evening was her time and she treasured it.

The homes in the Shattuck clearing formed three sides of a square that opened in back, away from the river to the west. They were all alike; rough log rectangles divided into two earthen-floored rooms, with pitched roofs covering low lofts. Her father's faced the river, Samuel's the clearing from the south, and Benjamin's from the north. Between them were the barns and gardens.

The other women would be busying themselves in their cabins now, waiting for their men to come home from their futile pursuit of that gray wolf. Samuel's wife Judith would look up with a devoted smile but would not speak. She rarely did. And then only to say that something was sweet – or that a request was no inconvenience at all. Life for Judith was completely unruffled and she moved through it with a steady good humor that made Suzanna love her, but avoid long periods of time alone in her company. But Judith was the only person in existence who could abide Samuel's moodiness and unwavering certainty about his own views, without being torn apart by them. She had done it by carefully avoiding opinions of her own.

Maggie, bless her heart, held an unstudied but freely expressed view on everything. She was as fertile as a cottontail with three children under four years and chattered about them and other matters from the moment she arose until Benjamin refused to listen to another word at night.

"He says to me, 'Maggie, good night' and I know it's time to be quiet," she told Suzanna one morning as they hoed potatoes. "Even then, I can hardly contain myself. I just have so much that needs to be said."

Suzanna marveled that Maggie found so much to say with so little happening about her. Fortunately the other women had not seen the wagon move upriver, or Benjamin would surely go without sleep tonight.

But Suzanna had seen it and might also have a sleepless night. She longed for company. No – not for company, but for companionship. She had seen in the face of the young rider a man of deep thoughts and new ideas. As she looked northward into the deepening shadows over the Chariton, she wondered who and where he was and what he was doing.

. . .

The howl of the timber wolf that turned the heads of the Shattuck men was also heard by the Whitlocks as they pulled their wagon beneath the leafless arms of the oak forest. David's mare, unfamiliar with the sound, sensed the danger in it and reared with shaking head as he struggled to hobble her beside the wagon. The mules shifted nervously and pressed together, crunching iron-shod hooves into the crisp leaves and hickory husks that blanketed the ground.

David quickly cleared a circle to bare earth with a flat bladed spade and brought water from the river. Camp setup had become a well-rehearsed routine and each family member worked quickly and without conversation. Lydia pulled a heavy tarp from the wagon bottom, draping it over the side until its fringe folded against the leaves. As David returned from the river with the last of four large stones for the fire circle, she gathered black oak twigs and piled them in the square formed by the rocks. Encouraged by gentle breaths, a spark from her flint smoked a twisted handful of grass into flame and she pushed it beneath the twigs. As the fire grew, David hoisted a heavy iron grate from the wagon and balanced it firmly between the stones.

As larger branches spit sparks and orange flame up through the grate and spread the glow of the campfire into the deepening night, Lydia knelt beside the blaze skinning
two cottontails shot earlier in the day along the trail. She deftly removed the feet, sliced around each neck and down the belly, then stripped the skins away like removing tight fur sweaters. As the flames died into coals, she spread sections of pink meat along the grate's edges and placed a shallow iron skillet beside them, its bottom coated with gray-white lard scooped from a brown earthenware crock. From cloth sacks, she sliced fresh potatoes and onions into the melting fat, then filled a smoke-blackened kettle

with water and sat it beside the sizzling pan.

While she worked on the vegetables, Lydia watched her husband hobble the mules in the narrow grassy area that separated the forest from the river. Wolves would not bother the mules. The predators could not spring onto their broad backs like a panther might, and on the ground the powerful teeth and unfettered hind legs of the mules were a match for any attacker. Lydia also knew that wolves would not get within a hundred yards of the team without the forest erupting in a cacophony of ear-splitting shrieks and brays.

The mare was a different matter. If frightened, she could snap the leather thongs hobbling her forelegs like pieces of cotton string and would bolt into the trees where the wolves could pursue her until she dropped. Lydia prayed silently that the wolves would not come tonight. Trouble with the mare would only rekindle another fire...one set when David had returned home from Independence with the mare instead of another mule. John met the boy in front of the cabin with fists firmly planted against his hips, and jaw set.

"She's not fit to pull her own weight, let alone a heavy log," the cooper growled, looking at the mare. "I told you to get a work mule."

"I didn't want a mule. I wanted a good horse."

"I don't give a damn what you wanted."

She had started to intervene. "Please John. Your language...."

"Quiet," he snapped. "This is between me and the boy. And damn my language."

"You told me the mule was for me – for the work I'd done," David said firmly. "I didn't want a mule."

"You don't decide what you want. Take him back."

"It's a mare. And I won't take her back."

More quickly than Lydia had seen her husband move in many years, the man had stepped forward and slapped a broad palm across his son's cheek and ear, staggering the boy backward into the dust. She had stepped forward, but saw David's eyes flash with indignation rather than well with tears, and withdrew to let the men finally meet each other. David had scrambled to his feet, fists clenched, then realized he was no match for the man's great physical strength.

"You have told me," he said, brows dropping and voice unsteady, "that I will be mocked for my beliefs; that how I deal with those who mock me will be the measure of what kind of man I am. I gather that standing up for what I believe only applies when it doesn't interfere with what you want."

"This is not a matter of belief, but of obedience," John Whitlock growled. "I gave you the barrels and I told you to get a mule."

"You gave me the barrels? I built the barrels myself... from raw bolt to finish. And you told me to buy *myself* a mule. I chose not to have a mule, but a horse."

"But look at that animal! It isn't even a strong horse. What good will it be to me around the shop?"

"Perhaps I misunderstood," David said, gaining control of his voice. "I didn't realize I was buying you a work animal, but one for me to use." The men stood facing each other in silence, the son warily watching for a swing of the meaty hand, the father trying to parry the last verbal thrust. Finally the older man turned and tromped off toward the cooper's shop at the rear of the cabin. Lydia looked at her son, her face expressionless.

"Be careful that you don't become too impudent with your father," she said and stepped back into the house. The purchase of the mare had never come up again. She hoped it wouldn't tonight.

As Lydia crawled beneath the wagon to scrape the ground clear and spread blankets, she wondered what had changed her husband so. He had been such a gentle man to begin with. And jovial. At their first meeting she had stopped along a busy Philadelphia street and watched with unashamed admiration as he single-handedly unloaded casks and barrels from a flatbed wagon. While two other men were struggling to lift a hogshead, the young cooper had rolled a larger puncheon onto his shoulder and carried it into a shop as if it were a mere six gallon keg. He later admitted that he had seen her approaching and had done it to impress her, but that carrying all ten from the wagon, one after another while she watched, had almost finished him. Perhaps it was this pride... this stubborn, obstinate pride of his that had gradually hardened him.

I'm a self-made man," he told her, when he learned she was a teacher. "Self-taught and self-disciplined. You'll never hear me misuse a word or phrase and I haven't spent a day in school since I was ten. And I'm as well read as you, I would think."

He wasn't. But his intellect and curiosity went refreshingly beyond the dull patter of the other men who wooed her and his frankness amused her and put her at ease.

"You're unfittingly tall for a woman, don't you think?" he had asked one evening as they walked beside the Schuylkill.

"And you unfittingly broad for a man," she replied.

"Being broad is a fine feature in a man," the young cooper said, throwing back his thick shoulders and strutting ahead of her like a proud young bull.

"It is for those who like their men broad," she answered. "And perhaps there are those who enjoy a tallish woman."

"And I am one," he laughed, whirling toward her and scooping her up with a squeeze that crushed her own laughter to a dizzy gasp. "We are the height and breadth of a perfect match."

And so it had seemed for those first years. He was indeed a curious man. At night he read to her, and she to him from whatever book they had found most recently – until she was given the book by the two Mormons.

"There are some things one just doesn't meddle with," John said as she tried to entice him into listening. "And one is a man's beliefs. I know what I believe...the same as my father, and his father before him. There's no changing that."

"But if you are so certain, what's the harm in listening? There are some ideas here that are really quite fascinating. And at some point back there, one of your fathers' fathers must have chosen to be a Methodist."

He shook his head. "We've been Methodists since Christ himself. I've said my piece on it and you do as you wish."

She had, and had become captivated by the complex logic and bold assertions of the new faith. She felt no change in their love, but a change in their freedom to express it. There were times when he obviously deeply felt and resented the religious gulf that separated him from wife and son and the gulf had grown with the Mormon problems.

There had been other changes. As David grew and showed great skill but little interest in his father's trade, the breach widened.

"He thinks me a common laborer," John grumbled as he came in from the shop one noon. "He thinks he's too good for coopering."

"The boy just has other interests," she replied. "He seems to lean toward professions that rely on thought and learning, rather than manual skills."

"Ah-hah! And you're as bad! Do you think I just turn off my brain at the beginning of the day and do my work like some dumb sot?"

"You know that's not what I mean. I know you are a master at your craft. And I think you know that he has great admiration for that and much of your natural skill. But his interests are elsewhere."

"As long as he's in this house, he'll be a cooper. Once he's free of me, he can do what he damn well pleases. But his thinking is going to land him in trouble. The boy needs a trade to fall back on when he finds out the world doesn't need more philosophers." John's fears had almost proved prophetic.

When Lydia joined the Mormon movement, David had followed. Her devotion had taken them – John begrudgingly – to the Colesville settlement in Ohio and then to Jackson County in Missouri. This last move had embroiled the family in Mormon problems with the Missouri frontiersmen that the cooper wanted no part of. But as mob activity increased against the new settlers, David had argued for every effort to make peace with the angry residents of the area. His father called him foolish, warning that to stay in Jackson County was to court disaster. It was while David met with local elders of the church to draft a petition for legal aid that the Whitlock cabin had been pillaged and burned.

Lydia shuddered now as she remembered fleeing the burning house through ankle deep mud to a neighboring farm, then on north to Haun's Mill. Again, when Colonel Jennings had come to the Mill to propose a treaty between villagers and the state militia, David had encouraged the elders to accept the agreement.

"This is our chance to show these people we don't mean trouble. That we can live in peace with them." The cooper shook his head as he packed tools, provisions and clothing into the wagon. He lifted Lydia up onto the wagon seat and snapped the reins over the backs of the mules.

"We'll be in Millport. When you realize you've again been taken for a fool, that's where you'll find us. If I were you, I'd tie that horse of yours somewhere back in the trees."

The mob attacked the Mill the following morning and David reached Millport by mid-afternoon, the mare lathered and panting from the frightened dash to safety. As a concession to his father's suspicious nature, David had tied the mare in the forest and did not argue when the cooper refused to gather again with the body of the church. Another stranger to Millport, a Benjamin Parrish, told them of the stand of white oak north of the Chariton crossing on the Hill Spring Trail. Parrish had planned to homestead the land himself, then decided to go farther west across the Missouri. John Whitlock gave Parrish two small oak kegs, the two men clasped hands, and the family took to the trail the next morning for the Parrish timber.

As Lydia hunched beneath the wagon to spread blankets over the bare earth that would be her bed, she knew that they were now close to the stand of white oak. If they had not raised the suspicions of those Shattucks, no one would bother them now. She bowed silently and clasped her hands against her breast. Forgive me, dear God, she thought, for turning away from you into this place.

David bent to help her crawl from beneath the wagon, then lifted a new percussion rifle from the wagon bed and pushed its hooked lever forward to open the breach. She disliked guns, particularly this new one with the spring loaded breach that flipped upward to accept paper cartridges. John called it "The Hall's" and had purchased it because he said it saved enough time in loading to be worth two of any other rifle. The seam along the front of the breach was loose and spewed smoke and hot gas up into the face of the user. She shivered every time she saw it fired. Someday it would cost one of them an eye.

A charge was already in place and David snapped the breach closed and stood the weapon against a wheel within reach of his bedroll. Lydia walked with him to the cook fire where her husband scooped sizzling potatoes onto one of her rose-patterned china plates.

"I wish you wouldn't use those, John," she said. "We have the wooden ones and I'm down to only a few of the china.

"Not going to get any other use up here," he said matter-of-factly. "If we don't put them to good use, they'll just sit in that trunk forever."

"They are one of the few things left that we brought from Philadelphia. I would like to keep them nice, even if I don't use them."

"Fine by me...but it's already messy for tonight. Tomorrow we make it a show thing."

David lifted the lid of a small square trunk and took out two stained walnut plates, handing one to his mother. "It's going to be a cold one tonight," he said, spreading vegetables across the flat wooden surface to cool. "Snow can't be far away. If the clearing's as good as Parrish said, we should be able to put up a sod hut in a day."

His father grunted doubtfully and they finished their meal in silence. The night was clear and moonless, glimmering softly with a band of misty stars arching across the heavens, the autumn constellations shining with crystal sharpness. An owl called farther upriver and was answered by another directly above their heads while beneath the dark pillars of hardwoods, dry leaves rustled with the movement of small night animals.

Darkness pressed in upon the circle of firelight, choking it slowly with the chilling fingers of a northerly breeze. It encircled Lydia in its lonely arms, drawing her gradually away from the two men who ate silently beyond the glow of the last, struggling embers. What had become of Mercy Taylor? Of Elsie Ryder? Their friendships had been brief, but of a warmth and closeness that develops in times when faith and fear throw women together with little else to support them. In less than a year, she had grown to love them more dearly than any friends before and now they were gone. Perhaps to Quincy. Perhaps to God. In either case, they were closer to humanity than she was.

The rising howl of the wolf jerked the smothering blanket of loneliness from her shoulders and pulled her to her feet. She took the china plate from John's outstretched hand and poured steaming water from the kettle over its pearly surface. With a square of cotton cloth that John had left draped over the wagon side when he took the plate from the trunk, she wiped and wrapped it and returned it to its place.

David scraped the coals into a heap beneath the grate and covered them lightly with soil to hold their heat through the night. As Lydia busied herself with the pots, she realized that despite the trying day, she was not sleepy. Her body was tired and itched to be washed, but she was not sleepy. As the men crawled beneath the wagon and pulled at dusty boots, she returned again to the iron grate and poured the last cupfuls of steaming water into the skillet. From the chest that held the wooden plates, she drew another square of soft cloth, then peeled her dress and underclothing to the waist and stood in the moonless night rinsing away the travel and irritation of the long week since she had heard another feminine voice.

To the west two wolves moved quietly through the forest toward the river, stopped and sorted again the mingled scents that drifted up from the Chariton. There was the musty odor of horses and the pungent sharpness of wood smoke tainted with cooking flesh. They trotted another two hundred yards, heads low and glowing eyes piercing the forest night, then raised their noses again to the breeze. This time the scent of horse was mingled with others that the wolves knew and feared; the sharp, salty smell of man. The smell was strong. These men were not within their walls of fallen trees but were in the open. The wolves milled with momentary indecision, tested the air again, then turned south parallel to the river toward the site of their easy kill of the night before.

3

DAVID

Morning's half-light, gray and muted, pushed back the forest edge as the Whitlock wagon lumbered into a wide semicircular clearing along the river's west bank. It was a meadow much like the one in which the riders had startled the family the day before, but broader and without brush. In hundreds of seasons of sudden spring thaw the usually placid Chariton had become a gravel-churning torrent, shearing into a gently rising slope that now formed the north edge of the clearing. Like a newly sharpened hasp, the river had ripped away at the hill in a wide, sweeping arc, leaving a steep bank of ten feet where the slope had once been gradual. The last receding waters, heavy with silt and the seed of thick, deep-rooted Iowa prairie grass, blanketed the clearing with fertile loam. Lightning-sparked fires had swept the meadow with enough regularity to keep the birch, columbine and sumac from filling the clearing, and it now lay knee high in coarse brown grass.

David reined the mare to a halt beside the wagon and surveyed the expanse of grass with mild surprise. It was just as Parrish had described it, high enough above the river that a normally heavy melt would not flood the meadow, but with banks that sloped on both sides of the Chariton into a shallow ford. The steep embankment at the north end of the clearing, now overhung with brush, was what they had most hoped to find. It would save a full day of building.

John Whitlock snapped the reins across the mules' backs and urged them forward toward the hillside, muttering under his breath. David rode ahead into the center of the meadow, dismounted and tested the sod with the toe of his boot. Though late in the season, the grass was healthy with tightly woven roots and would hold the soil nicely when cut. He led the horse to the wagon where John Whitlock now stood erect in the bed.

"Parrish was telling it just as it is," John said. "We'll square this bank and butt up against it as the back wall." He lifted the square-bladed spade from the wagon bottom and handed it to David. "You work on that while I un-strap the plow and cut sod. Lydia, you might as well start cutting thatch."

The work was again rehearsed. While John Whitlock unharnessed the mules and hitched them to the wooden plow, Lydia lifted a long-handled scythe from the wagon and began to cut the grass with broad even sweeps, working her way from the hillside out toward the center of the meadow. David scrambled around the end of the steep bank and climbed to its top.

The hill, overhung with a tangle of leafless columbine and brambles, ascended ten feet in less than a yard. He paced off four strides along the upper edge of the face, marked the ends of his steps and chopped away the autumn-bared vines with the side of the spade. Scoring a straight line into the bank-top between the marks, he began to dig an even twelve foot ledge down into the hillside, throwing the dirt onto the grass at the base of the slope.

Below, his father directed the mules and plow to the wagon track, turned them back toward the woods at a right angle to the river, and dug the point of the iron plow share into the earth. As the gray beasts strained forward, he cut a straight deep furrow into the rich loam, swinging the team around at the trees and returning with a parallel furrow two and a half feet from the first. With a third strip cut the same distance from the second, he stopped to pace off the twenty-stride length of the furrow.

"David, throw down the spade," he shouted. David, who now stood knee-deep into the bank on a narrow earthen shelf, tossed the shovel down and plopped backward onto his seat on the hilltop, spreading his fingers wide and twisting the straining muscles of his forearms.

His father examined the sod strips, then made two deep slices between the plowed furrows, a pace apart. As the first brightening rays of morning sun seeped down the thick trunks that bordered the meadow on the west, he thrust the blade into the furrow where the plow had begun to roll the tightly matted grass, undercutting a yard long block of sod. With powerful arms, he lifted the piece onto the ground beside its rectangular hole and measured its depth with his palm.

"Twenty paces by about six inches," he announced, looking toward Lydia who had stopped her cutting and leaned near the bank against the bowed handle of the scythe.

"What size do you want the room?" she asked, studying the shelf that David had made in the hillside. "Four paces each way?"

"Inside," he said.

She measured the bank with her eye. "It's about ten feet high, so we will want to make the roof eight feet or so in the back and six over the door. We'll figure seven feet as an average." She closed her eyes and tilted her chin upward as if lifting her eyelids to the new light to better read their insides.

"That's eighty-four square feet per side, and you have sixty foot strips, by six inches. Thirty square feet. We'll need three strips per wall and, let's see...another one hundred forty-four divided by...." She lapsed into silent computation.

David watched her with amused admiration. She had taught him to do figures, but he required chalk and slate to work out a problem like this one. His mother did them deftly in her head.

"Twelve twenty-yard strips, counting the roof," she said after a moment.

"Are you certain? I don't want to be short."

"This is the second one we've built in as many years. I had it right last time and I should be getting better."

John reddened without comment, threw the spade back up to his son and returned to the mules.

Lydia turned to David whose feet dangled a few yards from her shoulder. "You've been unusually quiet about our coming up here. I expected you to have stronger feelings about staying with the church and trying to work out some kind of settlement."

"I was wrong," he said simply. "The Mill proved that."

"'Mistaken' may be a better word," she said. "Wrong sounds so hopeless and I don't believe you think it hopeless."

"More than I used to. At least enough not to argue about it."

"Things have a way of turning back on themselves, given time," she said. "I promised your father when we left Independence that if there was more trouble, we would do things his way. Perhaps he's right about our being better off away from the others. Time will tell." She looked absently across the stretch of freshly cut grass, her shoulders rising and dropping in a long sigh, then returned to her mowing. For a moment David watched the rhythmic swing of her curved blade, listening to its swish as it sliced through the thick brown grass. His father was not right. But David was not certain what was and until he knew, he would keep his peace. He scrambled to his feet and dug again into the bank.

Before the sun was midway to its peak, the clay wall was squared down to the meadow and a flat dirt floor rose six inches above the grass of the clearing. As his father used the spade to slice blocks of sod from the earth, David searched the nearby woods for roof timbers. He located and felled six straight hickory trees of eight inch diameter, stripped limbs and bark from the trunks and cut them into seventeen foot lengths. With the aid of the mules, he dragged the logs to the cabin site and with iron wedges, split the trunks lengthwise in half.

With a long, fingered branch, Lydia raked the cut grass into brown bundles and gathered willows from the river bank. Together they emptied the wagon beside the flat square of earth, re-harnessed the mules and as Lydia drove the team, the men methodically loaded the bed with heavy sod blocks. The cooper easily hoisted each square up to David who struggled them into place.

By noon, two loads were moved and stacked in overlapping brick patterns, thick earthen walls resting solidly on the flat foundation. The blocks butted snugly against the hillside, running perpendicular to the bank to form two side walls of the dwelling, then parallel with the clay wall in what would become the southern face of the house. The front was broken in the center for a doorway and when the walls reached chest high, two additional gaps would be framed for windows. As the men stacked blocks, Lydia forced dirt between the sod sections to tighten the wall and tamped the earthen floor with a thick, blunted limb. The work was hard and quiet, each Whitlock moving without hesitation from task to task, stopping only to mop the sweat and dirt from their faces with damp sleeves.

They paused briefly for a lunch of dried venison and thick, dark bread coated with lard, washed down with water from a small stream that emptied into the river a short distance above the clearing. The meal too was silent and hurried, each of them lost in private thoughts.

As the sun began its downward slide, Lydia gathered wood for a cook fire to simmer a pot of beans that had been soaking since morning. David returned to the wagon to gather sod blocks and the cooper turned to the pile of belongings that now rested outside the rising earthen wall. At one side was a stack of pre-cut lumber, all of equal widths, but varying in length from over five feet to no more than fifteen inches. Beneath the pile was a rough plank door, its iron hinges already in place. While residents of Haun's Mill had been contentedly making peace, the skeptical barrel maker had cut and augured planks for both door and window frames, expecting that he may soon find use for them at a time and place when making them would be much less convenient. David had laughed and called him "cynic."

He lifted the two longest planks into place on either side of the door opening and with the shorter lintel plank under his arm, struggled onto the waist-high wall and placed the board across the two uprights. Four round holes through each end of the lintel lined up perfectly with holes in the tops of the side pieces. With a heavy oak mallet he drove tough wooden pegs into the holes, then pounded two smaller strips diagonally across the upper corners, squaring the frame and fastening it rigidly into place. By the time David and Lydia returned with the third load of sod, the windows were framed and John was hanging the sturdy plank door on its iron hinges.

"You thought me a cynical old fool when I made these," the bearded cooper said as his son approached. "What do you think now?"

"You're a cynic...but not foolish," David said, lifting a block from the back of the wagon and throwing it into place. "...though I don't find much consolation in your being right."

"If you're expecting consolation, life's going to sorely disappoint you. You'll be wiser to hope for a bit of good luck. You might find that my cynicism improves my good luck."

David hoisted another square onto the rising wall, started to speak, but thought better of it. He had found little consolation over the past three years and his father's cynicism seemed to have kept them alive.

By mid-afternoon the walls were complete, sloping upward from six feet over the door on the south wall to just over eight where the sod met the clay bank. A simple fireplace and chimney were gouged out of the solid earthen wall of the hillside, the chimney tapering upward, then jogging to the left into a shallow flue trap before climbing straight again to the top of the bank. While Lydia faced the chimney with clay and willows from the river bank mixed with coarse meadow grass, John and David hoisted the split logs to the top of the walls and surfaced the roof; a layer of split hickory logs chinked with brush, mud and long willows, covered by a grass thatch and a final layer of thin sod shingles. Where the turf roofing joined the hillside, John cut a slot into the bank, running the final row of sod blocks into the notch and tamping around them tightly with smaller pieces of the earthen mat. Runoff from winter snows and spring rains would now course down the overlapped layers and onto the ground.

They gathered in front of their newly completed shelter, John Whitlock wrapping a dirt-stained arm about his wife's waist while David leaned back against the wagon. The ground for ten paces behind them had not been plowed, leaving a grassy stretch of meadow to keep mud from the door. For thirty feet beyond, the clearing now displayed a broad brown swath of bare earth. In early spring it would again be plowed and planted with hemp, potatoes, onions, beans and corn. Until this new crop ripened, they would live from their dwindling stores and from what they could kill and forage from the forest.

At John's insistence Lydia led them into the earthen room, dark and close despite the open doorway and windows. As the afternoon slipped toward evening, high thin clouds had given way to lower, rolling billows of deepening gray, carried by a cool breeze out of the northwest. There was the smell of rain on the wind that added to the closeness and mixed with the pungent sharpness of freshly split timber and raw earth. David set a fire on the raised clay hearth and touched it to flame with coals from the cook fire in the clearing. Lydia placed the iron grate between the hearth stones, moved the boiling kettle of speckled beans over the flame and cut chunks of salt pork into the rolling brown liquid. While John carried their supplies into the new home, David spread bedding out on the tamped floor. They would not make furniture until a cabin was finished. The trunks would be their chairs and cupboards, their laps tables, and the ground their bed.

As they sat to their meal of beans and bread, the wind quickened and whirled brown leaves from the forest across the naked strip of meadow. Before the rain reached them, the icy edge of the wind caught it and threw it in frozen pellets against the brown mare and gray mules that huddled in leather hobbles against the east walls of the dwelling.

John Whitlock dipped a thick crust into his plate of beans.

"We should offer thanks," Lydia said. "The Lord has been good to us today."

Her husband lowered his plate.

"He has indeed," he said.

4

THOMAS

The wolves had come just after midnight; dark shadows slinking between the sleeping cabins. The cattle shuffled nervously in the enclosure behind Samuel's house – a young bull and two cows, one with a twelve week old calf. In an adjoining pen, four black horses paced from side-to-side and a pair of yellow oxen struggled to their feet, lowered their thick-horned heads and pawed the bare clay.

Above the corral on a crudely constructed platform of lashed poles and rough split planks, Thomas Shattuck stirred in his bedroll and reached for one of three rifles that lay beside him. He had not expected the wolves to return so soon. During the day he and his sons had almost chased down the one he called the Gray and his mate, losing them just before running across the wagon. It was almost as if the wolves had led them into the clearing, knowing that the resulting chaos would divert the hunters from the chase.

Quietly stretching cramped arms, he squinted into the blackness looking for the wolf leader. The old man knew he would not see him. The killer would remain in the shadows, sending in the pack to harass, attack and weaken, appearing only to finish the kill and feed on the spoils. It was not cowardice, but cunning that kept the gray wolf in the shadows. Though strong and vicious, he had lived to be the pack leader because of his cunning. To have a chance at him tonight, Thomas knew he would have to sacrifice one of the animals and he could not afford to lose the other calf.

The Gray and his pack had given notice that the Shattucks had infringed upon their territory the month the family moved onto the river. Thomas had risen one morning to milk and found the brown cow slaughtered and stripped to red bones. She hadn't even bellowed during the night. A Sac hunting party, passing the cabin as Thomas and Samuel dragged the carcass from the pen, paused along the river bank on bare, stocky ponies.

"Wolf," one said in a short bark, pointing to the butchered animal. With sign and single words, the Shattucks learned of the gray giant and his pack that roamed the forest from the Grand to the Chariton. On that morning Thomas Shattuck swore that he would rid the Chariton of the killer and for six years he had tried and failed. But he knew the wolf better than any man, red or white.

As Thomas now watched shadowy forms slip closer to the penned cattle, he hoped only to protect his livestock. If he weakened the pack or wounded one of its members to the point that he could follow its bloody trail into the forest, it would be a bonus.

Three wolves crouched in the opening between cabins, crawling, stopping, crawling again. Thomas sighted on the animal farthest from his tower and the night exploded with a flashing report. The wolf howled and dropped and Thomas snatched the second weapon and fired at another silhouette. The fleeing intruder hopped and barked sharply but continued into the night. Shattuck pulled the third rifle to him and lay motionless, eyes and ears probing the darkness. Acrid black smoke stung his eyes and nostrils. Below, the cattle continued to shuffle and low but the woods were silent, hushed of the sounds of night birds and insects.

A yellow lantern spread the darkness below the platform and Samuel appeared between the cabins, wearing only his trousers.

"Did you get him? Did they get to the animals?" Thomas pulled himself to the edge of the platform and clambered stiffly to the ground. "Didn't even get a look at him. Same as always. There's one of them over here."

Together they skirted the corral and inspected the fallen wolf. It was a small male, strong and thick furred from good hunting.

"And I think I wounded another.   Over here somewhere."
Samuel lifted the lamp higher to widen the circle as his father
crouched forward, then knelt beside a bloody stain on the grass.

"Looks like we might have a trail in the morning," he muttered.

Samuel grunted. "Might as well come in now, though.   They
won't be back tonight."

The old man shook his head. "He's a clever one. I'd lie in there
thinking he was going to out-smart me and come back...knowing
I'd think he wouldn't. I'm staying out here till morning."

He climbed again to the platform, certain that Samuel was right.
The wolves would not return. The night forest had already begun
to rustle and hum and an owl hooted from the edge of the clearing.
Thomas reloaded the two fired rifles, placed them neatly in line at
his side and wrapped himself again in the blankets. Far north of
the clearing the deep, throaty call of a wolf rose on the night air,
sharp yapping barks, swelling into a long, chilling howl. They
mocked him, he thought, and curling beneath the thick covers,
pillowed his head on a rolled quilt but did not sleep.

. . .

Samuel's hound sniffed at the dried blood on the damp morning
grass, zigzagged across the clearing until he found other stains,
then trotted northwest toward the woods with the men at his heels.
The eastern sky was just showing the first hint of dawn but the
dog's nose saw for them and he led confidently across the fields
toward the deep shadow of forest.

"I still think we should take the horses," Samuel said as they
reached the trees. "If Brutus gets a strong scent, we'll never stay
with him."

Thomas Shattuck ducked beneath a limb and scrambled after the
dog. "If the Gray took the pack where I think he did, we couldn't
follow with horses. Anyhow, I thought that hound was trained to

stay close."

"He's trained all right. But if the scent gets fresh, no telling what he'll do."

"If we come across them, we won't want to be on horseback," the old man said. "The horses would spook and I don't want to be on one with him tearing through these trees. Best to be on foot."

Brutus followed the trail of blood for nearly a mile, tracking west away from the river through thinning trees and thickening brush. The ground became more rocky; steep banks of shale and rough limestone outcroppings. At the bottom of a narrow ravine, the dry streambed was darkly stained and the dog paused to sniff and circle.

Thomas knelt beside the purple patch, touched it gingerly, and scratched at his white beard.

"A lot of blood here. This one was hurt bad and can't have gone far. They're headed where I expected though." He stood and looked northward along the wash.

"This the place you were telling about? Where the brambles make a cave-like tunnel?"

The old man nodded. "'bout half an hour above here. Looks like the dog agrees with me."

Brutus raised his head and sniffed, then pressed his nose again to the rocky bed and headed up the ravine. Before the men could follow, he stopped abruptly, short hackles
bristling between his shoulders and a deep snarl rumbling in his chest. Samuel leapt from the wash toward the nearest trees and Thomas crouched with weapon raised, edging toward the growling hound.

"Can't be the pack," he muttered. "We're too far south. Must be something else bothering him. Snake, maybe."

"He don't set like that at no snake and it's too cold for snakes," Samuel said. "And if the wolves was moving ahead of us, he'd be after them. Must be something stopped up ahead."

With the old man beside him, the dog stalked toward a sharp

turn in the wash then froze again, growling through bared teeth. Samuel circled tensely above, peering down into the cutaway stream bed, then relaxed and waved his father around the turn.

"Here's your wounded one. You got him in the side and he bled to death."

The wolf, dusty brown, lay on a flat, water-smoothed slab of bedrock in the middle of the ravine. As the man and dog approached, he quivered suddenly and raised his matted head, growling weakly. Brutus leaped forward but the animal could not respond and dropped his head again to the cold stone.

"Not gone yet," Samuel said from above. "Best let Brutus finish him off."

Thomas drew back the hammer on his rifle and fitted a cap over the stem.

"You ain't gonna shoot him? Let the dog have his sport."

"This isn't sport. We're hunting," Thomas said coldly. "The animal's dying. Nothing to be gained by letting the dog tear him up."

"If you shoot, it'll spook the others. Brutus will crush his throat and be done with it. It's good for him. Sharpens his instincts."

"We're not going to surprise them, one way or another. If we get close, they'll know it. And I'm not so certain we want a dog around with those kinds of instincts." Thomas raised his rifle and shot the wounded wolf through the head.

"I can't fathom you sometimes," Samuel said, jumping down into the wash. "You been bent on riddin' the river of these wolves ever since we came up here. And sometimes I think you've got soft on them."

The old man's face hardened beneath his short beard. "Does he look any better off to you than if the dog had tore him to bits?" He turned and started again up the stream bed. "If we find the pack, the dog will get all the sport he needs. And us too, for that matter."

As they moved north along the wash the brush closed in on both sides, turning to a tight tangle of wild rose and blackberry. The dry streambed now cut shoulder deep into the floor of the ravine. As it turned suddenly west the brambles dropped over it into a low, tangled archway. The men paused before the tunnel and the dog started in, then balked and returned to their sides.

"You don't need to worry about his instincts," Thomas chuckled. "He has enough sense not to go up in there." Samuel studied the mass of bare, thorny vines that stretched chin-high over the narrow wash.

"You ever gone up yourself?"

"Just once. Before I knew the dens were in there. They were empty – lucky for me. But fresh."

"Where does this come out? Did you find the other end?"

"There ain't no other end. A hundred yards ahead or so there's a rock wall that the water pours over during heavy rains." Thomas pointed to the tangle of thorns. "This cover runs right up to it."

Samuel crouched and peered up into the lair. "How do they keep out of the water? Must run pretty fierce in a bad storm."

"The dens are dug high up on the bank, just under the roots of the brambles. They're smart ones, this bunch. About as safe a place to live as you'll come across. The only way we'll flush them out is to send the dog up after them."

Samuel looked skeptically into the tunnel, then at the restless hound. "Brutus, go!" he commanded, pointing ahead. The dog trotted forward again, sniffing, then hesitated.

"Go!" Brutus dropped his head and obediently continued forward beneath the arched brambles.

Thomas Shattuck scrambled up the bank to his right and into a stunted red oak while Samuel continued to squat in the stream bed, squinting after the dog.

"I'd be getting up out of there, if I was you. If he finds them, he'll be coming out with them hot on his tail. Wouldn't want to be in the way."

Samuel climbed the opposite bank, found a tree roost of his own and the men primed their weapons. Squirrels raced along the limbs above their heads, leaping from branch to branch with noisy chatter.

"Don't think nobody's home," Thomas said. "Squirrels don't seem bothered and we'd have heard something by now."

His son frowned. "That rifle shot scared them off. They wouldn't be staying around to see who was coming."

"They'd stay right up there where we couldn't get them," the old man said, scratching again at his beard. "They've gone somewhere."

Brutus reappeared, sniffing back and forth across the dry bed with new confidence, and the men descended from their roosts.

Thomas looked up at the sun that was breaking above the trees to the east. "No use going on from here. The wolves could be anywhere. Looks like we'll have to leave them for another day."

They left the wash and scrambled up the side of the ravine, hiking east toward the sunrise and the river. As they neared the Chariton the sharp crack of splitting hardwood sounded in the morning air and they hesitated, circling south and east until they stood in the shadows of the bare forest, a stone's throw from a broad clearing that arched away from the river in a wide semicircle. Two men worked in the open meadow beside a rough earthen square and farther toward the trees on the south, a woman sheared the long grass with broad even sweeps of a scythe. The younger of the men, his damp shirt clinging to a strong, sinewy back, stripped limbs from the trunks of straight hickory logs. The older was darkly bearded, thick and solid as an aged oak cask, and plowed the meadow sod into long even strips behind a team of gray mules.

"The Mormons," Samuel whispered, crouching beside the dog among the leafless bushes. "I thought they might take a look at the place and go back south."

Thomas Shattuck sniffed under his breath. "I don't know much about them, but I know they're not quitters. Look at that bank – and the floor already in place. They'll put it up in a day, just like they said."

"That's what makes them so dangerous," Samuel said bitterly. "There's no getting rid of them."

Thomas frowned. "What makes you so set on getting rid of them?"

"They're not Christian folk. Heathens of a kind. I just don't like them bringing their ideas up into this part of the state."

"Like I say, I don't know that much about them. But they look like they plan to stay, and I'm not interfering with them."

Samuel stood, looking darkly at the men through the veil of trees. "Sooner or later, they'll be trouble. For us, and for others up here."

"When that happens, we'll deal with it," the old man said. "Till then, we'll leave them well enough alone." He turned and walked briskly south away from the clearing.

5

JACOB

Jacob Randall paused on the low step of the Cole County Courthouse and looked up with distaste at the squat, two story stone building that served as temporary home for the 1839 Missouri General Assembly. The courthouse was a wearisome structure, a thick pile of gray limestone quarried from nearby bluffs, with heavy doors and deep lifeless windows. Inside, a swiftly remodeled courtroom had become the temporary senate chamber, darkly paneled and furnished in the somber fashion of the day. It did nothing to redeem the building and was a fitting setting for the debate that was about to begin.

In front of the courthouse, Jefferson City's Monroe Street bustled with the commerce of morning market. Wagons carrying cloth, tobacco, fresh fish and barrels of molasses strained up the hill from Jefferson Landing on the Missouri River, stopping to unload at the Market House at the corner of Monroe and High Street. The crisp January morning rang with the cries of impatient teamsters and the clatter and rumble of full oak barrels rolling along wooden docks. The air smelled of chimney smoke, fish and warm manure.

Jacob normally enjoyed the busyness of the market. It reminded him of his own store in Shelbyville and of Monday mornings when settlers came to town for their weekly provisions. But on this particular morning the sounds and smells surrounded him without notice. He gazed westward along the brow of the hill, past the white tower of the Methodist Church to where workmen already scrambled like foraging ants over the rising brick and stone walls of the new capitol building. The only bit of foresight and inspiration that Jacob was willing to credit to Governor Lilburn Boggs was the politician's insistence on the construction of a new capitol before the old one fell down around its lawmakers. The old building was not given the chance to collapse, but burned to the ground with the mortar on the corner stone of the new capitol barely dry. Some blamed the blaze on poorly attended office fires – others on over-heated political enemies. Jacob credited it to the fact that Boggs had under-appropriated for the new building with his initial $75,000 request and was paving the way for the additional $125,000 he now claimed was needed to complete construction of the edifice. Jacob was certain that even this new amount would fall short.

But despite Boggs, the new capitol was going to be magnificent. From where he stood on the steps of the courthouse, Jacob could already discern the classically handsome lines of the structure and imagine the domed tower rising nobly above the broad span of Missouri River that spread below the bluff on the building's north side. In this city that had been described by a European visitor only seven years earlier as little more than a frontier village, there was uncommon pride in this new capitol and Jacob shared it. He hoped this Mormon business would be resolved by the time the legislature moved to its new quarters, leaving its staining blot behind on the cold and indecorous Cole County Courthouse.

He pushed the thick geometrically carved door open with difficulty and entered the dim entryway of the stone building. The Senate chambers were on the second floor, with the House meeting in a larger downstairs room. As he climbed the wide central staircase, a twinge of anticipation mixed with the foreboding premonition that both he, and in his judgment the state, would suffer from today's debate.

Still, the discussion would be spirited and stimulating, an improvement on the argument over the formation of a state bank which had filled the preceding week and become mired in technicality and political interests. The newly rekindled Mormon issue was a pleasant departure from the insufferable docket of petitions and resolutions that generally crowded the calendar. Jacob was well prepared and that added to his anticipation.

Despite his readiness, State Senator Jacob Randall expected that he would lose and he was not a man who liked to lose. Not so much because of vanity, he told himself, but because he thought his positions on issues to be well considered and correct. He was a slight, sandy-haired man with a thin brown mustache and a generously freckled face, one of the few vestiges of a long line of undistinguished, but feisty Scotch-Irish Randalls.

His father had been a non-conformist minister in the English colliery town of Jarrow, and Jacob assumed he still was, though he had not heard from his family since immigrating to America a decade earlier. In Jarrow among the dust-blackened pit shacks and sooty row houses of County Durham, the Reverend Randall's own uncertain faith in Congregationalism had guided his only son into the accommodating embrace of agnosticism. Much to the Reverend's relief, though not satisfaction, Jacob's agnosticism had remained congregational, accepting the basic rights of all to determine the nature of their own beliefs – or lack thereof.

Jacob acknowledged that one could not discount the existence of God without totally inventorying the universe and finding Him absent. He failed nonetheless to be convinced by the conventional arguments that declared God present. Instead, Jacob had adopted an ethic based on order, viewing those behaviors which maintained and enhanced the order in a society as being moral and defensible. It was a value system that had allowed him, he believed, to remain unencumbered by most of the pettiness and prejudice that seemed to shackle those who professed to be God's children.

The younger Randall's conversion to unbelief had been aided by an early obsession with the works of the Venerable Bede whose life, death, and burial in Jarrow in the eighth century served to distinguish the village from any number of other dirty north

English mining towns. Jacob had struggled to master Latin in his youth for no other reason than to read *Historia Ecclesiastica Gentis Anglorum* in its original form. The reading had shaken his very soul. In this writing of the first history of the Christian faith in England the Venerable Bede, Jacob concluded, had allowed myth and wistfulness to so color his perceptions of Christian history in Britain that he could not distinguish between fact and desire. Now the young Senator questioned that such distinctions existed in most Christian tradition.

On this particular morning Jacob had been thinking of Bede as he gathered together the documents collected since receiving the committee report on Mormon activities in Daviess and Caldwell Counties. Distinguishing between truth and myth was central to this discussion. As he climbed the steps to the Senate chambers, he reviewed in his mind the cases that had been presented to the legislature, first by the Governor, then by the Mormons. Boggs had come to rally his colleagues behind his efforts to raise money for his war against the sect, insisting they were a threat to the security of the state. Then the Mormons made their appearance – Young, Kimball and Taylor – arguing that it was they and their rights as free citizens that were threatened. Most recently, the Senate had heard from the House Committee on Mormon Activities. Jacob felt the entire affair smacked of dishonesty and collusion.

Randall despised Governor Boggs, which by his own admission tainted his objectivity. The Governor was a boisterous, extravagant man with an uncanny knack for suppressing and uncovering information as it suited his needs. He and Randall had tangled often and bitterly over the Shelby County senator's efforts to protect Sac and Fox Indian lands in the largely uninhabited and unrepresented northeast corner of Missouri.

These Mormons, on the other hand, had impressed Randall – particularly their Mr. Young. He was an imposing man with a thick brown mane, deep melodious voice and authoritative manner.

Though labeled a bandit and fanatic by a number of those before whom he stood, Young had presented the Mormon grievances to a joint session of the legislature with calm unwavering certainty.

"I close by expressing both my own confidence and that of my fellows in the justice and good graces of the state," he concluded. Randall's investigations since had supported Young's position. But the senate experience of the Shelbyville merchant led him to doubt the wisdom of the Mormon spokesman's confidence in legislative justice.

As Jacob entered the modified courtroom the Senate President, a round balding man named Cannon from Cape Girardeau, was gaveling the session to order. Randall slipped into his seat behind the semicircular row of dark walnut tables, surveying the others present as the opening formalities commenced. To his left, the western contingent had assembled in strength; Noland from Jackson County, Thompson from Clay, Turner from Ray, and White and Morin from Caldwell and Daviess. Formidable opposition. But Conger from Callaway and Rawlins from Howard were also present and visibly relieved that Jacob had arrived. The Reverend Willard Dennison droned a lengthy but empty prayer and the honorable Mr. Cannon again rose on the dais.

"The issue that is before this body again today is the Mormon War that continues in the northwest counties. His Excellency, Governor Boggs, has respectfully requested an additional $12,000 to feed and billet volunteers engaged in this action. The Chair recognizes Mr. Morin, who I believe has a petition from the citizens of Daviess County."

Jacob leaned back loosely in his chair and rolled an engraved silver pocket watch between his thumb and forefinger. The Senator from Daviess, a man of imposing size whose coarse black brows and mustache appeared to divide his face into thirds, stood stiffly, unfolded a worn square of paper and waved it before the assembly.

"Gentlemen," he said, his voice brassy and echoing in the small paneled chamber. " I have here a petition signed by thirty honest citizens of Daviess County, attesting to the atrocities enacted upon them by the Mormons. With your indulgence, I will read it to you."

Jacob turned the watch over, rubbed the engraving of his name on its flat silver back, and looked thoughtfully across the crescent of desks at Rawlins and Scott who nervously dipped pens into their desk wells and scratched notes to each other on scraps of paper. Morin cleared his throat.

"We, the undersigned residents of Daviess County do herewith plead with our duly elected representatives in the legislature to provide us with the protection and redress to which we are entitled as citizens of the sovereign State of Missouri. In recent months we have been under siege by the bandetti who call themselves Mormons, who have burned the town of Millport, burned Stollings' store in Gallatin, have driven us from our homes, pillaged our belongings and destroyed or stolen our crops. We are in a wretched condition; driven out in the winter night with nothing but the clothing on our backs, our means of subsistence taken from us."

Morin paused, the momentary silence serving to draw the attention of the assembled lawmakers again to his reading, then continued as his voice swelled with emotion.

"It appears that many citizens of our state, as well as a portion of our legislature (for reasons which we cannot comprehend) are disposed to take sides with this lawless set of fanatics. We beseech you to hear our pleas for aid, restore to us that which is rightfully ours, and recognize these Mormons as the murderers and scoundrels that they are. Respectfully submitted. The undersigned."

The senator slowly lowered the paper to his desk, dropping his eyes and voice with it.

"These are my people." His voice was husky and trembling. "My neighbors and my friends. They ask but a small payment from us, but have sacrificed so much. In good conscience, gentlemen, have we any choice but to approve the Governor's request by acclamation?"

The room sat in uncertain silence, fidgeting under the weight of Morin's impassioned oratory. Despite the January chill beyond the walls, the room was oppressively warmed by two large stoves in the front corners and hung heavy with the smoke of twenty cigars. Jacob grimaced, shook his head slowly, and leaned forward in his chair.

"Will the Senator from Daviess yield to a question?" The room relaxed as suddenly as it had silenced, rustling and coughing away the smoke and tension as Morin slowly raised his bushy head and glared at his questioner from beneath the black brush of his brows.

"Will you yield to the Senator from Shelby, Mr. Morin?" the President asked. Morin nodded resentfully.

"I cannot help but be moved by the conditions described in the letter just presented... as I'm certain all of us are," Jacob began. "I would guess that the concerns expressed in the petition would be shared by the officers in the militia assigned to the area. Would you agree, Mr. Morin?"

Morin hesitated, glancing quickly toward his supportive colleagues.

"I cannot speak for the officers, but I would assume so."

"Can you explain then," Jacob continued, lifting a paper from the top of the stack in front of him, "this message from General Atchison to the Governor which seems to contradict your thirty citizens of Daviess County?"

Morin sniffed nervously. "Atchison would write no such thing."

"Let me read it to you and you may inspect it if you wish, though it is only a copy. Then perhaps you can comment on its authenticity." Jacob leaned back again, rubbing the large watch as he held the page before him with his free hand, reading in a clear even voice.

"I quote. `Things are not so bad in that county as represented by rumor, and in fact, from affidavits. I have no doubt your Excellency has been deceived by the exaggerated statements of designing and half-crazy men.'"

Jacob paused, waiting for the growing hum of whispered conversation to subside, then continued. "'I have found there is no cause of alarm on account of the Mormons. They are not to be feared. They are very much alarmed.'"

Morin leaned forward heavily onto his hands and growled across the room.

"That is an outright fabrication. A despicable lie. We have heard nothing from the Governor about such a letter."

Jacob nodded thoughtfully. "Indeed we have not. But I have no doubt that Atchison will be back in Jefferson City soon. I'm sure he will confirm his words. Or would you prefer that we call in the Governor to ask him about it, and about his reasons for not sharing it with us?"

Morin looked toward the bench as if asking the President to restore discipline to the proceedings and credibility to his argument, but Cannon returned his gaze without sympathy. He had apparently decided to let the debate move freely.

"Where did you get this copy, Mr. Randall?" Morin sputtered.

"From Atchison himself. He sent it to me."

"Atchison is a fool and a disgrace to his rank."

Jacob raised a surprised brow as a murmur passed through the chamber, relishing Morin's ignorant blundering into his snare. "And General Doniphan? Is he a fool and a disgrace?"

The Daviess County Senator looked up sharply but made no response.

"From what I gather," Jacob said matter-of-factly, "Doniphan... and Lucas, for that matter... have both refused to lead their troops against the Mormons and have returned home."

"Are you questioning the word of these good citizens, Mr. Randall?" Morin waved the petition and turned to squarely face the Shelby senator. "Let the record so indicate!"

"Let the record indicate that I merely point out what appear to be contradictions," Jacob said calmly, turning to one of Morin's associates. "Allow me to draw your attention to a letter written by a good citizen of your county, Senator Thompson, that was presented before the House and printed in the *Republican* not too many weeks ago. A sentence or two if I may." He drew another sheet from his pile and read:

Humanity to an injured people prompts me to address you thus: An unfortunate race of beings inhabiting Daviess, Livingston and Ray Counties are being treated by our fellow citizens in such a manner as would make humanity shudder, and the cold chills run over any feeling man. Their women are being insulted in any and every way, and the poor devils are being plundered of all means of subsistence, driven from their homes leaving the poor Mormons in a starving, naked condition. These are facts that I have from authority that cannot be questioned.

Senator Thompson rose a few seats to Jacob's right. "I am aware of the letter you reference there," he said evenly. "I also know the Mr. Arthur who wrote it to be a troublemaker and a Mormon sympathizer. To believe him above the men of Daviess County is to place sedition above patriotism."

Jacob leaned forward onto his elbows, tugging thoughtfully at his short mustache.

"It is very difficult to know what to believe above what," he said. "We have been hearing about these Mormon problems for five or six years now and for the first four years, I don't recall hearing about any violence from these people at all. We have chased them from Jackson to Clay to Ray County, and now to Daviess and Caldwell. I do not deny for a moment that on occasion they are now choosing to fight back. But perhaps they have decided they have given enough and aren't moving again."

"I am a bit surprised to learn that you have such fond feelings for these Mormons, Mr. Randall." Austin Noland, the attorney from Jackson County, sat near the center of the semicircle of desks, smiling coolly at Jacob. "But then, you don't have any in Shelby County and I vaguely remember that you were also fond of the Sac and Fox savages who were ransacking farms up your way. Are you planning next to champion the Negroes of the state?"

Jacob steadily held Noland's gaze and returned his unfeeling smile. The Jackson County senator was the most dangerous man in the room; shrewd, disarmingly handsome, influential...and calculatingly brilliant. Noland was a close friend of Boggs and was viewed as one of the most powerful men on the west side of the state.

"I appreciate your concern for my allegiances, Mr. Noland," Jacob said pleasantly. "And in truth it brings us to the very heart of the issue." Again he drew a sheaf of paper from his desktop.

"It was in your county that the first concerns about the Mormons were raised. The concern at that time was not that they were murderous or villainous fanatics, but that they were – and I quote from one of your Jackson County papers – 'eastern men, whose manners, habits, customs, and even dialect, are essentially different from our own. They are non-slave holders and opposed to slavery, which in this peculiar period, when Abolitionism has reared its deformed and haggard visage, is well calculated to excite deep and abiding prejudices in any community where slavery is tolerated and protected.'"

Jacob rose slowly to his feet and surveyed his colleagues with a shrug of resignation.

"I am an eastern man whose manners and customs differ from many of yours. God knows that my Geordie dialect differs and I believe it to be common knowledge that I am not a slave holder. Am I next to be driven from my home?"

He reached within for that resonance of voice and trace of controlled emotion that might touch an uncertain conscience. "I think I speak for many when I say that we came to this edge of civilization because we were people with differences, unsettled by the rigid and conforming mores of our eastern brethren. Have we now assumed that same intolerance and cannot abide the presence of conflicting views and ideas? *God save us if we have!"*

Again the chamber sat in subdued silence. Noland spoke, quiet and confident.

"'God save us', you say, Mr. Randall? May I assume then that you are a believer?"

Jacob flushed and turned to face the attorney. "I am indeed," he said.

"And in what, exactly, do you believe, Jacob?" He spoke the name with intended emphasis.

"I believe in the equality of all men, in loving my neighbor as myself, in being slow to judge and quick to forgive. Perhaps you recognize the principles."

"But are you a *believer*, Mr. Randall? Do you believe in the Holy Trinity and in the saving grace of our Lord?"

Jacob struggled to maintain his composure, looking to Conger, Rawlins or Scott to rise and lend their orthodox support to his position. The three senators sat silently, eyes resting on their desks.

"I'm not certain that I see the relevance of your question, Mr. Noland," Jacob said. He had stolen the floor from Morin and could not declare Noland out of order. And it was never wise to challenge on procedure – not with your back against the wall.

Noland smiled thinly and picked a piece of lint from his wide lapel.

"The question being debated is one of belief. These Mormons, as I understand it, do not accept the Holy Trinity. If you hold similar doubts, I would suggest that it might give you a certain sympathy. I ask again, are you a believer?"

"As I remember the discussion that we had with the Mormons before this assemblage, they did believe in God... and in Christ and in The Holy Spirit. It was the concept of them being three-in-one that they objected to. And I believe this is a question that was debated among Christian theologians well into the fourth century."

"We are not in the fourth century," Nolan said acidly. "And let us disregard the Mormon aspect for the moment. How do *you* view the Godhead, Randall?"

"I cannot say that I accept all statements of orthodox Christianity as unchallengeable," Jacob said. "That has nothing to do with my sense of justice."

Noland surveyed the three senators who had in the past spoken on behalf of the Mormons, and now cowered behind their polished desks. The narrow smile passed again across his perfectly formed lips.

"Perhaps, Jacob, you are more like these Mormons than we had imagined. Mr. President," he turned in his seat to face the bench. "I call for the question."

6

SUZANNA

Suzanna Shattuck stood in the shadows of the log room, aware that she could not be seen by the men who talked outside the open doorway. She wiped coarse bread dough from her fingers with a crumpled apron, edging sideways to better see the young man who leaned forward intently on the wagon seat talking to her father. She had heard the wagon coming down river long before it was in view, just as she had heard it two months earlier when it first appeared on the Chariton trail. The wheels still had not been greased.

The sound of the approaching wagon had touched her with the same shiver of excitement she had felt when Maggie's first baby uttered its birthing cries; anticipation, fear, and a sense that things were changing in ways that would never allow them to be the same again. As the pair of gray mules entered the clearing where the stubble tops of timothy and redtop now showed only in brown patches through the smoke-darkened snow, she forgot for the moment the ball of dough and followed the wagon slowly with her eyes as it approached the house.

She was pleased, looking at the young man more closely, to see that he was much as she remembered. Samuel said he was Mormon. But he looked no worse than other men ...and better than most. She had never seen a Mormon, but knew that they were strange folk. Not exotically strange, as a Chinese person might be. But strange in a sinister sort of way. Sallow complexioned, with deep sunken eyes and a lean, unfriendly countenance. This man was lean but otherwise looked very ordinary. In fact, well above ordinary. And much more at ease than the last time she had seen him. His face was strong and sensitive and Suzanna judged him to be a year or two older than her own seventeen years. Possibly as old as Benjamin.

As she craned now to see him more clearly with his wagon beside the block where her father split kindling, Suzanna noticed that he displayed a certain quiet and reserve that she thought uncharacteristic of north country men. He spoke so that she could not hear him clearly only twenty yards away and seemed attentive to everything about him. He gestured to the rear of the wagon which, from her view point, appeared to contain only two large oak barrels, then pointed to the mules and back behind him up the river. Though relaxed, he seemed ever aware of the cluster of Shattuck cabins, the snow-covered fields that stretched behind them, and the surrounding woods. She wondered fleetingly if he could see her, finding a new excitement in the thought that he might, but still not stepping forward into the light from the doorway.

Thomas Shattuck leaned loosely over the handle of his axe, then shook his head slowly and waved an arm down river. The driver's face showed resigned disappointment and he stood in the wagon seat, partly to stretch his trail-stiffened limbs and partly to peer down river in the direction of her father's gesture. He was taller than he had appeared on horseback – and perhaps not as thin. He turned toward the cabin and nodded in its direction, smiling faintly as he spoke to her father. The smile softened his face even more and Suzanna decided that he was, in fact, quite a handsome fellow after all.

Thomas Shattuck also looked at the cabin and nodded curtly, placing another short oak log on the chopping stump. He split it with a single deft stroke, the axe cracking sharply through the cold wood. The young man sat, spoke a brief thank you that Suzanna read from his lips, and flicked the reins over the backs of the waiting mules. The wagon creaked forward and she moved with it across the room until it disappeared into the woods along the river.

She quickly spread a damp linen cloth across the wooden bowl that held her partially kneaded dough, threw a knit shawl over her shoulders and walked out into the cold morning. The path to the chopping block was trodden into packed ice and she skated to keep her balance.

"Who was our visitor?"

Her father lifted half of the divided log onto the stump, swung the axe evenly, and quartered the piece with an easy stroke.

"One of the new people from upriver,"

"One of the Mormons?"

Thomas Shattuck dislodged his axe from the scarred stump and leaned again on its handle.

"Who says they're Mormons?"

"I heard Samuel and Lyman talking."

"We don't know that." He hoisted the other half of the log to the block. "The boys were guessing."

"But you think they are too, don't you?"

He swung the axe and popped the section in two. "Why do you say that?"

"I watched you. You were abrupt with him. Not friendly. Anyone else you would have invited in for a warm and a cup of tea."

"He had work to do. No time to be wasting here." Suzanna watched him skeptically as he split one of the quarters.

"What did he want?"

Her father answered sharply, irritated. "He was looking for hay to buy. They moved up here without anything to winter over their mules... and a horse the boy's got."

"We have hay," she said. "Since the wolves got the calves, you said we would have extra."

"All he's got to trade are barrels. We need that hay to trade for tools."

She stepped farther around to his front, watching his face.

"We could use a good barrel. And I've never known you to put needs above helping a neighbor. We could trade a barrel for tools, just as easy as hay."

The bearded man whipped the axe down sharply through the upright section of oak, burying the blade deep into the block and leaving it there. He lifted a foot up onto the stump and leaned forward onto his knee.

"Yes. I think they probably are Mormons. But that's none of your concern... nor mine neither."

"Either," she corrected before she could check herself.

"I've told you not to correct me," he snapped. "Your mother did enough of that, rest her soul."

"But if it's no concern of ours, why are we shunning them?"

"They're trouble. Trouble comes to them like flies to a running sore."

Suzanna turned to look down the Chariton after the wagon. "He looked harmless enough to me. In fact, he seemed quite nice."

His face was sober and he wrested the axe again from the stump. "It's not the people. They seem decent enough." He drove the blade into the top of another log section with a snap of his wrist and lifted it onto the chopping block. "It's their ideas that's dangerous. They're heretics. Believe in prophets and a gold bible come from an angel. Strange things."

Suzanna studied her father's face without reply. She enjoyed talking to him about such things. Her brothers and their wives never discussed. With them it was either this way or that, good or bad, to their liking or against. But her father was thoughtful, slow to make judgments and free to ponder new ideas.

"Strange is often no more than different," she said finally. "We accept some strange things when all is said and done."

"Not so strange that they get us run out of the state and our houses burned down about us," her father said, bringing the axe around with a crack that echoed against the wall of trees on the far side of the river. "And what's so mystifying to you about what we believe?"

Suzanna did not need to consider the question. "The Pinnexes over on Locust Creek? Their baby that died with the jaundice before it was christened? And was declared damned to hell? That's what strange is to me."

"Some things are not for us to understand," he said. "But you just forget about the Mormons. If we leave them alone, they'll leave us alone. And we'll all be the better for it."

She knew the discussion was over, but stood for a moment hoping he would continue. When he didn't, she returned to her bread, kneading it firmly with strong, slender fingers as she thought about the tall young Mormon and wondered what could make him so objectionable. She suspected her father was more concerned about her brothers than himself. He would never turn a stranger away, no matter what the person's beliefs. But he would also do what was necessary to keep her brothers from becoming more hostile – and he would never tell her what he was really thinking.

The day passed without the Mormon's return. As she sat at the table that evening with her father and Lyman she heard again the dry screech of the wagon moving upriver. Lyman looked at Thomas expectantly but the man continued at his meal without expression. Suzanna wanted to go to the window to see if he had found hay but stayed at her place. The wagon passed without stopping, grinding slowly northward into the evening.

After supper was cleared the older boys came to the cabin; first Ben and then Samuel. They came to talk and whittle wooden spoons and small toys for Benjamin's children, leaving the women to their own company. They talked of news that Samuel had picked up during a trip to Gallatin. Some months before...Samuel wasn't certain how many...a congressman from New Hampshire named Culley had killed a Kentucky legislator by the name of Graves in a duel. President Van Buren's reaction had been to advise the congress by message to "act more gentlemanly," adding to the ire of his growing opposition and fueling interest in bringing William Henry Harrison to the presidency. Suzanna listened intently as she wiped and put away the last of the dishes.

"This Mr. Harrison. Would he be good for the country, do you think?"

Samuel looked up from his whittling. "Not something for you to worry about. Why don't you run over and see how the ladies are doing."

"I would think it's just as important to me...," she began, but her father frowned her to silence.

"We're having a bit of a talk here, Suzanna. Why don't you go on over to Ben's." Without them looking up again, she slipped a heavy shawl about her shoulders and left the house.

Maggie sat beside the fireplace in an oversized maple rocker that her mother had given her when she married and left Brunswick. Her wooden needles clicked methodically through a long brown stocking, fashioned from a ball of wool that tumbled freely in a basket beside the chair. Judith sat across from her, listening to Maggie's patter and stitching a delicate bouquet of violets onto home spun linen that she had stretched tightly across a wooden hoop. As Suzanna entered, both smiled and beckoned in unison to a third chair that faced the fire between them.

"Looks like I've been expected," she said. Maggie laughed a bright cheery laugh that shook her ample body. She had entered her marriage a plump, buxom girl and had added girth with each child. Though her chair was wide, she was wedged comfortably between its arms as if she too had been carved from the maple.

"When the men get together, it's no use staying over there," she said. "Judith was just saying that any moment you would be coming through the door."

Judith nodded without speaking, the nod seeming little more than the swaying of her own rocker. She was as slight as Maggie was ample, narrow shouldered and breastless under her homespun dress. Suzanna sat between them, lifting her skirt and extending booted feet to the fire.

"Their talk interests me. But I don't think I was welcome."

The women looked at her pleasantly and worked in silence.

"I saw one of the new strangers today," Suzanna said finally, stopping their activity with an abruptness that both amused and satisfied her. "It was a young man. And a very nice looking one, at that."

Maggie slowly returned her chair to motion. "I hope you didn't speak."

Suzanna raised a brow. "And why not? He looked harmless enough."

"Benjamin thinks them to be Mormons. Who knows what they might do."

"And what *might* they do?" Suzanna drew her feet back from the fire and vigorously rubbed her boot toes. "All I hear is 'Don't! Beware! Stay away!' But I hear nothing about what makes these people so dangerous."

"I wouldn't worry yourself about that," Judith said quietly. "Samuel knows about them, and he thinks them heretics."

"I think Samuel knows nothing about them at all," Suzanna objected. "He repeats what others have told him and that could be far from the truth. And you, Maggie. What do you really know about them?"

Maggie smiled sympathetically. "Suzanna, you are such a thinker. It will get you into trouble someday."

Suzanna shook her head slowly. "Maggie, don't you see? We're in trouble already. All of us. A new family has moved upriver and we're treating them like they have the cholera. What has happened to this family?"

Maggie and Judith exchanged perplexed glances. "Your father asked that we leave them alone," Judith said. "We won't bother them, and we'll trust that they won't bother us."

Suzanna stood and stretched awkwardly. "I guess I'm more tired than I thought. And tomorrow is a wash day." The women stopped their work but did not stand.

"Suzanna," Judith said. "Don't be foolish, will you."

"I think perhaps I'm the only one who isn't being foolish," Suzanna said seriously and pulling the shawl about her, left the cabin for the quiet solitude of her sleeping loft above the low murmur of the men's conversation.

7

DAVID

David lay motionless in the fresh spring grass, the barrel of his rifle thrust forward through a screen of red birch that shielded his spot on the west bank of the Chariton from a deep clear pool a hundred feet downstream. The river was already warm. Runoffs from melting snow had crested in mid-March and thunderstorms now rolled almost nightly across the April sky, showering warm southern moisture onto the forest and river and splashing deepening green throughout the north Missouri woods. As days lengthened, they wooed pink and white blossoms from thickets of wild cherry and plum, scenting the air with light perfume. The earth beneath David's legs and stomach still radiated with soothing warmth, though the afternoon now stretched in long shadows across the flat surface of the river. Soon deer and turkey would slip from the woods to drink. David was waiting.

The soft embrace of the earth drew his head down onto outstretched arms, his thoughts wandering idly through the hazy fringes of sleep. Winter had come late and departed early, attacking in brief blustery flourishes. Though cold and slushy, December had allowed the Whitlocks to finish a simple two-room cabin with a high loft, a shelter for hay bartered from homesteaders west along the Hill Spring Trail, and a solid windbreak shed and corral for the animals. In the barren woods, wolves howled and yapped from sunset to before dawn, their tracks marking the snow on the fringe of the meadow. But the abundance of deer and weaker livestock had discouraged them from trying the wills of the strong and pugnacious mules and the mare knew enough to stay near the pair when the wolves came. In the sod hut, now filled with a lathe, shaving bench, and hoop puller, David and his father had split oak logs into thin boards, planed and shaped them with the draw knife into precisely symmetrical staves, then bowed and banded them into water-tight barrels.

It had been a winter of accepted isolation. No other being, friend nor stranger, wandered north of the Hill Spring to the Whitlock clearing and the family had not dared venture to the nearest town for fear of recognition. As months wore by the small log dwelling became David's prison, confining and oppressive. The family avoided each other; David logging the surrounding forest, his father cutting and shaping the timber in the workshop, Lydia tending the house.

In January and February David took loads of kegs and white oak buckets south to Brunswick on the Missouri River and to Palmyra and Hannibal on the Mississippi. The first journey was cold but uneventful; eight days over frozen, clear trails. As he left for Palmyra the only real blizzard of the winter pelted the forest with freezing rain, followed by driving sleet and snow. It had taken a week to reach the east Missouri town and ten days to return. Both homecomings had been times of celebration, breaking tense monotony for those who had stayed behind. As he hailed the house, the wagon laden with food stuffs and dry goods, tools and kitchen wares, the door had burst open as if his mother had been waiting during his absence with her hand at the latch.

"I thought they must have found you out and killed you," she wept on his late return. He laughed and hugged her gently, then peeled away the heavy tarp canvas that covered the supplies.

"They despise us as a group but don't seem to think we exist as individual men," he said. "When I said I came from the Chariton River north of the Hill Spring, they called me a fool for living in this wilderness, then did their best to help me get a good exchange for my load. I seem to be quite a fine fellow when my beliefs are hidden."

His father had entered the cabin from the workshop and pumped his hand vigorously, more emotion than David had seen from the man since the family reached the Chariton.

"Did you get the steel band strips?" he asked, then stalked out to the wagon to see for himself.

As David's dozing mind sorted through the memories of winter a branch snapped beyond the river, startling him back to consciousness. He scanned the far bank of the pool, propping on his elbows and lifting the butt of the rifle to his shoulder. The willow tops rustled, separating as the animal pushed silently through them toward the stream. David tightened the rifle against his cheek, feeling the surging rush of the hunt, and set the bead at the barrel's end on the spot where his prey would emerge onto the bank. He could see it now... faintly through the willow screen. Light brown. A deer. The willows parted and his finger tightened, releasing suddenly as his sights centered upon a long row of white buttons. He raised the bead slowly, tracing up the bodice of a snug brown dress. At the end of the barrel was a lightly tanned oval face framed in loose, shoulder length brown hair. The rifle dropped quietly to the grass and he gazed from his hiding place at the woman. She stepped from the willows as quietly and alertly as a young doe, her dark eyes moving quickly up and down the smooth stretch of water. Her lips were parted in an amused smile and she moved with a light easiness that showed her to be at home along the river.

David drew a long deep breath and released it silently. He had almost squeezed. Almost dropped her as she stepped onto the bank. He wanted to rise – to let her know that she had come close to drawing his fire. But he felt a sense of intrusion, that she expected to be alone and would resent his being there.

She sat on a grassy tuft, unfastened high worn shoes and pulled them from her feet, then rolled off long stockings and placed them in the boots. She slipped her feet into the cooling waters of the river and stretched backward, rolling her shoulders to release the tension of the day. Then, as if remembering that other things were waiting, she leaned forward again, deftly released the row of white buttons on her dress, stood and peeled it away, dropping it about her ankles onto the sandy bank. As David watched with confused excitement, she untied her white cotton bodice and let it drop to the ground. Her face and arms to the elbows were already lightly browned by the spring sun, her legs and upper arms white as the chokecherry blossoms that bloomed behind her.

She was beautiful. Soft... yet molded by the daily work of life in the woods with firm round breasts tipped with light brown circles that blossomed as she stepped into the water. As she moved, muscles rolled smoothly in her legs and arms, a creature of nature come to the pool to drink and wash. He felt his own body quiver as the warm earth pressed against his chest and groin and the sense of violation again swept over him. He wanted to bolt and run but could not move, transfixed by the sensuousness of the woman who shivering slightly as the chill of approaching evening sent tingling fingers across her skin.

A moan swelled in David's throat and he buried his face against his arm, stifling an urge to burst from hiding and rush into the pool to touch her. A new heaviness pressed him against the earth like a dead weight, leaving him gasping for air. She stooped innocently to splash water up across her hips and breasts, unaware of his caressing eyes. He was a voyeur. A peeper. He had been aroused before, had admired women and imagined how it must feel to be close to them. But he had never felt what he now felt, looking at this woman.

Dragging the rifle after him, he squirmed backward on his stomach until she disappeared from view, then rose to a crouching run, twisting dizzily through the trees until he was far above the pool. A white-tailed buck raised its velvet antlered head from the water as David burst into the river, thrashing through the waist deep water oblivious to the bounding retreat of the stag. He clambered up the far bank, continuing his run until the cabin came into view through the trees. Soaked and out of breath, he burst into the log room and stood panting before his startled mother who was spreading a linen cloth over the rough-hewn table.

"Someone's coming," she said quickly, fear widening her dark eyes. He shook his head, stammering.

"A woman," he panted, still gasping for breath. "Down river."

Lydia straightened and studied her son's face. "Are they coming this way?"

David shook his head.

"What's wrong then? Why are you so out of breath?"

He leaned heavily against the table without answering, head down and chest heaving.

"Your trousers are soaked," she said, moving to the window that faced the river, a faint smile touching the corners of her lips. "Get up in the loft and dry yourself off."

"I'm all right now. It just gave me a start." He climbed the ladder to the low loft and stripped away his wet clothing. He was ashamed of his thoughts and feeling, of the surge of passions that had turned to panic. He had been out of control. He wanted to shout and shake himself. And he wanted to see this woman again.

8

SUZANNA

Arranging to meet the Mormon, Suzanna decided, was not going to be a simple matter. With any other neighbor she would stop by with warm bread and a basket of fresh wild strawberries, exchange the bits of news that rare visits to other homesteads carried throughout the woods, and reluctantly accept an invitation to dinner. But her father's forbidding her to visit the new cabin a few miles up the Chariton made that impossible. Any meeting would have to appear to be by chance.

Thoughts of the tall young man on the wagon seat had filled many of the idle hours of winter, occupying her as she sat before her loom, mindlessly threading the wooden shuttle back and forth through the warp and tamping lengths of wool or linen firmly into the weave. Around her, Maggie's endless chit-chat hummed like summer cicadas in a cottonwood grove.

At night he walked into her dreams, his strong hands and deep intelligent eyes reaching out to her to lead her to places she had been only in her imagination. She extended the dreams into her days, seeing him pass in the cold silent fog of a February morning with a wagon load of barrels, learning from her brothers that he was bound for Hannibal. She rode beside him through the gray winter mist, huddled close on the wagon seat until they reached what she imagined to be a bustling port city overlooking the frozen Mississippi. They walked hand-in-hand through the town, stopping in brightly decorated shops to savor exotic smells and taste strange and wonderful foods brought upriver from St. Louis and New Orleans.

Samuel had been to Hannibal and described it as no more than a

72

brown shabby row of unpainted cabins perched precariously on a low muddy bank above the river; a stopover for traders and river rats. But as Suzanna and the tall Mormon approached it in her dreams, a city of busy, warmly lit streets lifted out of the mist where ladies in fashionable costume visited pleasantly beside white frame houses.

A severe storm set in the first week of his absence – icy rain, then bitter winds flinging the first heavy snow of winter noisily against the cabin's shuttered windows. She curled beneath her quilts at night, shivering as drifts piled against the flimsy shelter of their fantasy wagon, his strong body wrapped around her to shield her from the raging blizzard. As the week passed and the storm intensified, Suzanna genuinely began to fear for him, this man whom she had never met but whose soft, down-filled body she hugged close at night as the wind howled outside through the naked oak and hickory.

She awoke suddenly one morning, the dying whistle of the gale broken by cold iron screeching against dry wood and knew that his wagon was pulling slowly up the river trail. She smiled and snuggled deeper into the eiderdown, drawing her pillow more tightly against her cheek.

Now as she walked back from the river breathing deeply of the sweet scent of chokecherry blossoms, she toweled her brown hair with a soft cotton cloth and planned their accidental meeting. For a week now she had watched bees work the crabapple bush beside the cabin. On warm days the busy insects streamed in an incessant flow from north of the clearing, crawled over the pink blossoms with systematic efficiency, then launching pollen-laden bodies back into the air, flying due north into the woods. She had followed a short distance, judging from their number that a large honey tree stood somewhere between her cabin and the Mormon homestead. It would take some time to find – long enough to arrange a chance meeting with the stranger with whom she had spent so many winter hours.

"There's a honey tree north of us somewhere," she announced that evening at dinner. "I think I'll see if I can find it in the morning." Her father did not respond and she accepted his silence as consent.

She awoke before dawn, dressed by candlelight in heavy stockings, underwear, and a pair of coarse men's trousers. Bending awkwardly beneath the low pitched ceiling of her bed loft, she wriggled into a thick pullover shirt with a high round collar that extended up under her chin. She folded the material down around her throat and pulled a drawstring in the shirt's long hem tightly about her hips. Over the tedious winter months she had sewn the shirt and coarse, elbow-length gloves, quilted to above the wrists with ticking to protect her from angry stings. Each year she improved her outfit and with each honey discovery she suffered less.

From a low wooden chest beside her bed Suzanna drew a wide circle of loosely woven linen cloth, also fitted about its circumference with a looped hem and drawstring. She climbed silently from the loft, draped the linen net over a broad brimmed straw hat that hung on a peg beside the door, and lit a fire for breakfast.

By the time the men were fed, the dishes washed and returned to the shelf and a lunch of brown bread and thick white cheese laid out on the table for her father, the sun was above the trees and the bees hummed methodically over the crabapple. Suzanna tucked the padded gloves into a wide wooden pail, added a flat oak ladle and selected the lightest axe from three that stood beside the door. With hat and veil under her arm, she stepped out into the morning sunshine.

Heavy dew still shimmered on the spring grass; tiny silver ornaments on green stems. A family of cottontails, the young ones no more than dun balls of fluff, hopped quickly out of her path and into a clump of thistle. She breathed deeply, savoring the fertile aroma of new leaves and damp earth. He would be about his chores now... or might be starting into the woods to cut timber. She would locate the tree, then cut over to the river and follow the trail north to the new homestead. Before reaching the meadow where she guessed the Mormon cabin stood, she would slip back into the woods and approach it through the trees.

Suzanna crossed the field of timothy, waving to her father and brothers who worked to clear new pasture behind the cabins. Chimneys smoked with morning fires but the women were still busy inside and did not see her go. They would not volunteer to go along anyway, happy to share the honey and eager for the sweet-scented wax that rose to the top of the kettle when the comb was melted. Both feared the woods and the pesky bees and preferred to let Suzanna roam the forest alone. She had discovered nothing in the woods more dangerous than a surprised bobcat that hissed and disappeared as quickly as she chanced upon him, but she fed their fears with tales of large paw prints and strange noises, welcoming the freedom of her solitary walks.

The forest floor was dry and soft, its green umbrella catching the dew high above the path. She moved quickly into the shadows, her feet springing against the spongy earth. New spring undergrowth veiled the trail ahead but she knew each dip and turn and moved swiftly, watching and listening for the stream of humming insects. As she rounded the thick gray trunk of a live oak she stopped abruptly, drawing a sharp startled breath. He crouched before her in the trail, a battered rifle half-raised to his shoulder.

They looked at each other for a moment without moving, then he rose cautiously, lowering the weapon to his side and stepping slowly backward. She watched his eyes and saw them drift fleetingly to her loose shirt, then snap back to her face with flushed embarrassment. As he retreated, his foot caught a raised root and he began to stumble, twisting as he fell to catch himself with his free hand, then rising again in a crouching run, dodging back through the brush into the trees.

"Wait!" Suzanna's shout was sharp and pleading and he stopped abruptly, standing upright with his back to her. "Please don't go. I didn't mean to startle you."

He turned awkwardly, the same embarrassed tint coloring his neck.

"You didn't startle me exactly.... I just wasn't expecting to run into anyone up here. I almost shot you."

She smiled faintly, pleased that when he was this close she liked the face even better. His features were clean and sharp and less exaggerated. His eyes remained riveted on her own as if afraid to wander and she looked down with amusement at the baggy shirt and trousers.

"I'm following the bees," she said, holding up her pail. "Looking for a honey tree."

He smiled stiffly and showed her the rifle. "Hunting. I almost bagged you."

She nodded without moving closer, wondering if hunting was his reason for being so near the Shattuck cabins. "You won't find much game down here – at least not this late in the morning," she said.

The color rose higher on his face and he looked behind him up the trail.

"I've been following deer sign. It seemed to lead this way." Again they stood in awkward silence.

"I know where your tree is," he said finally. His voice was more relaxed, with a note of eagerness. "I heard them humming about it as I came down the trail. I'll show you, if you like." She nodded and rearranged her plan.

"That would be nice. You're from up the river, aren't you?"

"About a mile." He watched her approach as if studying her movement, then took the axe and bucket without asking and walked briskly along the path with Suzanna scrambling in her baggy outfit to keep pace with his long easy stride. He stopped suddenly as they reached a small clearing where the path dipped into a noisy brook, stepping aside to allow her to come up beside him.

"Guess I haven't introduced myself," he said, more at ease now that the cabins were well behind them. "I'm David Whitlock."

Suzanna smiled. "David.... I like that."

"Well, actually it's Claiborne. But even *I* don't like that – and usually don't tell anyone. David's my middle name."

"We're not such strangers. I've seen you go by on your wagon. I'm Suzanna Shattuck"

Again they stood and studied each other, now without awkwardness. His tallness, she decided, was really more a matter of lankiness. And eyes that she had imagined to be dark brown had instead a light brown sunburst around the pupil, radiating into deep luminescent gold and green. He also studied her face as if he had seen it at a distance and was anxious to confirm how he remembered the detail.

"I hope I'm not keeping you from your hunting," Suzanna said. He glanced up at the sun slanting in leaf-dappled patterns through the trees from the east.

"You're right. It's getting too late. The game will all be bedded down. Maybe I can help...."

"If it won't interfere with your work...."

His expression clouded and he looked across the stream in the direction of his family's cabin.

"Guess you could find a honey tree while hunting," she suggested. "Show me where it is, then go get a bucket. I think there will be enough for both. If the swarm is a big one, there's quite a bit by this time in the spring."

He easily jumped across the small stream, extending a hand to Suzanna as she hopped across behind him. She thought there was a soft intended pressure as he touched her and she glanced up expectantly. He was looking ahead up the path, following the trail of bees.

"For a bucket of honey I think I can take the morning off. My father won't like it. But he'll eat the honey."

A hundred paces beyond the stream he stopped again, raising a hand to quiet her. Through the trees from the left came the steady droning monotone of a large bee colony and yellow-black insects buzzed overhead, ignoring the hunters on the path. Suzanna touched his arm, beckoning him to stay, and pushed cautiously through the underbrush. The drone grew, intensifying until she could feel its vibration. The broken carcass of a dead maple loomed through the trees, its side displaying a wide, brown-stained hole ten feet above the ground where a rotted limb had fallen away. Crawling bodies swarmed over the discolored wood, darting in and out of the trunk, lifting effortlessly into the air and streaking into the forest.

Suzanna measured the tree with an experienced eye, scanned the ground around the maple and estimated the height of the opening, then returned to the trail where David squatted expectantly.

"Not an easy one, but we can get it," she said. "I'll need two straight saplings about three times my height and as thick as your arm. And two pieces a yard long... and a bit thinner. Could you cut them before you go?"

While David worked in the woods across the path from the dead maple, Suzanna placed the straw hat squarely on her head, draped the linen veil over it and tightened the string around her throat. By the time he returned with the saplings, she wore the long padded gloves and had tied both cuffs and trouser legs snugly about her wrists and boot tops with hemp twine.

"You'd better cover up everything you can before you come back," she said, looking up at David through the thick veil. "They're going to be madder than a turned-over June bug by then." He nodded and peered curiously through the mesh.

"Can you see out well enough to know where you're going?"

"Well enough. You can see a lot better from the inside. And you might want to find one of these for yourself."

He lifted his rifle from a stump beside the path, waved into the faceless cloth as though she could not hear him if he spoke, and turned up the trail. She smiled as he broke into a trot, judging his haste to be an eagerness to return.

With axe in hand, Suzanna hoisted one of the long poles under her arm, dragged it through the bushes to the base of the gray trunk and hacked and kicked an eight foot arc of clear ground beneath the hive. She returned to the path for the remaining saplings and with the long poles side-by-side, lashed a short section between them two paces from one end. The poles formed a crude ladder that she lifted against the trunk, with the cross step resting just below the open hive. Spreading the base slightly, she pushed the poles firmly into the earth and tied the second crosspiece midway between the first and the ground.

The threatened insects matted her veil and arms, jabbing venomous stingers into the coarse material. She hung the pail and wooden ladle on the protruding arm of the top step and gathered dry twigs and brush into a small heap beneath the ladder. With clumsy, padded hands she groped in the bucket for her flint, sparked the twigs into flame and piled damp leaves and moss onto the growing fire. Bees thickened on the linen screen, crawling over each other in a living mass. She bent into the billowing smoke, brushing them from her clothing, then returned to the path where she sat motionless until the last of the irritated bees abandoned their attack and returned to the smoke-shrouded hive. Feeling her way carefully over the veil cloth to insure that it was free of insects, she untied the draw string and lifted it from her face. Nothing moved along the trail.

Suzanna feared suddenly that he would not return. Earlier as they talked, she had begun to feel that he had also seen her before, glimpsing her standing in the shadows of the cabin, and that he had come that morning to see her again. But now, she wasn't so certain.

"You are a fool and a dreamer," she thought, folding her arms tightly about her knees and lowering her chin onto them. "You are a plain backwoods girl and he thought you a silly sight in your men's trousers and baggy shirt. He must be up there telling his parents an amusing tale about now."

His muffled footsteps on the soft path drew her sharply from her thoughts. He was still trotting but slowed as he approached the honey tree. Suzanna's heart and body rose quickly as he strode into view among the trees, a small oak bucket in one hand and a wad of linen cloth in the other. His head was now covered with a brown, broad-brimmed hat. She laughed nervously and shook her head, feeling again the rush of excitement of their first meeting.

"You haven't done this before, have you," she said.

His face reddened and he held up the cloth and a ball of string.

"I brought this to cover my face."

"I think you'd better stay here while I take care of things," she said, placing the veil back across her face and tightening it about her neck.

"I didn't come back to watch. I'll do my share."

"I don't think you'd better watch either. You're going to get stung. What about your hands? And the neck of your shirt is open."

He grinned and pulled a pair of rough leather gloves from a hip pocket.

Suzanna again shook her head in mock exasperation.

"Help me get this stuff on," he said, draping the cloth over his hat and bunching it about his throat. She helped him tie the netting and tightened the leather gloves about his wrists.

"You stay back and don't move any more than you have to. There are still a dozen places the bees can get to you, and this shirt is too thin. They'll sting right through it."

She led him to the base of the smoke-shrouded maple, pointing for him to sit on a fallen trunk while she climbed into the billow of blue smoke. The bees that had coated the stained opening were gone, swarming into the hive to frantically fan the air to protect their brood from the smothering cloud.

Gripping the axe in her left hand she shinnied to the lower crosspiece, feet firmly wedged against the lashings of the step, the hive opening even with her veiled face. Bracing her knees against the poles, she deftly scored the trunk above the opening with deep diagonal cuts from the keenly honed axe, then split the surface between the scored marks with long vertical strokes. With a quick snap of her wrist she buried the axe head in the trunk below the ladder, stooped to pick the pail from its peg below her feet, and pressed it between her hips and the trunk. As she tore the first strip of wood from the side of the maple the bees attacked from the open wound, coating her headgear, chest and legs. Suzanna turned the strip of trunk in her gloved hands, examining the intricate labyrinth of hexagonal comb that covered its inner side to determine if it bore honey or brood cells. It glowed golden brown and she scraped the wax into her pail with the oak ladle.

Enveloped in smoke and stabbing bees, Suzanna ripped strip after strip from the trunk and scraped thick honey into her bucket until the entire face of the hive was open. Lifting the pail to her chest, she scooped into the open trunk, pulling out dripping sections of honeycomb until the bucket was half filled.

"Switch," she called to David, who sat transfixed on the log where she had placed him. "If you're going to get some of this, I need the other bucket." He jumped up quickly and reached for the empty container.

"Slowly. Slowly," she said softly. He carried the bucket to the tree and took hers from her outstretched hand, yelping suddenly as one of the insects, distinguishing him by his movement from the rest of the forest, found an opening in his sleeve and thrust home a painful barb. Another pierced his shirt along the shoulder and a third burrowed into the netting around his throat, climbing onto his face.

"Put that bucket down beside the fire and walk away very slowly," Suzanna instructed. "Go wait by the stream and I'll meet you there. If they chase you, lie in the water."

He moved more quickly than directed through the thick foliage to the path, breaking into a run in the direction of the brook. Suzanna scooped chunks of the rich comb from the tree, easily filling the smaller bucket, and lowered it to the extended stump at her feet. She scrambled backward down the ladder and stood squarely over the smoldering leaves, scraping bees from her clothing.

Dislodging the axe from the trunk, she hung the containers over the handle and carried them back to the path, walking quickly toward the stream until the tree was well behind her. She left the pails beside the trail, covering them with her veil cloth, and hurried on to find David.

He lay submerged in a shallow pool just below the path, his nose, swollen eyes and a tuft of hair all that protruded from the cold water. Suzanna quickly knelt at the edge of the stream, reaching out gingerly to touch his forehead. Little Micah Lawrence had once been stung by a swarm of mud daubers and had died within the hour. He had been a small boy, but....

David opened his puffy eyes and smiled. "You were right. They got me," he said, splashing up onto his feet. Suzanna stood beside him and turned his face with a gentle hand.

"One sting on the bridge of your nose. Where else?"

"A couple on my back... and one on my wrist." He extended a swollen forearm.

"Take off your shirt," she ordered. "We need to get the stingers out and put some mud on the spots to draw the poison." He looked at her skeptically.

"I have brothers at home," she laughed. "You won't embarrass me."

He stripped away his shirt and she led him across the stream to the grassy patch where he had stopped to introduce himself earlier in the morning. After examining his wrist and extracting a tiny barb, she sat him cross-legged on the grass and knelt behind him. Three large red welts ran together from his spine to his left shoulder blade. She touched them, feeling for their centers and the stingers. His back was broad and firm; fuller than he had looked under the cotton shirt, and she suppressed a desire to press her cheek against his smooth, taut skin. Only one barb remained and she grasped it easily with her nails and pulled it free.

"Did you know about the war up here?" she said, feeling his back tense suddenly under her hand. She quickly scrambled around to face him and squinted at his swollen cheek.

"The Honey War, I mean. People were still trying to figure out where Missouri ended and the Iowa Territory began and some settler from over east of here cut down a couple of bee trees in the disputed strip. It was a few years back and caused all kinds of fuss, with the militia up here and all." She lifted and turned his chin to profile his swollen face against the sky.

"This one's still in here. Hold still now." She cupped her left hand against his cheek, pinched the spine between her fingers and plucked it from his nose, rocking back on her heals to inspect her work. "I think you'll make it," she said. "You'll look funny for a couple of days and be kind of sore."

"It was worth having you fuss over me," he said, rising awkwardly and reaching to help her up. Again she felt the light pressure against her hand and shivered beneath the heavy clothing.

"I need to be getting back. My father wasn't too pleased about me coming in the first place." He stooped to gather up his wet shirt. Suzanna hopped the narrow stream.

"I'll get the buckets. You should follow the brook down to the river and take the wagon trail back to your cabin. The bees will still be pretty mad." She hurried up the trail, realizing how badly she wanted to see him again and not wanting to rely a second time on chance.

"I hope we meet again soon," she said as she returned with the buckets. "Do you think...?"

"Sunday afternoon?" he asked quickly. "Could you come to our...."

"No."   She shook her head more firmly than she wanted. "There's a place about half a mile up this stream where the spring rises and tumbles over a little bank. It's my favorite place. Could you meet me there?" He looked at her thoughtfully.

"If it's in the afternoon. About one o'clock?"

She nodded and he held her eyes with a long, smiling gaze, then quickly turned and strode down the bank of the brook and out of sight among the trees. Suzanna watched his strong, bare back until he was gone, then clenched her padded arms tightly about herself and squeezed out a high laughing squeal. Sweeping up her pail, hat and axe she walked briskly back along the trail, the heady aroma of honey filling the air about her and all the world smelling of sweetness.

9

ROGERS

Gray mist lay heavily over the Grand River; lifting, rolling, lifting again, spreading its vaporous shroud across a well-worn road that ran beside the deep cut of the river bed. Beyond the trail, four armed horsemen hunched forward in chilled silence, peering into the slowly shifting fog.

"Something's gone wrong," one said in a thick whisper. "They was supposed to be on the trail before dawn. Should have been here by now."

"With this fog, they're probably wandering about lost," said another. "Might be back to Gallatin by now."

"Or we've been sent on a fool's errand," said the third, his voice sliding over the words with the slow easiness of the deep south. The last rider sat erect in his saddle fingering the handle of a long corn knife that hung in a crude scabbard from his belt. He was a head taller than the others and watched the mist-covered road with a single dark eye, the other withered into a thick scar that twisted from the brim of his broad hat down past the corner of his mouth into his beard.

"We was told right," he said, his voice rasping in the heavy air. "They're bringing five of them south with five guards. The guards won't put up no fight."

"Who's with them, Sheck – other than Smith?" the first asked. "If that man Rigdon...or even Pratt.... If they ain't with him, we ain't gettin' rid of but half the problem."

Sheck Rogers continued to gaze into the fog. "Smith's brother and three others. That's all I know. If we need to hunt down Rigdon and Pratt later, we will."

"I thought they was tryin' them at Gallatin. Plannin' on hangin' them there on the spot," the Southerner said.

Rogers' voice showed irritation. "Judge Birch got some pressure from downstate. Some little do-gooder raised hell in the legislature and they're moving them to Boone County for the rest of the trial. That's why King got hold of us. He don't want them making it to Columbia."

"I still say something's wrong," said one of his companions. "They had plenty of time to get this far by now."

Rogers urged his mount forward into the mist, the others falling in behind in close file to keep each other in sight. For nearly an hour they walked their horses along the faint grassy fringe of the road, straining to hear the sounds of a wagon moving on the trail ahead. The vapor thinned as the morning lengthened and as they turned westward along a gradual bend in the river, a white military tent and empty two-horse wagon materialized before them out of the fog. The tent was silent, the only horses a team of hefty plugs still tethered beside the wagon.

The four riders approached the tent, reined in their mounts and surveyed the ghostly camp without speaking. Motioning the others to remain silent, Rogers swung stiffly out of his saddle, walked slowly around the empty wagon and threw back the canvas flap of the shelter. The sour stench of vomit and liquor-staled breath poured from the tent and he stepped backward, scowling. Five militiamen, weapons at their sides, stretched on their bedrolls in drunken sleep. Between them three clay jugs lay emptied on the matted grass.

Sheck Rogers crouched and with both hands, grasped the soiled jacket of the guard who lay closest to the flap, jerking him roughly from the ground like a rag doll and shaking him to consciousness. The man belched sourly and struggled for his footing, staring with stupid red eyes at the intruder.

"Where are the prisoners?" Rogers growled. The guard shook himself free of the clutching hands, wiping his damp mouth with a stained sleeve.

"Who's asking?" he said hoarsely. Metal scraped against metal and the long blade of the corn knife probed menacingly beneath the guard's stubbled chin. The other guards stirred, sitting bleary-eyed or staggering awkwardly to their feet.

"Where are the prisoners?" Rogers repeated. The guard strained away from the blade.

"Gone," he croaked. "The prisoners escaped."

Roger's free fist smashed up against the man's upstretched face, sending him reeling across a companion into the taut canvas side. From the rear of the shelter a hammer clicked loudly back into firing position and the guard captain stood unsteadily, staring coldly at the man who filled the tent opening.

"Touch one of my men again, Rogers, and you're dead." Sheck Rogers hesitated, scowling back at his challenger, then slowly returned the knife to its sheath.

"What's going on here?" he snarled. "They didn't escape. There was one of you for each of them. You damn well turned 'em loose."

"There's men in this state that has more to say about what happens than you and Judge King," the captain said. "They don't like the way you handle things."

Rogers glared into the barrel of the cocked rifle. "The Governor wants the Mormons exterminated. That's what I do."

"We know what you do, Rogers. The Governor wants them out of the state and that's where they're going."

"They're worse than Injuns, and worse than niggers. They breed like roaches and if we don't kill 'em all, they'll be back. Then there'll be hell to pay."

"They're gone, Rogers. A full night ahead of you. We had orders they weren't to stand trial in Columbia nor fall into your hands. If Smith gets killed on this trip, we'll have real trouble. Every damn Mormon left will come swarming back to Gallatin and they won't be coming to build no Zion. Now get out of here before

I spare both the Mormons and the rest of us your filthy company."

Rogers studied the captain with his dark, single eye then spit onto the grass between bedrolls and backed slowly out of the tent. "You handle it your way. I'll do it mine. But don't ever cross me again." He mounted, turning to the other riders. "I'm going north. If I can't find Smith, I'll get some others that hasn't left yet. Who's with me?" The three looked at each other nervously, then shook their heads.

"We was willing to help you get Smith but we're not just going up looking for some," the Southerner said. "Let them leave." Rogers sneered, wheeled his horse and spurred northward along the river through the lifting mist.

He rode through the muggy morning past Diahman and Jacobs' Ford, pausing only to water his horse. As he turned onto the square at Gallatin, conversation stopped as villagers watched him pass in silence, then hunched together whispering, glancing over their shoulders as they retreated into nearby doorways. He dismounted at Stollings' Store, glared menacingly at the cluster of men and women who watched from across the square, then turned to examine the smoke-blackened brick of the storefront.

As he entered the woman behind the counter slipped through a curtained opening into the back and was instantly replaced by a squat, balding man with a red, darkly veined face.

"The Mormons aren't here, Rogers. Judge Birch sent them down to Columbia."

Rogers face twisted with rage. "I was waiting for them, but the guards let them loose. We had them...." He slammed his thick fist down against the shop counter.

"They're leaving," the shopkeeper said. "All of them. Maybe it's best this way."

"Leaving's not enough. They burned you out, Stollings. Look at this place. It still smells of smoke and your new shelves ain't half stocked yet."

"We're getting back on our feet. Folks have chipped in and we aren't really sure who started the fire. They had their faces blacked over and...."

"The damn Mormons did it," Rogers snapped. "And they did this to me...." He fingered the scar below his empty socket.

"Let them go, Rogers. People around here are tired of it. The sooner it's forgotten, the better we'll all feel about it."

Rogers looked with loathing at the red-faced shopkeeper. "You wanted them bad as I did. You're one what said there would be no resting till they was all gone. You're bad as them, Stollings."

"They are all going," Stollings repeated slowly, his face deepening to purple. "Two or three months and we'll be rid of them altogether. It's the best way."

Rogers snorted and backed away from the counter. "They won't make it out of the state," he said.

. . .

As evening fell on the cluster of cabins that bordered the Grand River at the tiny settlement of Adam-ondi-Ahman, the cooling air turned moisture rising from the land and river again into shrouding mist. Candles flickered through the windows of the southern-most dwelling, a single-room cabin that stood away from the others in a grove of shag-barked hickory. As the fog thickened, a lone man approached the cabin on foot through the trees, hunching forward against the chill of the evening. He knocked furtively at the rough door. Inside a chair scraped roughly on the plank floor.

"Who's there?" The voice was tense and guarded.

"A brother with good news," the figure whispered back.

"Where have you come from?"

"Down in Daviess County. From Far West."

"How do I know you to be a friend?"

There was a moment of silence. "I bring news of Brother Joseph. Him and the others escaped as they was takin' them to Columbia. If all is safe here, they need shelter."

There was muffled whispering inside and the latch pulled noisily back. As the door cracked slowly open, the stranger burst it wide with a heavy booted foot. Before the startled occupant could react, a cold black muzzle pressed against his chest and exploded. Beside the low hearth his wife arose screaming, cradling her infant daughter against her breast. The long blade and single eye of the stranger flashed as he grasped the hair of the screaming woman. The doors of other homes flew open along the river and men scrambled for weapons.

When they reached the grove the cabin was a blazing pyre, flames tinting the dense fog with flickering red, igniting the loose bark of the hickories into crackling bursts of sparks. The men of Adam-ondi-Ahman took to horseback, searching the trail southward, riding together in threes and fours. They found no one.

10

SUZANNA

Suzanna needed a pool, a still place in the brook in which she could see her reflection. But the stream at her feet ran swift and clear and she could see only the smooth pebbles along its bottom. She had spent as much time in front of the glass on the cabin wall as she dared, knowing that too much preening would raise suspicion. Her father had already commented that she seemed "a good bit more cheerful than usual," unaware that "cheerful" did not even approach the excitement that was growing within her like the onset of a spring cold; chills, sudden rushes of warmth, racing heartbeat. As she waited now for David Whitlock, the warm flush and quickened pulse returned and she raised her face and breathed deeply of the warm morning.

He had not yet arrived but it was early. In front of her across the opening in the forest, a sun-sparkled spring bubbled from the top of a limestone bank, cascading in lacy patterns down its white and yellow face. At the base of the bank the stream divided into two lively rivulets that looped away from each other to the edges of the small clearing, joining again near where she stood to form the brook that tumbled past her feet toward the Chariton.

Between the circled arms of the spring spread a small oval island, the grass brightly spotted with spring flowers. Suzanna lifted her skirts and hopped across the stream onto the island, breathing again the flower-scented air. The grass beneath her feet was deep and soft, fed by the nourishing waters of the spring. This was her private place; her refuge from the tedious routine of the cabins. She had spent hours stretched out on the soft green carpet, reading in the books she borrowed from neighbors of places she had never seen and dreaming of someone who would take her to see them.

Today her dream was more immediate. She wanted to spend the afternoon with David. She had lied to her father, telling him she was going to search for the delicately flavored, spongy mushrooms that popped from the rich forest floor each spring following the first warm rains.

"In your only good dress?" he asked, looking up from the yellowed parchment Bible that spread across his lap.

"It's warm outside. And Spring. And Sunday. And I feel like looking nice," Suzanna said brightly. "And there's nothing else to wear this dress for. No parties or celebrations."

"But to gather mushrooms? You'll get it all tore up and muddy."

"Mainly I just want to walk and be by myself," she said. "It's so beautiful out."

Thomas Shattuck shrugged and returned to his Sunday reading. "It's your dress and when it's ruined, it's ruined."

As she hurried along the wooded path and up the bank of the stream to the spring, she tucked her skirt about her hips to keep it from snagging and now stood on the small island, smoothing the wrinkles from it when she heard him coming through the trees. She straightened and shook her head lightly, loosening her hair, then turned her back to the sound until she knew he must be standing at the edge of the clearing.

David did not have to lie to get away.

"You've work left to do," John Whitlock growled when his son announced that he would be gone for the afternoon. "You've been worthless around here since those cursed bees got to you."

"We don't work today," David said matter-of-factly, clearing his dishes from the noon table. "It's the Sabbath."

"You don't seem to work much any day of late," the cooper

grumbled. "Don't know what's gotten into you. What are you going to do out in the woods by yourself? Talk to angels?"

"John. You may not believe as we do, but don't make light," Lydia said sharply. "And why shouldn't he have some time to himself?"

"He should be spending his time learning to shape a better stave. He's not going to make a living on the sieves he makes now."

"We don't work on the Sabbath," Lydia repeated. "You agreed to that."

"I'll get them done tomorrow," David said. "But this afternoon, I'm going out into the woods."

He walked into the sunshine past the corralled animals and sod hut, then swiftly up the river bank until the cabin was well behind him. Turning away from the river into the trees, he skirted the clearing to the west, making his way southward along deer trails that passed on the far side of the raided honey tree. As he saw the tall gray tower of the dead trunk, he paused to listen for the drone of bees but heard none. Their nest plundered, the insects had gathered and swarmed into the forest seeking a more secure home.

Another hundred paces and he met the stream; clear and bubbling, running eastward toward the Chariton. He turned deeper into the woods, slowing, drawing long breaths to calm his pounding chest. Ahead light streamed into a break in the forest and he glimpsed the powder blue of her dress through the trees. She was standing with her back to him, arms raised as she twisted a delicate white flower into her hair. She seemed for a moment a part of the clearing, the flower springing naturally from her brown tresses and the gathered skirt flowing as softly over her hips as the water of the spring, mingling at her feet with the flowered carpet of the island.

"Suzanna," he said, surprised at the reverence in his voice. She turned and with a graceful sweep of her hand, showed him her woodland retreat.

"Isn't it beautiful?"

He nodded absently, his eyes fixed on her face, and stepped across the brook to join her. She flushed lightly and reached to touch his face with tender fingers.

"You're still swollen a bit. Does it hurt?"

"Not that I notice."

"I'm glad you came. I've been thinking about you."

He laughed nervously. "You knew I would."

She nodded, folded her skirts beneath her and sat down amid the bright bouquet, extending a hand to draw him down beside her.

"I want to know about you," she said, tucking her feet back under one hip and leaning on her hand. He sat cross-legged before her, nibbling on a long shoot of grass.

"Not much to tell. We moved up here last November from Caldwell County. I'm working as an apprentice cooper with my father."

"Are you a good cooper?" she asked, tilting her head to one side.

"I'm getting better. My father doesn't think my work is as tight as it ought to be. I think it's as good as his and he just doesn't want to admit it. But he doesn't like much that I do." He frowned and looked past her at the cascading stream.

"This is a strange place to be a cooper – up here in the woods...."

David looked back at her, studying her eyes. They were deep and golden brown and shined innocently.

"Not really. You can either live in town and have the wood brought to you, or live where the trees are and take the barrels to town. The barrels are easier to move."

She laughed and seemed momentarily satisfied, then twisted around suddenly to face him, also sitting cross-legged with straight back and hands folded in her lap.

"Are you a Mormon?"

David felt the blood rush from his face and knew that she was watching him carefully. He smiled faintly and plucked another grass stem.

"That's a strange thing to ask."

"You are, aren't you?"

He leaned backward onto both hands. "Why is that important to you?"

"Because if you aren't, things will be simpler." David arched an enquiring brow.

"Simpler?"

"My family isn't too fond of Mormons... especially my brothers. And I want to be able to see you."

David tossed the first grass stem aside and put the new one between his lips. "And if I am?" he asked.

She looked at him intently. "If you are, things will certainly be more interesting." She was, he thought, an exceptionally lovely woman. And there was an honest curiosity in her frankness that disarmed him.

"It appears that things will be interesting, then," he said.

Suzanna smiled a satisfied smile and also leaned back onto her hands, again tilting her head slightly as she studied him.

"You must be terrible people to have everyone so worried about you." Her eyes laughed as she spoke. "Are you like Muhammadans or something?"

David leaned forward again, picked a yellow flower from beside his knee, and began to pull the petals from it one at a time.

"I don't know much about Muhammadans. But we used to be Methodists. My father still is. We're pretty much like Methodists in most ways – and like you... at least if you are like I think you are. We believe in God and all that."

"And in the Holy Bible?"

He nodded.

"And in the saving grace of our Lord?"

"Just the same."

Suzanna let her arms collapse and stretched out on her back, hands behind her head, and gazed upward into the cloudless sky.

"If we're alike, what makes you different?"

David pulled the last petal from the flower, tossed the stem aside and picked another. She had been thinking about this for some time, he decided, but didn't seem too troubled by it. Maybe she would understand....

"We believe in a prophet," he said simply.

She turned her head to look at him quizzically. "And that's so different? I believe in the prophets. Jeremiah and the like."

"No. I mean now. That there is a prophet now."

Suzanna propped again on her elbows. "You mean *now*? Right today?"

David nodded.

"Who is it?"

"His name is Joseph Smith. I've met him."

She nodded slowly. "I've heard about this Smith. He's not a well-liked man. At least people seem to want to get him out of Missouri. What does this Mr. Smith tell you that's so special?"

David stopped picking at the flower and considered the question. "Mainly that terrible corruption and falsehood entered into the Church after the time of our Lord... and that the truth has been restored through him."

"By *him*, you mean this Smith?"

Again David nodded.

"Funny that God would pick someone named Smith," she said. "I would think a prophet would be named...well, something more prophet-like."

"Had to be named something," David said, finding the comment silly and irritating. "If he'd been named Shattuck, people would say, 'Who ever heard of a prophet named Shattuck?'"

Suzanna looked over at him and smiled, seeming to enjoy his irritation. "Then you think that you have the truth, and nobody else does?"

"Not exactly. There is truth in all religion. But we believe we have the complete truth."

"Hmmm," she mused. "I hope you don't tell that about too widely."

"Widely enough. It's an important thing to let people know."

She nodded thoughtfully. "I can see why folks haven't taken too kindly to you. Is that the major thing? That you think you are the only people with all the truth?"

"Well," David said, clearing his throat nervously. "The prophet has also told us that Jackson County is a land set aside for us as a people... that we are to build Zion there."

Suzanna's smiled broadened, then she chuckled softly. David felt his face redden and the muscles in his jaw tighten.

"I'm glad you think that's so funny. I thought I could talk to you."

"I'm sorry," she said, the smile vanishing into an embarrassed frown. "But what is this Zion?"

"Zion is a place for God's people to live. Sort of a refuge for them."

Suzanna rocked into a sitting position, the frown relaxing. "No wonder you're having trouble," she said. "Think about it for a minute. You all move into a place. `Good morning,' you say. `We are here to tell you that we know the truth and you don't.... And by the way, did we mention that God has given us this land for our Zion? Just thought you should know.' It doesn't make for very happy neighbors."

"That isn't exactly how things have gone," David muttered, wishing he hadn't admitted to her first question.

"How then?" Her eyes had regained the smile. "From what I hear, they certainly haven't gone well. Your 'refuge' has run into a bit of trouble."

"We haven't gone about announcing that Jackson County is going to become our Zion," David said, hearing the defensiveness in his voice. "And we haven't forced anybody to leave, or do or believe anything. To us, Zion is where people who want to live in peace come together. Zion can be in the middle of others. We buy the land and pretty much leave other people alone."

Suzanna leaned forward and reached for his hand. He let her take it and felt like the air had suddenly been sucked from his lungs. His lips were dry and he flicked his tongue over them, hoping she couldn't feel his nervousness.

"I was teasing and it wasn't nice," she said. "As I tell my father, we all have strange habits and beliefs. 'Different' just means its someone else's belief. Perhaps you're right... in which case my laughing is especially bad. But it really is a lot for people to accept."

"Truth has always been a lot for people to accept. And does it really seem so strange to you?" A new passion swelled in David's voice. "Doesn't it seem to you that all the world is... is wandering about without any guide? That somehow what God wants of us has been confused by all the ritual and pretense? When I first heard this from my mother it all sounded so right."

"It would be nice," she admitted thoughtfully. "God telling some man right now what he wants us to do. Maybe that's what makes it seem so... so convenient. I think sometimes that religion is not supposed to be full of simple answers. That we're supposed to struggle with it."

"Why?" David challenged. "Why would God want it to be confusing to us?"

Suzanna shrugged. "My father says when he reads that if it's too clear, he doesn't take time to think about it and what it means. Maybe God wanted us to struggle with meaning."

David nodded absently, wondering what else her father said. "Perhaps he has to struggle with meaning because much of the clarity has been lost," he suggested.

Suzanna thought for a moment without expression. "Are there many of you who follow this prophet?" she asked quietly.

David smiled thinly, feeling his eyes moisten. "People have been accepting it by the hundreds. What's more, people have been dying because of it. Does it seem that strange to you?"

Suzanna shook her head silently, still holding his hand. A heavy lump rose in David's throat and he choked it back, swallowing hard.

"I lay in the bushes behind the smithy in a little place called Haun's Mill... shaking so bad I couldn't stand... and watched them butcher a wounded old man with a cutting knife." He swallowed hard again as the emotion rose, looking away from her and blinking back the moisture in his eyes.

"They... they shot a little boy to death. Eight or ten of them shot him while he crawled on hands and knees at their feet. He was just a little boy.... a boy who didn't have anything to do with all of this...." She reached up and turned his face toward her, gently wiping away the tears that now streamed down his cheeks.

"I didn't know these things," she whispered. "This killing of people. I knew the Mormons were shunned. Were disliked, but...." Her voice trailed away with a wandering thought.

"Do you believe this prophet?" she asked after a moment.

"I think so," David said quietly. "And my mother does. And she's a serious, thoughtful woman. My father? He doesn't. But he reacts instead of thinks. He says sometimes that if it isn't true, it ought to be. And he finds the book very hard to explain."

"The book?"

"Oh, yes." He laughed nervously. "I forgot that. The Book of Mormon. The Prophet received it from an angel...."

"Oh...the golden Bible Samuel spoke about."

"Samuel?"

"My brother. He's had an interest in the Mormons on occasion. Not a very good one, I'm afraid."

David frowned and looked down at his hands. "Ah, yes. I remember Samuel. We met on the trail our first day up here. But the Book of Mormon isn't a Bible, but like it. It talks about another people that lived here at the same time the Bible was being written."

"Here?" Suzanna patted the grass in front of her. "Right around here, you mean?"

"Well, not just here. But in America. The Indians come from them."

Suzanna's golden eyes reached deep into his own. "And you believe this?" she asked.

He looked away, gazing into the trees beyond the brook. "I've read through it – and it amazes me. I think 'Where could this have come from?'" He placed the hand that she wasn't holding against his chest. "I pray and ask God and sometimes I feel this warmth. I think that's what belief is all about...."

"Sometimes when I pray I feel it too," she said. "Do you think maybe it's in the praying...?"

He didn't reply, and they sat silently for a moment.

"And you believe this enough to be killed for it?" she asked finally.

David shrugged. "Is there reason to be killed for anything?"

"Well, I suppose. But I don't believe there are many such things."

"And what are they – if there are some? The things that are worth dying for?"

She thought for a moment. "Things without which life wouldn't be worth much. Like my family... or maybe being free to live in a certain way."

"And believe as you want? Is that the same thing?"

"I suppose," she said in a way that he knew she was still considering the question.

They again sat silently among the flowers, studying each other's thoughts and faces. The clear spring spread over the white limestone bank behind Suzanna, tumbling past them on either side.

"Why are you up here," she asked finally. "If this is so important, why...."

David felt the tremble in his chin that had stopped her question and looked away from her again. The chill of fear and shame that had chased him through the woods to his horse behind the blacksmith's shop at Haun's Mill crept again along his arms and back.

"Let's walk," she said suddenly, standing abruptly and pulling him up beside her. A path led northward from the clearing, barely visible in the new spring foliage. David straddled the brook and reached to help her cross, grasping her waist and lifting her easily. Beneath the blue cotton dress he felt her firm, slender stomach, seeing her again beside the Chariton pool. He released her quickly, turning ahead of her into the woods.

"I don't know much about you," he said. "Why are *you* living up here away from everybody?"

"We came when my mother died. From Ohio. Father just didn't like being at the old place anymore. It made him unhappy." The path widened and she stepped up beside him, slipping her hand again into his. "You don't mind, do you?"

David shrugged loosely, shivering slightly at her touch, but pressing her hand. "You're not a shy person, are you?" he said.

Suzanna laughed. "You haven't been here long enough. There's no being shy up here. You ask what you want to know."

"Can I ask then...." He stopped and licked lips that had again become sticky dry. "Do you have... someone you specially care about?"

Suzanna smiled, the sun finding strands of gold in her brown hair and dancing in her eyes. "I think so," she said.

11

JACOB

The success of the Shelbyville Mercantile and Exchange had convinced its proprietor, Jacob Randall, that another store farther north toward the Iowa territory would be a wise and profitable investment. Despite Jacob's commitment to legislative duties, his Shelbyville store had flourished due in part to its exclusive position on the southern edge of Missouri's vast northern wilderness, and in part to the ingenuity and business sense of its tenacious owner. From Jefferson City, a two day journey to the southwest, to Hannibal two days eastward on the Mississippi, Randall's Mercantile was the only source of dry goods, tools, salt and coffee. Along with a shop in Brunswick, Jacob's Shelbyville store served as supplier to the growing number of homesteaders settling northward along the Salt and Chariton Rivers.

Randall had also learned that his northern location placed him perfectly to take advantage of a lucrative fur trade with trappers, farmers and small bands of Sac and Fox Indians frequenting Shelbyville to exchange beaver, muskrat and fox pelts for goods and supplies. In Jefferson City and St. Louis the furs traded for twice to three times the Shelbyville rate, a profit viewed by those who traded with Randall as reasonable payment for Jacob's journeys south to the cities.

The merchant had also found it profitable on his trips to Jefferson City to swing southwest along the Salt River to load one of his wagons with soft black coal, surface mined by two enterprising homesteaders in Monroe County who exchanged it for Jacob's goods. He sold the coal to boat crews on the Missouri who preferred the more efficient and space-saving fuel to wood.

It was the lure of furs and coal that led the Englishman northward during the spring of 1839. Systematically, he traveled the postal routes and Indian trails that connected the scattered settlements of north Missouri, estimating travel patterns, anticipating community growth and judging distances from the vast layers of bituminous coal rumored to stretch from the border with Iowa down both sides of the Chariton River. He had surveyed Smith's Trail the previous autumn, winding northward from the Missouri near Jefferson City through rocky, wooded hills to a point just below the confluence of the Mississippi and the Des Moines. In March he traveled the Great Trail, leaving the Salt River south of Shelbyville, crossing a new postal route above the settlement of Macon, then wandering northwest to the headwaters of the Grand River.

Between these two routes, the less traveled Hill Spring Trail left the Great Trail near Gallatin, running almost due east to Hill Spring at Locust Creek, across the Chariton River and eastward to meet the Smith's Trail above Palmyra. It was at the Chariton crossing of the Hill Spring Trail that Jacob Randall rested his weary horse in April of 1839, surveyed the surroundings, and decided that this was the spot for his new trading post. Here the Chariton flowed southward through a broad wooded vale, bordered both east and west at the Hill Spring crossing by a wide grassy meadow. He had learned from other travelers on the trail that settlers upriver to the east were already digging soft coal from the forest to heat their cabins, and the tributaries of the upper Salt, Chariton and Grand were rich with beaver and muskrat. By midsummer with the help of two brothers from the Hill Spring settlement, Jacob had completed a long log building and stocked it with the essentials for wilderness living, adding a few of the niceties that drew settlers and Indians to the post to trade.

Turning care of his Shelbyville establishment over to his clerk, Jacob moved into two rooms behind the Chariton Trading Post; a bedroom with bed, straight backed chair and wash table, and a kitchen boasting the only iron stove in the territory. On the first day of July to the sound of lively fiddles, mouth organs and a breathy but enthusiastic bugle, settlers gathered to celebrate Randall's first day of business: Grogans, Dickersons and Pinnexes from Locust Creek; Martins from Lesley's Ford; Shattucks from due north upriver; and Cochrans and Wrights from east of the Chariton. They were tough, hearty people with the blunt frankness and reserved appreciation for each other's company that grows with hardship and isolation. Jacob liked them, and they accepted the little Englishman with unrestrained enthusiasm.

"Ya need yourself a good woman if ya plan to stay up here in these woods," Able Grogan said, appreciating a plug of tobacco purchased at half-price as part of Jacob's opening. "Ya see other folk sometime once a month. Sometime less. That can be mighty lonesome."

"I've had a good woman, thank you," Jacob said pleasantly. "And when I get lonely I just think about her. She was taken by the cholera in '33 when we were living in Palmyra."

Grogan's rugged face reddened and he looked awkwardly at his boots. "Beggin' your pardon, Mr. Randall. I wasn'y meanin' to...."

Jacob slapped him firmly on the shoulder. "We had some good years and I still miss her, but I don't mind people asking about it. There were six hundred people living in Palmyra when the cholera came, and it took over a hundred of them. That's what got most of us over to Shelby County – running from the plague, in a manner of speaking."

The merchant's willingness to sit and talk frankly about whatever a man had on his mind brought settlers to the trading post more often than they needed supplies, and by mid-August business was brisk. Jacob occasionally found himself chuckling with unabashed pride at the wisdom of his choice of locations. The Dickersons, whose poorly conceived efforts at farming the previous year had forced them to rely on trapping, found much greater success at their new endeavor and came in weekly with rich, soft pelts. A broad, thick seam of coal, thrust above ground by some prehistoric cataclysm, had been discovered on the Cochran homestead at the base of a twelve foot shale and limestone embankment. Jacob agreed to purchase four wagon loads of the black fuel per month and though the Cochran pit was now producing only two, the coal filled a wagon that would otherwise have returned empty during bi-weekly trips to Shelbyville for supplies.

Martins had cleared nearly twenty acres of timber and had half of it in corn, with the best river bottom land yielding fifteen bushel to the acre. They had also begun to raise hogs for more than their own use; narrow, long-legged creatures with high sharp backs, pointed snouts and ears, and foul dispositions. When the first long cold spell came, the Martins butchered their boars, hanging the carcasses outside to cool quickly, then cutting and packing them in salt. With increased travel westward across the Hill Spring to the Great Trail, salt pork had become one of Jacob's principle trade items.

The Chariton location had also provided the post with an unexpected bonus. The day after Jacob's opening, a noisy wagon rumbled down the faint track that bordered the west bank of the river loaded with white oak barrels and buckets that were as fine as any the merchant had seen. The tall young man behind the team of gray mules jumped lightly down from the wagon seat and thrust a strong callused hand into Jacob's.

"David Whitlock," he said. "You interested in trading for barrels?"

Jacob surveyed the load in the wagon with unveiled admiration, lifting a three-gallon keg from the bed and inspecting its perfect seams.

"This is fine work. Where did these come from?"

"My father and I make them at our place upriver. Well, actually, my father makes most of the barrels and casks and leaves me to make the kegs and buckets," David grinned. "He doesn't trust me yet to shape the larger staves. We can make hogsheads, barrels, firkins, blood tubs, three and six gallon kegs... even can make a puncheon if you need something that big. All white oak. They don't leak, and will last forever. Can you use them?"

Jacob looked at David Whitlock, then across the Hill Spring Trail and up the Chariton wagon track.

"You make these up there in the woods?"

David nodded, still smiling. "We missed your opening yesterday, but were glad to hear about the trading post. We're about five miles upstream."

"I'll take these and any more you can make," Jacob said. "I can trade some here and take the rest down to Shelbyville. I've had a hard time finding good coopering like this. It's getting to be a lost art, I'm afraid."

"In part exchange, could you bring us up some banding strips for hoops – and some hoop nails? We're about out." David hoisted a firkin under each arm and carried them to the long covered porch that fronted the store. "And maybe a few books and newspapers." Jacob agreed, and with each trip south took barrels and buckets to the growing number of settlements that lay between Shelbyville and the Chariton Trading Post, often arriving at his mercantile store without so much as a bucket remaining.

As Jacob now stood on the porch of the outpost in the humid August afternoon watching the heavy wagon creak its way down the river trail, he was particularly pleased to see young Whitlock seated behind the mule team. Of the homesteaders who frequented the Chariton store, Jacob found David to be the best company; bright, educated and amiably argumentative. The curious young man devoured the literature the merchant brought him and returned it with lists of questions and comments, some suggesting that he had already debated the issue with someone else before talking to Jacob.

As David reached the post and climbed from the high seat, a

lighter wagon appeared along the Hill Spring Trail from the west, pulled behind a single plodding ox with a heaviness that told of hours of travel on the sun-scorched road. The two men stood together and watched it approach, studying the stooped driver and slight, darkly clad woman who sat beside him. Behind them in the wagon bed, bundled together as if warding off a winter wind, three children huddled in worn blankets and a brightly patterned quilt.

The wagon halted in the middle of the trail thirty paces from the porch and the man climbed stiffly from his seat. Carefully he lifted a square box from the wagon bed beside the children and walked resolutely toward the trading post. Jacob stepped from the porch and greeted the stranger.

"Why don't you draw your wagon up here and rest a bit. That ox looks worn out."

The man hesitated, looked Jacob and David over carefully, then nodded to the woman who drew up the reins and directed the animal over to the building. David moved toward the wagon.

"Let me help you little ones out," he said, reaching toward the oldest of the children, a girl of about twelve with a round pale face and matted blond hair. Instinctively the children shrank from him, pulling the blankets more tightly about them.

"Thank you, but we'll stay in the wagon," the woman said quietly, glancing from David to the children, then straight ahead at the wall of the trading post. "The children aren't feeling well."

Jacob watched the scene at the wagon with curious interest, then turned back to the man who stood several feet in front of him.

"What can I help you with?" he said pleasantly. The man held up the box.

"Would you be willing to trade this for some provisions? Some beans and flour... and perhaps a little powder and lead, if you think it's worth it." Jacob took the box, surprised at its weight, and examined it carefully as David returned to where the two men stood in the open sun. It was a small chest of dark, richly grained wood, a foot square and half as deep. Its top and sides were intricately carved in deep relief with a delicate grape and leaf pattern. The merchant released the small brass clasp and raised its lid, showing a plush interior of purple velvet.

"This is obviously a valuable little chest," he said, looking back to the wagon where the slight woman gazed stoically at the log wall, her chin and lip trembling almost imperceptibly. "It wouldn't be right for me to accept this. Perhaps you have something else I could consider for trade."

"The wagon, the ox, and a rifle, "the man said. "Those and the chest." Jacob looked uncomfortably at David who intently watched the man's face.

"That's a beautiful quilt the children have," David said. "I'd love to have one like that myself. Maybe I could trade one of the barrels I brought in today for that quilt, and you could exchange the barrel for your supplies." The man hesitated, turning to his wife who sat rigidly, as if holding her breath in expectation.

"The quilt's not worth too much. Martha just made it a few months ago from old scraps. We need a bit more than it would bring."

"Looks like about a one barrel quilt to me," David said. "May I look at it?"

"I imagine you can." The stranger led the men to where the children still huddled together in the wagon. The frail woman had turned, her face and eyes brightening as the men talked.

"Alice, can you share the blankets with the others for a while?" she said gently. The girl slowly unwrapped herself, handing the quilt to her father. Her feet and legs were bare and a thin night dress clung in the oppressive heat to her gangly frame.

David took the quilt and stretched it at arm's length in front of him. It was a block design, each deep blue square centered with a white octagon which radiated red star points from its eight sides. The needlework was painstakingly fine and the batting thick and soft.

"No, I don't think this is a one barrel quilt." He folded it neatly and draped it over the wagon side. "A barrel and a six gallon keg. But that's all I can afford." The woman turned and spoke to Jacob, her voice still low but expectant.

"What would that be worth? A barrel and a keg?"

Jacob looked at the empty wagon bed and at the three children hunched in their night clothes beneath the torn blankets.

"Where are you folks headed?"

"Quincy," the man said. "We... have family there."

"Quite a few people came through here in May when I was first building this place. All headed for Quincy. There must be quite a gathering going on over there."

The man looked quickly up at his wife, then steadily at the merchant. "Wouldn't know about that. We're pretty much on our own."

Jacob nodded slowly. "Well, Mr. Whitlock here makes the best barrels in Missouri. I figure one of them and a keg would buy you a fifty pound sack of beans, ten pounds of flour, a smoked ham, the shot and powder you need... and a bit left over." He handed the carved box up to the woman on the wagon seat who wrapped it lovingly against her breast.

"I have a couple of blankets in here and could throw in a small bag of salt and maybe a pouch of tobacco. Would that seem fair to you?" Jacob said. The woman's eyes clouded, then suddenly overflowed with tears as sobs shook her thin body. Her husband stepped quickly to her side and took her hand.

"That would be awful generous," he said, his voice wavering. "You might give Mr. Whitlock here the tobacco. That's not something we use much." Jacob began to reply, then looked suddenly over at David. He had never known the young cooper to order tobacco either.

"We'll find something else instead," he said, leading the man into the trading post.

They loaded beans, flour, pork, powder and lead into the small wagon while David wrapped two new blankets about the children.

As the stranger climbed again to the wagon seat, Jacob handed the woman a small bag of salt, a large fold of linen cloth and a spool of yellow thread, a thin needle thrust through the roll.

"Bless you," she said and tears again welled in her shining gray eyes. The man reached down and firmly shook Jacob's hand, then David's.

"You are good men. We know you've been specially generous and will remember this kindness." He turned the ox and wagon onto the trail, heading east.

Jacob watched them cross the ford and disappear into the trees on the far side of the Chariton.

"I thought they were all gone by now," he said.

"Who's that?" David was also following the retreating wagon.

"Mormons. I thought they'd all left the state."

"You think they're Mormons?"

Jacob nodded. "When I was first traveling the Hill Spring Trail looking for a spot to build this place, they were moving east across here toward Illinois by the hundreds. Many had less than these folks."

"Why has this family waited so long? I'd think they'd have gone with the rest."

Jacob looked at his young friend. "You tell me. Perhaps they didn't want to give up their home. Maybe they tried to hide somewhere and were found out. Who can say?"

"You were good to them," David said.

"And you, Mr. Whitlock? A barrel and keg for one quilt?"

"I like the quilt." David glanced over to where it draped over the hitching rail. Jacob chuckled and walked to the Whitlock wagon to carry barrels into the store.

"I've been meaning to ask you," he said, hoisting new oak kegs onto each shoulder. "How would you like to manage the post for me?" David paused, a heavy thirty-six gallon barrel balanced on the edge of the wagon bed.

"I've got to get back to Jeff City," Jacob continued, "and I'd trust the store to you."

David lifted the barrel, shaking his head. "I'd never get my father to agree to it. He's convinced he'll make a decent cooper out of me yet, and won't give me up until he succeeds. I've promised him another year."

"Any other ideas? I need someone reliable and don't want to bring a man up from Shelbyville."

"Would you take a woman?" David lowered the barrel easily to the porch and returned to the wagon while Jacob stood in the shade of the awning, watching him.

"Your mother?"

David shook his head. "Suzanna Shattuck. She lives just below us about three miles upriver."

"Ah. I've met her. The pretty girl that was at the opening."

David laughed. "There was only one pretty girl? Well, that would be her. She'd be reliable."

"I doubt she could stay here overnight. Or handle the blizzards in the winter."

Again David chuckled. "She could handle the blizzards. And who's to bother the place overnight? She could go home."

"You seem to be pretty well acquainted with this Suzanna," Jacob said, leaning against a post that supported the porch canopy.

"Not that I'd mention to her family," David smiled, climbing onto the wagon seat with a final armload of provisions and taking a roll of newspapers from Jacob.

"Ah hah! A little secret romance."

"Call it what you want. Just don't mention that she was my idea." David turned the mules toward the river, flicking the reins over their backs.

"I guess you won't be wanting that tobacco you were given," Jacob said. David pulled the mules to a halt and looked at the merchant.

"No, I don't think so."

Jacob nodded. "Enjoy your quilt," he said.

. . .

The gavel rapped sharply against the dark walnut bench of the Cole County courthouse as Mr. Cannon struggled to restore order to the Senate.

"*Mr. Randall*!" He pounded again. Three rapid raps. "*Mr. Randall*! I cannot allow outbursts of this nature."

Jacob stood trembling and crimson-faced, jabbing an accusing finger across the curved row of desks at Austin Noland who reclined with calm amusement as Jacob sputtered. "*You... you hypocrite*! You speak with the tongues of angels but...but inside are ravening wolves... whited sepulchers!"

"You're mixing both your scripture and your metaphors," Noland chided.

"But I am not confusing your condoning the pillaging and murdering that's going on upstate with Christian charity," Jacob retorted.

Noland leaned back farther in his chair and laughed aloud as the president banged again with the gavel, the sharp raps drawing Jacob suddenly from the senate chamber back into the close dark bedroom behind his Chariton trading post. He shook the sleep from his head, groped at the foot of the bed for his trousers and stumbled through the store to the heavy wooden door which still vibrated with blows from outside.

"Patience! Patience! I'm coming." He threw back the heavy lock bar and pulled the plank door inward. A silhouetted figure filled the open doorway looming darkly against the moonlit night sky, his face a shadow under a flat, broad-brimmed hat. Behind the man two others sat motionless on sweating, blowing horses, holding the third mount between them.

"Who's in here with you?" the man demanded. Jacob glanced reflexively back over his shoulder into the black room.

"I live here alone," he said, steadying his voice.

"You live out here alone? What are you? Some kind of Injun lover? There's nothin' up here but Injuns."

"I'm a merchant. I run this trading post for the people who have homesteads along the river."

One of the men on horseback spoke. "There are three wagons out back. You live here alone with three wagons?"

"I told you," Jacob said slowly. "I'm a merchant. I use them to carry goods up

from the south." He wondered vaguely why he was submitting to this interrogation. The dark figure before him turned to the others, the low full moon momentarily illuminating his rugged face. A thick scar ran like a piece of knotted rope into his ragged beard.

"Search the place," he ordered, and the others dismounted. Jacob forced himself forward into the doorway.

"No you don't!"

A burly forearm smashed across his chest, throwing him backward into a wooden display rack of sperm oil and tallow candles. The rack snapped under his weight and he crashed to the floor amid broken dowels and tangled wax and string. With the leader standing over him, a long chopping knife dangling in a leather scabbard from his belt directly over Jacob's face, the others pulled crude torches from their saddles, lit them into smoking flame and tramped noisily through the store and back rooms.

"Nobody here but him," one said, dousing his torch in a barrel of dried beans. The man with the scar pushed Jacob roughly with a booted foot.

"Get up," he ordered.

Jacob rose slowly, untangling the web of looped wicks and tallow.

"Who's been by here today?"

Jacob was silent, still unraveling the mess about his feet. A strong fist grasped the front of his loose night shirt, jerking him upright and slamming him into the frame of the doorway. The long knife flashed from its sheath, its broad curved point pressed firmly under the Englishman's chin.

"Who went by here today, Injun lover?"

"No Indians have been by here in weeks. Most of them are settling up by Ottumwa on the Des Moines." Jacob strained away from the blade.

"I ain't talking about Injuns. Did anyone pass? Heading east?"

"A number of people stopped. Some passed without stopping. I didn't see everyone."

"A man and a skinny woman with children? Did you see them?

"I saw them," Jacob said. "They came by early. They'll be almost down to Macon by now."

"You're a liar, Injun man," the man hissed, twisting Jacob's shirt more tightly and jabbing the blade into his skin. "They was going east to Quincy. They wouldn't have turned down river."

Jacob twisted to relieve the pressure of the steel against his neck.

"Must have been a different family then. This one went south toward the Macon road." The man released him suddenly and pulled the knife away, stomping out into the night with the others behind him. They hunched together between their horses, talking in low guarded tones, then swung suddenly up into their saddles.

"You'd best not be lying, Injun man." They whirled their mounts toward the river, paused in the shallow ford for the horses to drink, then galloped east along the Hill Spring Trail into the first glimmer of early dawn.

"God of the Mormons," Jacob said, still trembling on the dark porch. "Protect your people."

12

JACOB

"Suzanna Shattuck?"

She started upright from the pool, water running from the long strands of flax in her hands down onto her sleeves and dress front. The small, sandy-haired man smiled apologetically and stepped closer through the knee-high grass.

"Sorry I startled you. Your father said I would find you here. I'm Jacob Randall from the trading post."

"I recognize you, Mr. Randall...from your opening celebration." She dropped the stalks back into the soaking pond and wiped her hands against her hips. She had not been close to him at the opening and he was slighter than she remembered, his face more animated and friendly. "Can I help you with something?"

The Englishman stepped up beside her, looking curiously into the shallow, rock-lined pool. "I don't mean to disturb your work. But what are you doing?"

Suzanna suddenly became aware of her appearance; dress clinging and hair damply matted in the heavy morning air.

"I'm afraid you didn't catch me at my best, elbow deep in stale water." She collected the handful of stems that she had tossed aside and held the damp fibers out for him to examine.

"These are flax. We strip the seeds off to press for oil then soak the stems in this pool until the pulp rots away from the fibers...like this." With a thumbnail she scraped the decaying stalk, separating pasty brown matter from long light strands. "When these are dry, the hackle board will take off all of this brown, leaving the thread for spinning." She pointed across the river at a patch of tall nettle.

"Until we planted flax, we used those. The strands are coarser, but strong."

Randall fingered the fine fibers. "Do you do the spinning too?"

Suzanna laughed lightly. "Not if I can avoid it. I like this part much better. And my brothers' wives like the sitting work. It's good we're not all alike."

"I think I came to the right place then," Randall said. "I have something of a business proposition for you."

She smiled cautiously, examining the man's freckled face with mild curiosity. "You want us to make linen for you? I'd better warn you that it's awfully heavy and not very soft. I hate to wear it myself."

Randall laughed. "There's a product idea in there somewhere. But for now I'm looking for something other than linen. You may not be aware of it, but I represent Shelby County in the state legislature."

Suzanna nodded. "I remember you saying that at the opening."

"I have to be heading south again shortly and I need someone to keep the store for me. You were recommended."

Suzanna's forehead furrowed. "I don't know a bit about keeping shop. Who possibly would have...?" Her eyes narrowed skeptically. "Who suggested me to you?"

"Let's just say 'a friend,'" Randall said. "This person thought you both able and dependable. The most important qualities, in my judgment. I can teach you the rest."

Suzanna's thoughts leapt to David Whitlock. It was David, she was certain. But why hadn't he mentioned it on Sunday at the spring?

"I'm a bit surprised no one said anything to me – about the recommendation, I mean." As she spoke the merchant's eyes laughed playfully, seeming to read her thoughts.

"There probably was no opportunity. The suggestion only came up yesterday. Rather a sudden thing when I mentioned that I needed help."

She turned back to the pool, knelt to lift another handful of limp stalks from the water and spread them on the bank.

"It was David Whitlock, I imagine. I saw him go by yesterday on his way to the crossing."

The merchant sat at the edge of the basin on a large flat stone. "It was indeed – though he made me promise not to tell anyone. I can't see any harm in it, now that you've guessed. And just as he said, I can see that you are a young woman who says what she has to say."

Suzanna looked up sharply. "I hope you're not making light of me, Mr. Randall. I see no sense in saying what I don't mean. Or not saying what I do. It takes twice as long to get to the point."

"Oh, quite the contrary, Miss Shattuck. I meant it only as a compliment. Mr. Whitlock displays a great deal of admiration for you and presents you as capable of doing most anything well. I respect his judgment. That's why I'm here."

Suzanna felt her face redden, more with warmth than embarrassment. Her meetings with David each Sunday afternoon at the spring were now the center of her weeks. She passed each day only to get through the next to Sunday.

"He's a nice man. I talk to him sometimes when he passes."

"He particularly asked that I not mention his part in this to your family. I hope my visit won't cause you any embarrassment."

Suzanna started to turn, caught herself and struggled to control her voice. "Did you mention him to father?"

Randall shook his head. "I said only that I was looking for help at the post and that you were recommended. I told him the job wouldn't require you staying overnight, but he still wasn't very keen on the idea."

Suzanna drew another handful of stems from the pool. "Did he say anything else?"

"Not really. Only that he didn't like the idea of you being there on your own. But he said I could visit with you."

"No. I mean David. Did he say anything else?"

Randall smiled. "He was careful about what he said, just as you are."

Suzanna sat back on her heels, looking seriously into the finely featured face and lively eyes of the Englishman. "Do you know David well?" she asked.

Randall shrugged. "As well as I know anyone up here.... Perhaps better than most."

She looked away across the river, weighing the moment. "He thinks a lot of you," she said finally. "He considers you thoughtful and honest. I see some of the books and papers you bring to him. There's more to David than one might think... at first acquaintance."

Randall leaned back, twining his fingers together about his knee. "I realize that more all the time. There are things that are important to him that we don't talk about much. But I'm beginning to understand them. And you seem to know a great deal more about him than you would learn by watching him drive by...."

Suzanna flushed again. "He's...." She paused and gazed at her own reflection in the pool, anxious to share her thoughts with this man who already seemed to know so much. "We meet sometimes. He's a very interesting person. I like being with him very much."

Randall sat upright again. "You will learn one thing about me, Miss Shattuck, if you choose to work at the trading post. I try not to pry, but I'm also the picture of caution and discretion. You will also learn – and I don't say this in any sort of a threatening way – that very little escapes my notice."

She turned toward him and he smiled wryly.

"I'm a small man as you can see. I almost have to look up to you. That has taught me to defend myself with my wits. I really can't afford to miss much."

Suzanna returned his smile. "David said as much. He thinks you're wonderfully observant."

The Englishman grinned broadly and rose from his seat, offering Suzanna a hand. "I wouldn't go that far by any means.

Nor would many of my colleagues. But it's nice to hear. Now, what about the business offer?"

"We'd better talk to Father." She stood from the pool and walked briskly toward the cabin with Jacob Randall hurrying behind her.

Thomas Shattuck sat on the chopping block waiting for them to return from the river.

"I don't like it, Suzanna," he said as they approached. "It's not the kind of thing a girl should do."

"You need to be accepting, father, that I'm not a girl anymore," she said. "And women do it all the time in town. It's very respectable and keeping shop is what you said mother wanted to do."

"This is different. You won't exactly live above the shop. And you'd be by yourself down there most of the time. There's all kinds of people coming along that trail, and in bad weather...."

"Pardon my interrupting," Randall said cautiously, "but if the weather is bad, I won't expect the girl to go. No one comes by and there's little sense in opening up."

"And as for being by myself," Suzanna added," I've been roaming these woods by myself since I was ten years old. What could happen to me there that can't happen up here? Even less, I should think."

Thomas Shattuck looked at her grimly. "I don't like it. But you're right. You're getting to be a grown woman and I can't make up your mind for you. You do as you please about it." He rose abruptly and walked into the cabin.

Suzanna stood with the merchant in uneasy silence then drew a long breath. "Can I come down tomorrow and see what it would require before I tell you for certain? I've never really had a chance to see much of the shop."

"Are you certain? I don't want to encourage you against your father's wishes. And if you'd like a bit more time...."

Suzanna shook her head. "If he was strongly against it, he

would have said so. We're alike that way. He just doesn't like to think of me as growing up and getting away."

"Tomorrow it is then." Suddenly the Englishman's face darkened. "I need to warn you in advance and should really mention this to your father. I had a rather unpleasant visit last night from some ruffians who threatened me. They thought I was harboring fugitives. I don't expect any more trouble from them but needed to say something about it."

"Fugitives?" Suzanna looked toward the house. "You mean slaves?"

Randall shook his head. "Mormons. They were hunting down a family of Mormons."

Suzanna wiped her hands against her dress to keep them from trembling. "What did you tell them?"

"What *could* I tell them? I don't think I'd know a Mormon if I saw one. I told them that many people stop by, but none I know to be Mormons. If I thought they would return, I wouldn't be asking this of you. But I'm afraid they have other mischief on their minds."

"Where did they go?"

Jacob Randall nodded off across the Chariton. "On east. Came by just before dawn this morning."

Suzanna looked evenly into the open face of the merchant. "You haven't discouraged me and I'll mention it to father before I come in the morning. But I'm very able to take care of myself."

Randall smiled and took her hand. "David said you were. I think he made a good recommendation. And meeting you again has helped me understand him just a little better."

She watched him mount and ride south along the wagon trail, feeling a share of her burdens leave with him. He knew more about David than he said. More about both of them. It was a burden she had needed to lighten for a long time.

She returned again to the pool, picking absently at the rotten pulp and wondering at her father's response to Mr. Randall.

Thomas Shattuck had never spoken about his worries for her but she had felt him watching her more of late, catching her in her silent moments. Like Jacob Randall, he was an observant man. And she was beginning to love David Whitlock with an intensity that couldn't be hidden. As for the ruffians...she would at least save her father that worry.

. . .

In the shallows of the ford where the Hill Spring trail dipped into the Chariton a blue heron strutted on stilt legs, stepping, pausing with one foot raised, stepping again. Jacob watched the bird from one of the porch chairs, feeling the first warm fingers of morning sun touch his face. Since opening the store on the Chariton he had become an early riser, finding that he preferred the hours just before dawn to those that followed sunset.

The crane stopped, poised above the water, then thrust downward with its coiled neck and rapier bill to spear a fish. There was a raw beauty to the woods that Jacob never tired of watching. He had seen some of that rawness and beauty the morning before as he talked to Suzanna Shattuck. She was a striking woman indeed. Not lovely like his Betsy. Betsy had been blessed with a face that painters dream of, perfectly formed and colored. She had been lovely. But lovely was too soft for Suzanna Shattuck. She was beautiful... in the same way that these woods were beautiful. Natural and unspoiled, imperfect but with a harmony of imperfection that was alive with an energy that could be felt, just by being close to it. She was at once graceful and strong, feminine and imposingly independent. When he had taken her hand it had been slender and warm, but callused by the swing of an axe. David Whitlock was a man of discriminating taste.

Betsy would have liked them both. He felt little guilt anymore about her death. About being spared. He had managed to fit it all into his sense of order, judging that what was meant to happen in the great cycle of nature must necessarily happen. He could not have prevented the spread of cholera down river with the soldiers from the Black Hawk War any more than he could he have prevented a woman like Betsy from insisting on giving the sick her care. It was her nature, just as it was the nature of Suzanna to take this position at the trading post. The sun and its planets had been placed in motion by some great accident of this same nature, beginning a chain of happenings that now brought him to this moment and would lead him unavoidably on to the next.

He saw Suzanna coming before he heard the horse, its hooves muffled by the grass between the wagon ruts. She rode astride a black mare, her dress tucked neatly beneath her and her brown hair catching the gold of morning sunshine. If fifteen years younger – or even ten – he might try to give young Whitlock a run for it, though he guessed whatever race there might have been for this prize was already won.

Jacob rose from the straight oak chair as she swung easily from the horse, surveying the front of the trading post.

"I haven't been back down here since you opened," she said. "The men always like to come for supplies."

"There's not much to see. I stock mostly basic items. Tools, kitchenware, and shoes. Salt and coffee. We'll have to talk about fair exchange, if you decide you want the position."

"I decided last night," she said candidly. "I'm here to learn what I need to do. When will you be leaving?"

Jacob laughed, pushing open the door to lead her into the dimly lit interior of the trading post. "Tomorrow, if all seems agreeable with you."

"Whew!" she said, grimacing. "This place could use some air... and a bit of dusting. Did you put all the windows in to keep them covered up?"

Jacob's laugh became an embarrassed chuckle. "I'm a man selling to men. If you can attract some of the ladies in here to buy by brightening up the place, it's fine by me. I can send up some goods that will appeal more to the women."

She walked through the store, opening packages and poking into barrels, counting and cataloging with a careful eye. As she lifted a pair of boots from the floor to study the soles, she turned to him suddenly.

"What do you do in Jefferson City? I was wondering as I rode down."

"I'm a legislator," Jacob said simply. "I help make laws for the state."

"When you make them, how do you decide what to do? Do you decide what you think is right or what the people in Shelby County think is right?"

Jacob smiled, liking her all the more. "You've put your finger on one of the basic questions of representation. Do people elect a man to directly represent them? Or do they choose him to exercise his own best judgment?"

"Yes, that's the question. What do you do?"

"I'm inclined," Jacob said, surprised at the turn in the conversation, "to favor the latter. I usually do what I think is right, regardless of what others might want."

Suzanna hesitated, placing the boot back on the floor.

"Yesterday you called the Mormons 'fugitives.' Are they fugitives by law?"

"Not by legislative law," he said grimly. "But by an edict from the Governor."

"From the papers you gave David, I saw that it has been talked about in the legislature. What have you said about it?"

"Ah. If only my own people were as concerned! I have tried to defend the Mormon position – with little success, I might add."

"Can anything be done?" There was the faintest pleading in her voice, a shadow of desperation on her sun-browned face. "It seems so... unjust in a country such as ours to make people fugitives because of what they believe."

"I'm not certain. At times I fear that the cause is a lost one. But

I haven't given up. In fact, during my stay here I've gained a new resolve of sorts."

Suzanna's look was questioning.

"Before now, it was simply a matter of principle," Jacob said quietly. "The rights of the downtrodden, so to speak. I've championed the Indian and the Negroes... and most recently these Mormons. But now it's become more of a personal matter."

Suzanna nodded slowly. "It's a very personal matter to me, Mr. Randall. Do what you can to help."

Jacob again wanted to take her hand but resisted, looking with admiration into that beautiful, thoughtful face.

"If you'll take on the trading post, I'll do my best with the legislature."

Suzanna smiled and turned again to learning her new business.

13

DAVID

The winter of 1839 arrived with a vengeance that seemed intent on making amends for the season's mild showing of the year before. Plummeting temperatures in mid-October stripped the forest bare, a harbinger of wet, smothering snows that accumulated in inches, then feet until the cover reached mid-thigh in the open meadow surrounding the Whitlock cabin. As temperatures dropped again new snow froze to grinding pellets, whipped by north winds across the hardened snowpack. Slender-legged deer broke through the crust, floundered until they froze in place or were torn to pieces by light-footed wolves.

Inside the sod cooper's shop, now barely visible beneath drifts that piled against its earthen sides, John Whitlock's mood darkened with the weather. He had delayed bringing in winter timber to be cured, working feverishly on a load of kegs for Jacob Randall's November delivery to Shelbyville. By working long into the night he and David had made the delivery without a day to spare, beating the merchant's departure and the first blizzard of the season by only a few hours.

As David now carefully shaped a stave with a long draw knife, another storm raged about him in the cramped workshop as his father paced and rumbled across the packed floor.

"Damn snow, coming this early! The last load didn't get us enough to make it through the winter. We're low on hay and this is the last of the seasoned oak. Even if we can get a log in, how can we cure it? The curing racks are covered under six feet of drifts." He stopped pacing and glared at David.

"And what have you done to help? You've been worth nothing this whole summer. I send you out to hunt; you spend all day and come home empty. We're almost out of meat."

David continued to pull the draw knife along the edge of the stave, stopping with every few strokes to check the symmetry with his gauge.

The bearded man smashed a burly fist down onto the plank table.

"*Talk to me, damn you.* We've got to get another tree in."

"We're almost out of meat because we've spent the last two weeks locked in this hut," David said. "And I told you we were getting low on wood and suggested we send fewer kegs down with Jacob this time and spend a few days getting in some timber. You were the one who wanted to keep on working, saying we'd have time when we were done." He set the knife on the shaving bench, ran the gauge a final time over the strip of oak and placed it beside the blade. "But there's no sense worrying about it now. We can't go out in this. When the storm breaks, I'll see if I can get the mules into the woods. Maybe I'll see a deer."

"You'll never drag a log out through this. And how are we going to season it? The curing shed's collapsed under the snow and nothing will dry outside."

"What do you suggest?" David snapped. "We had to get that load to Randall's or we'd have lost a whole month. We needed the supplies and as it turned out, he hasn't made it back up here since. So it's good we got them done and down to him."

John Whitlock clenched his fists, sputtering in frustration as David rose and pulled on a heavy jacket.

"I'd better feed the animals. The wolves seem to be getting closer every night. We'll have trouble with them before long." He forced the door outward against the snow and ducked into a deep, sleet-blurred channel that connected the shed to the cabin.

Overnight the storm changed, turning again to heavy wet snow that fell in crushing inches throughout the following day and night. On the second morning the sun rose distant and cold into a clear, still sky, touching only the topmost layer of white and fusing it to an icy glaze.

Wrapped in layers of heavy woolen trousers tied tightly about his boot tops, David strapped a pole axe, buck saw and the newer breach loading rifle onto a flat wooden sledge, belted the cartridge and cap boxes to his waist, and shoveled his way to the stable. The mules stood still and sullen amid drifts that now reached to the shelter's sagging roof, blowing clouds of vapor into the air as David fitted them with frozen harness straps. His mare snorted and shook her head, pawing at the icy ground and nuzzling David's back as he urged the team forward into the shoveled path at the stable's gate. The team plodded grudgingly into the gap, then balked and bellowed as he fought to turn them toward the trees into the belly-deep snow.

David smacked the reins against their backs, cracking the air like frozen glass. The animals surged into the drifts, breaking and plowing with broad chests as David struggled behind with the sledge. Balled pellets clung to his woolen pants and layers of crust chewed at his legs. The stand of mature white oak nearest the cabin, ten minutes by foot when the ground was clear, now took him over an hour to reach, pausing every few minutes to scrape chafing ice from the mules' legs and rest against the exhausting snow.

As the team finally dragged the sledge into the stand of trees that David had been working before the snows came, he searched out a tall straight oak that grew away from the others near the center of an otherwise open glade. It was smaller than he liked to harvest, no more than twenty inches in diameter, but it branched high above the ground with a trunk that could easily be felled and trimmed in the clearing. With the smaller log cut into two sections, the mules might be able to drag it back through the drifts to the shop.

He kicked and scraped the snow from its base, then cut deeply into the trunk with the axe opposite the track he had plowed to the tree. The upper half of the V-shaped cut was tapered more steeply than usual and would act, David hoped, like the curve of a sledge runner as the animals pulled it. He hacked a third of the way through the trunk, then moved to the other side and scored it lightly six inches above the opposing notch. Setting the blade of the buck saw into the gash, he pulled and pushed rhythmically, slicing the sharp teeth downward toward the undercut.

Though the air was still icy and stabbed at his lungs, wisps of steam rose from David's face as he worked and his hair matted and dripped beneath his knit cap. His father had been right. The hunting trips had been rendezvous with Suzanna and he had neglected the store of venison. If only the snow had not come so early....

He felt the wood give as he passed the center of the trunk, pulled the saw free and threw himself backward into the snow to escape a kick-up should the trunk snap suddenly upward as it fell. Ripping fibers cracked in the forest air like a barrage of rifle fire, followed by staccato snaps and pops as brittle branches broke under the fall.

David scrambled to his feet and with the buck saw and iron wedges separated the bottom eight feet of trunk. The wood grain was close and even with no sign of disease. It would split well and without waste. He smoothed the slope of the cut to improve the runner effect, then drove iron spikes into the sides of the section closest to the team and looped sturdy hemp rope over the metal pegs.

As he tied the ropes to the harness rings the mules suddenly wheeled and brayed, surging against the weight of the attached logs. David shouted, grabbing for the cold-stiffened straps, but the animals pulled more violently, rearing with high pitched screams. The mule closest to David swung suddenly against him, knocking him backward into the snow. As he clambered angrily to his feet, a low guttural snarl rose above the cries of the team. At the edge of the clearing, crouched beside the deep path plowed by the mules as they approached the tree, stood a huge gray wolf, head lowered almost to the snow crust, black lips curled over menacing teeth. His narrow eyes, pale gray balls of ice, were fixed on the panicked team. The left side of his head and neck were streaked with hairless scars where claws and teeth had searched in vain for his throat.

David glanced across the rearing rumps of the mules to the sledge where his axe and rifle lay twenty feet out of reach. Slowly, speaking softly to the team, he crawled over the log section toward the weapons.

"Whoa now.... Eeeeeasy, there." The mules surged again against the strained ropes, jerking the log beneath him and pitching him forward toward the sledge. In front of him, a quarter around the clearing from the snarling gray giant, a smaller black she-wolf crouched, inching forward with head low and teeth snapping. The chill of the morning air reached through David's woolen clothing and raced along his back, drawing the blood from his face and hands. He slipped forward on his stomach toward the sledge, freezing suddenly in place as a brown wolf, then a fourth the color of wood ash appeared to his left, extending the circle.

David reached the sledge, grasped the rifle in one hand and the axe in the other, and inched backward on his stomach toward the terrified mules. As he reached the lashed trunk he pushed upward, rifle pointed waist high toward the slinking black bitch. With a swift flick of his wrist, he slashed the axe through one of the hemp cords. Another swing freed the mules from the log and they bolted forward toward the gray, wheeled away toward the black, then back again as their flight was blocked by two more snarling hunters.

David scrambled again onto the fallen trunk, edging backward along its length to the upper section where leg-thick limbs rose thirty feet above him from the snow. Beneath his heavy clothing, beads of perspiration ran down his ribs and pooled along his belt. As he moved, the wolves closed slowly around the team.

He climbed up into a wide crotch ten feet above the crusted surface and braced himself against the larger of the branches, breathing deeply to slow his pounding chest. Another wolf barked behind him; seven in all. They moved as if on cue from the gray leader, circling back and forth to keep the mules plunging from side-to-side through the exhausting drifts. David fitted a cartridge into the breach of the Hall's rifle and placed one of the tiny hat-like copper caps over the nipple, sighting on the scarred neck of the lead wolf. His heart was slowing and he noticed with mild surprise that his hand was steady beneath the barrel. As his finger tightened on the trigger, the team surged across his line of fire and he swung to the left, found the ash gray animal and fired a ball into its side. The wolf yelped, leapt skyward into a twisting loop, and fell quivering into a crimson stain. Rather than retreat, the pack rose as one from its crouching crawl and rushed the team.

David threw the lever on the breach, thrust another cartridge into its smoking chamber and snapped it back into place. With a new cap over the stem he sighted again on the leader - again losing him behind the thrashing mules. A large dark male crouched before the teams' snorting faces, holding their terrified eyes as the pack ripped at their flanks. The second ball shattered the wolf's skull, dropping him without a whimper. As David hooked his thumb again into the breach lever, a lean grizzled animal sprang from the pack and charged his position, leaping with startling speed across the snow pack, back arched and bristling. David had buried the axe blade into the broken stub of a limb above his head and groped for the handle, eyes riveted on the charging wolf. The rifle slipped from beneath his arm and he snatched for it desperately, jarring the cap box on his belt with his forearm and scattering unspent caps from the open container into the snow below. His hand found the axe and he yanked it free, swinging forward and down as the wolf flew upward toward his feet, jaws spread and dripping the mules' blood.

Steel and fur met in mid-air, the axe burying deep in the shaggy side above one shoulder. The wolf issued a wailing cry and clawed wildly at the trunk, suspended in air as David clung with one arm to his perch and the rifle and with the other struggled to wrest the axe from the thrashing body. The animal twisted free, pulling the axe with him, and staggered toward the woods, dropping into a faint before reaching the trees.

The four remaining wolves ignored their wounded member, dashing with quick, slashing attacks at the mule team, then darting out of reach as the mules turned. David reached for a cartridge, fit it into the breach and fumbled in his pouch for a cap. Desperately he probed the small leather box, finding only three of the fulminate charges.

A bellowing cry echoed across the clearing and reverberated among the surrounding trees. The scarred gray wolf had mounted one of the mule's backs, clamping iron jaws down onto her twisting neck and crushing her spine. Her legs buckled, dragging her harnessed partner down onto her quivering body. With feet now pulled from beneath him and tangled tethers keeping him from lashing backward with his wide, powerful teeth, her teammate also fell to the pack. The black bitch grabbed an ear and pulled his exhausted head sideways, opening the mule's throat to her mate.

David screamed and waved at the pile of animals, desperate to divert the attention of the attackers. The wolves seemed to sense his growing impotence and continued to rip at their prey. A soot-colored male slashed at the side of the mule nearest the tree and the next shot smashed through his shoulder, dropping him lifeless into the snow. Only two more caps. He loaded again, carefully fitting one of the pair over the smoking nipple, and fired. The shot was slow, the cap weakened and stale from lying in the bottom of the pouch as others were replaced above it. The delayed charge caught a brown bitch in the flank, sending her yapping and hobbling into the trees.

The mules were still, their dying breath hanging thinly over the field like the last smoke of battle. Above them the gray male and black bitch stood with braced paws, their heads lashing back and forth as they tore at the team's open sides. David snapped the breach open and thrust in another cartridge, groping into the corner of his cap box for the final charge. He drew down slowly on the gray wolf and squeezed evenly. As the hammer fell, the wolf raised his face toward the tree perch and licked his bloodied lips and teeth. The cap puffed harmlessly and the rifle was silent.

David rose erect in his perch, his chest swelling almost to bursting and eyes stinging with rage. He gripped the butt of the useless weapon in both hands and reared to hurl it at the wolves. As he twisted to throw, his foot slipped sideways in the tree crotch and he fell heavily against one of the limbs, forcing out the angry breath in a low grunt.

"Be smart," he muttered. "They haven't got you yet."

He squatted, searching the broken snow below where the falling tree had shattered the crust. He could see a cap. No... two caps. Dull copper dots against the white surface. With an eye on the feasting wolves and blood pounding in his temples, he slowly extended a leg downward along the back of the limb. The black bitch raised her head and barked sharply, spinning on the torn carcass and rushing the tree. As David froze in place, she slid to a snapping halt and growled up at him through crimson teeth. He gulped a quick breath and trapped it, inching again downward. Again she charged and he jerked back upright in the tree, braced his legs against the crotch and raised the rifle above his head to ward off the attack. She did not leap as the first had but stopped below him, slowly circled his perch, then crouched on her haunches. David slumped back against the oak limb and buried his face in his hands.

From the position of the sun, David guessed that it was nearly noon. He had been in the tree for over an hour. The gray wolf sat in glutted silence on the torn bodies of the mule team, watching him with pale eyes as he stiffened in the tree. Below, the black mate lay on her belly, head resting on her paws. If he could leap onto her back and smash the rifle butt into her skull, he could then deal with the gray one-on-one, swinging the rifle as the wolf charged. Or there may be that fleeting second that would allow him to snatch up one of the fallen caps and use the cartridge that now lay useless in the breach.... But what if it also misfired, with the gray almost on top of him?

His thoughts were broken by the distant sound of his father's voice, calling from across the clearing beyond the wolves. Both animals arose, ears and hackles erect, and the black returned to her mate.

"Stay away!" David's voice was shrill and hoarse and the wolves spun back toward him. "The wolves have me!"

John Whitlock appeared through the trees, hip deep in snow and carrying the old flintlock and the short, flat-bladed spade that had cut the sod blocks for the workshop. He stopped as he saw David.

"How many are there?"

"Two left. They got the mules."

Even at a distance, David saw his father stiffen.

"You let the damn wolves get the mules?" His voice rose as he pressed forward through the drifts. *"You let two wolves get the mules?"*

The wolves crouched and crept sideways, one left and one right, heads low and eyes fixed on the stocky figure that stood solidly in the snow, pulling the plug from his powder horn with his teeth. Their attention diverted, David slid from the tree and pushed quickly on his stomach across the snow crust to the dead animal that held the pole axe, reaching it before the wolves turned. As the burly cooper tapped powder into the pan of his rifle they hesitated, sensing new danger, turned back and forth between the darkly bearded man and the hunter who had already destroyed their pack.

The gray wolf crouched, growling, then turned with his black mate and loped southward into the frozen woods.

John Whitlock surged forward to the edge of the clearing, his face dark and eyes scanning the bloody scene. David stood beside the dead wolf, the stained pole axe in one hand and the impotent rifle in the other.

"Why didn't you shoot them?" His father's voice was low and intense.

David pointed to the broken snow below his tree perch.

"One of them charged me and I knocked most of the caps into the snow, fighting off the charge. I killed this one with the axe when she jumped at me, but when the caps ran out, the black kept me treed."

"*You dropped the caps?*" His voice rumbled across the clearing. "You let my mules get killed because *you dropped the caps?*"

David stood straight in the blood-stained snow.

"There were seven and I killed five of them. One with the axe."

"You didn't kill enough," the cooper snapped. "If you'd kept your head – and the caps – we'd have two mules alive and some way to get through the winter."

The steadiness that had surprised David in his tree perch slowly gave way to shivering trembles and he tensed his shoulders to smother them.

"I'll replace the mules," he said evenly.

"You can't even get a log out of the woods. How are you going to replace two good mules?

"I'll replace them," David repeated.

The two men stood above the mutilated team, smoldering silently.

"Get home."

"I need to find some of the caps."

"Get home. We'll settle this when I get your mess cleared up. I'll get the harnesses and forget the cursed caps."

David looked around the clearing at the bodies of the fallen wolves, then pushed through the snow to the deep track that he had broken earlier that day on his way to bring in the oak that would see them through the winter

. . .

Lydia stood behind him in the low loft.

"You can't leave this late in the day," she said. "It's already near dusk. Where can you go with this snow and so little light left?"

David thrust rolled clothing into a heavy cloth sack.

"I've had enough of him," David muttered sullenly. "I don't want to be here when he gets back."

"He loses himself when he's worried about how we're going to get by. You know how he gets...."

"I know how he gets... and I've had enough of it."

"I can talk to him. He'll have had time to cool down...."

David straightened and looked at her.

"I don't want you to talk to him. It's time I was going; maybe past time."

She did not speak but he understood the question in her eyes.

"I'll go south, I think. Down to Shelbyville."

She stepped closer, touching his arm.

"Go find the Church," she said softly. "You said the man at the trading post – Mr. Randall – told you they are gathering in Illinois. At Commerce."

David shook his head.

"I have to replace the team. If I go to Commerce and bring a team back here with me, trouble will follow. The time isn't right." He drew her to him, hugging her as a man does his best friend, and felt her tears against his neck.

"I'll be all right," he said. "It's time."

He lifted the sack to his shoulder and tucked a small bedroll beneath his arm, tightly wrapped in a brightly starred quilt. She stretched up and kissed his cheek.

"Remember who you are," she said.

David saddled the mare, tied the bundle to her back, and led her out of the covered stable into the deep snow and pale sun of the late afternoon. Lydia watched him from the doorway, a knitted shawl pulled tightly around her shoulders.

"You should have enough to keep the two of you 'till spring," he said. "I'll have the mules by then."

He forged ahead of the horse into the drifts and she reluctantly followed. At the edge of the clearing where the buried wagon trail slipped between the forest and the frozen river he looked back. His mother stood with raised hand but did not wave. He lifted his own hand then pushed southward along the Chariton, his thoughts turning to Suzanna Shattuck.

David trudged for nearly an hour on foot without covering a mile, then mounted the mare to find that her long legs moved with relative ease through the frozen cover. He passed the Shattuck cabin without apparent notice. Though Suzanna had been tending the trading post for three months now, the snow south along the trail from her homestead was undisturbed. Travelers would not be moving along the Hill Spring until the snows receded and settlers in the area were already stocked for winter. There was no need for her to open the post until early spring.

By dark he was still a mile above the trading post but pushed on into the evening, the events of the day dampening his desire to spend the night in the woods. Cold air cleared and sharpened the night sky as it had filtered and muted the day. A broad band of stars arched across the heavens, poured from the lip of the Big Dipper that bent downward overhead. David felt a sudden exhilaration and freedom and wanted to shout at the trees and sky, quieted only by his memory of the wolves and knowing that they had also come south along the Chariton. But he had done well against them despite his father's anger. David would replace the mules and then see what would come.

The moon rose bright and full as he reached the trading post, lighting the night with a glow that softened both the cold and the darkness of the building. With the mare secured in the stable behind the post, he tried the front door and found it locked. Without explanation, Jacob Randall had decided to install a regular locksmith's lock on the heavy door before leaving for Shelbyville, though he knew any settler in the area would leave behind his payment or credit slip even if the post was empty when he visited. Jacob had hidden an extra key beneath the ledge of the porch step, a key that he told all of his customers about, adding to the mystery of the lock.

David burrowed in the snow and found the key, entered the dark store and locked the door behind him. The bed in the back room was softer and warmer than his own thin cot and he soon drifted on the edge of sleep. As he slipped into unconsciousness he smelled the faint sweetness of lavender seeping into the room from the store beyond, saw the lithe figure of Suzanna step through the willows onto the bank of the Chariton, and faintly in the distance heard the low chilling howl of hunting wolves.

14

DAVID

Choking black dust clouded the narrow shaft, filtering light that seeped from the tunnel opening above into gray haze and coating the neckerchief masks and unprotected eyes of two men who crouched before the coal face. They hacked at the black rock with short-handled picks and shovels; coughing, spitting, each swing and scoop thickening the dust. The tiny particles seeped into openings in two pale oil lamps, flashing into flame and casting grotesque shadows across the ebony walls of the pit. The men rested, their low wooden cart full, and waited for the suffocating cloud to settle.

"Your turn to take the load up," said one; a squat dwarfish man with a flat, overly large brow and no neck. David Whitlock tugged at the knot that cinched the sooty kerchief across his mouth and nose, shook it vigorously and arched his aching shoulders. When he knelt with thighs and back straight, his hair brushed the timber-braced ceiling.

"You don't need to remind me," he said. "I'll be glad to get up out of this hole for a breath of air."

"Don't take too long. If we can get this wagon filled by noon, Cochran will take it down to the trading post tonight. And you know what that means." The dwarf grinned through stubby blackened teeth.

David glanced at him, his eyes white ovals in a black mask. "One of these times, Will, Cochran isn't going to stay overnight. He'll come back early, catch you three with his missus and shoot you on the spot."

"And you too, Whitlock. He'll figure we all been havin' a bit," the squat man chuckled. "You'll go right along with the rest of us."

David snorted, blowing puffs of black from both nostrils, and crawled around to the back of the coal cart. "I'll be gone by then. As soon as I get enough to buy the mules, I'm through with this place. Another two weeks, maybe."

"And you'll be gone none the wiser for it. No women. No drinkin'. No fun at all. When you come here three or four months back, we thought we'd make a man of you before you left. But you haven'y give us much of a chance." Will grinned slyly. "You got unnatural desires or something?"

"I've got natural enough desires," David said. "But I'm not wasting them on the likes of Missus Cochran. It's wrong – and it cheapens the whole thing."

"Ah.... Now that Suzanna down at the trading post. Nothing cheap about that bit o' all right. Maybe that's what keeps Cochran overnight when he takes the coal down."

David's hand shot out like an exploding piston, catching the dwarf by the collar of his greasy shirt and pinning him against the rock, then relaxing as Will laughed coarsely and spit a black stream past David's arm into the dust.

"There. That got yer blood a churnin'. Maybe you should drop in on Anna while you're up on top."

David released the deformed man and looked up the shaft toward the distant entrance. "You're a rotten one, Will. You and Frank and Eli. And Anna Cochran, too."

Will scoffed. "And you? You're a fine one, mate. A little slap and tittle never hurt a body. You'd do well to learn a thing or two before you have to find yer way around that Shattuck lass."

David turned to face him again, sputtering in his anger.

"That's... that's all you'd know. Nothing's important to you. One woman's the same as another and you think they just exist for you to take your pleasure with. You'll never understand what it's like to really care for someone." He dug booted toes into the packed floor of the shaft and leaned into the cart, starting it slowly up the incline toward the entrance. Will laughed coarsely behind him.

David rolled the cart out onto a muddy flat in front of the pit, stretched his legs and back, then pushed the load to the edge of a deep sloping trench that held a large wagon. He rammed the cart against a bumper log at the edge of the pit and flipped it over onto the growing pile of coal, coughing and blowing black from his nose as fine dust rose from the wagon.

With a water bag that hung on a post beside the wagon pit he washed the gritty taste from his mouth and drank deeply. Beyond the pit to his left, another cart path led through low brush to a wide surface trench where Frank and Eli worked the second coal seam with Ellis Cochran. Tomorrow they would switch; David and Will to the open pit to mine a yard thick layer that stretched four feet below the clay surface, the others into the tunnel to dig the deeper seam twelve feet below ground.

David surveyed the clearing, breathing deeply of the clean April air. Above him, a cap of blackened snow still covered the bank into which the shaft disappeared. Below the slope gray snow patches spotted the forest floor beneath budding oaks and hickory. Across the clearing, its chimney spouting black coal smoke into an overcast morning sky, the Cochran cabin stood with door ajar. As David drank again from the bag, Anna Cochran stepped onto the porch, dressed in men's trousers and a loosely fitting work shirt.

He threw the strap of the water bag back over the post and watched the woman. She was sturdy and bronze skinned, colored like the Sac and Fox with raven hair that waved in unruly wisps about her shoulders. Her large dark eyes were deeply set below heavy brows that arched above a narrow, straight nose. But she lacked the high distinctive cheekbones of the Indians... and their cautious reserve. She was not a beautiful woman. But there was a lusty healthiness about her that made a man take a second look. According to Will, she had come up river from New Orleans with

Cochran without ever marrying the man.

"It's not like bedding down some other man's wife," Will reasoned. "She's like a she panther. Taking whatever howls the loudest."

As David watched her, considering Will's description, she smiled and walked toward him across the clearing. "Well, Mr. Whitlock. I see ya got a load 'bout ready to go. Ellis will be takin' it down to the crossin' this evenin', I 'magine."

David rocked the cart backward off of the coal pile.

"Yes ma'am. Looks like he might."

"The other boys know how lonely I get when Ellis is away... how lonely I get for a little company." She leaned against the post, folding her arms tightly across her stomach to spread open the top of her shirt and expose the tops of her full breasts. "I keep waitin' for you to come comfort me."

David had never been this close to her and could smell her through the coal dust that coated his nostrils. Heavy sweet rose water and pungent musk. A fine dark down rimmed her upper lip, accentuating the fullness of her smiling mouth.

"I keep pretty much to the shed...." David choked in mid-sentence, gulping back a catch in his throat. "...when I'm not working."

"Aw... that is so dull and so...wasteful. The others tell me how you could use some cheerin' up. Some excitement. Why don' you come over with them tonight?" David pulled the cart away from the wagon pit and walked around it, away from her.

"Thank you, but I'm usually worn out when I finish work. I'll just stay in the shed."

"I could make you feel *so* good. Take the aches right out you' tired back. Maybe a hot bat'."

"I don't think so." He rolled the cart back to the shaft.

"Think 'bout it while you' down there," she said, her voice husky. David bent low over the cart and disappeared into the opening.

Two hundred feet down the incline, Will sat with his back against the coal face.

"Have some company up there?" His white eyes shone in the dark hole. David crawled around the cart, lifted his short handled pick, and spiked it violently into the soft black wall. Will laughed.

"You must be quick. But then, for a first time...."

"Shut up," David snapped. "I have to work with you but I don't have to put up with your evil mouth." Will laughed again until he coughed black into the dust, but stopped talking.

Cochran took the wagon to the trading post that afternoon and Will, Frank and Eli washed in the creek, slicked back their hair and went to keep Mrs. Cochran from getting lonely. David lay shivering on the narrow plank cot in the shed behind the cabin, listening to their muffled talk and laughter. Though the days were warming, night brought on a damp chill that soaked through walls and clothing, coating blankets and the shed's meager furnishings with a dusting of frost by morning.

Curling his knees against his chest and wrapping the star-patterned quilt tightly about him, David thought of Suzanna. She seemed so distant. Beyond his reach. She had come to the trading post the morning after he left home, arriving on horseback through the deep snow as he fixed a breakfast of boiled dried venison and potatoes fried in lard. She unlocked the door with her own key and walked unheard through the store to the kitchen, hugging him from behind and kissing his ear.

"I saw you go by yesterday. I couldn't come out. But I saw you. What are you doing here?"

David pulled her to him and squeezed her until she protested.

"Had a big argument with my father. We'd both had enough of each other. So I left" He waved an arm as if throwing a stick.

Suzanna's face clouded. "Do you mean it? You've said you had differences, but...."

David nodded. "Yesterday they became *big* differences." He related the events of his logging mishap.

Suzanna listened intently, nodding from time to time.

"I know about the big gray one. My father's been after him for five years now, but he's clever. He always seems to get away, just as they think they've got him."

"I'd have split his head, if I hadn't dropped the caps," David said. "But then, I probably wouldn't be here with you."

"You don't seem especially upset... about leaving home, I mean."

David laughed dryly. "I feel bad about the mules. They were a good team. But I've been aching to get away from that cooper's shop. I just wasn't cut out to make barrels. Anyway, it's time I got a place of my own." He hesitated, watching her face. "It's time we both found a place."

She smiled sadly and lifted his hand to her cheek. "That's all I dream about. But it's going to be so difficult." She dropped their hands into her lap and looked down at them. "You know how my family feels... that you should be left alone and not kept company with, I mean. And things have gotten worse."

David snorted. "What could be worse?"

"Samuel's been doing more talking about the Mormons. I guess they... I mean your people... are gathering again in Illinois and he's afraid they will come spilling back over into Missouri to take revenge. I've heard him say he thinks we should expose your family."

David pulled his hand away slowly, feeling his face flush.

"Will he do it?"

Suzanna shook her head. "Not as long as he wants to work the homestead with the rest of us. Father wouldn't allow it. And you know how I feel." She reached again to touch his arm. "To me it makes as much sense as anything else. In fact, I don't think God cares much what you believe if you live as you should. And I think father would agree. But most people seem to think it important that they are right and everyone else isn't."

David frowned. "And that's not all our problems. My mother

hasn't said as much but she's had such a miserable time with my father since joining the Mormons. She'll be worried about the same happening to us, with you not believing."

"Maybe I could believe... at least as much as I need to," she began, but let the sentence trail away as each became lost in separate thoughts.

"We could run off," Suzanna said finally. "To St. Louis. Or even beyond."

David shook his head. "And be hunted by the Shattucks the rest of our lives? Your brothers would skin me raw if they caught us. And I'm tired enough of hiding. Running away is no answer."

"What then? What can we do?"

"I don't know. But there's a way. I know there is."

He brightened and pulled her to him playfully. "What are you doing down here anyway? No one will come by in this weather."

"Taking stock," she said, mocking seriousness. "Every good shopkeeper has to take stock of her supplies when she gets the chance."

David laughed. "With the snow waist deep? You could count the supplies in this place in a spare hour on a good day."

"You and I know that, but not a backwoods dirt farmer. And what's this smelly broth you're boiling here?"

They spent the day talking and touching. As David sat on the kitchen bench in the early afternoon with her curled beside him, she lifted her face and kissed and nibbled his neck.

"I saw you once," he said suddenly, "when you were bathing in the river." She pushed away from him, studying his face with an embarrassed flush.

"When?"

"Before we met in the woods the day we got the honey. I was hunting."

Suzanna leaned back slightly, her forehead furrowed. "What did you see?"

David sucked in a quick breath and arched his brows. "Most of you, I guess. You were beautiful. The most beautiful thing I ever saw.... Then I ran off...."

She cocked her head to one side. "Why did you run?"

He grinned shyly. "I just didn't know what to do. It didn't seem right to me to just lie there and watch."

She laughed and squeezed his arm.

"That's what I love about you. No other man I know would even think twice about watching. Everyone says you're different. They should be different like you."

"I wasn't entirely different," David admitted. "I decided that I was going to see you again. That's why I was in the woods above your place."

"You? I was the one who was arranging to meet *you*. I saw you talking to my father in front of the cabin... though I wouldn't say that I thought you were beautiful. But nice. And I didn't see nearly as much." She turned on the bench to sit facing him.

"Would you really marry me if you could?"

He glanced back at her, embarrassed by her frankness.

"I'd marry you in a minute."

"Even if I didn't become a Mormon?"

He hesitated. "I'd hope you would. It can be so hard when one is and one isn't."

She leaned forward and took his face between her hands. "You've told me your Prophet started this all because he wanted answers to questions that bothered him. We need answers too. If we're patient, maybe your God will give them to us."

David turned his face in her hands and kissed her palm. "I'll ask," he said. "And I'll try to be patient."

· · ·

As David sat in the chilled silence of the mining shack remembering the day with Suzanna, he was running out of patience. She had known of Cochran's coal operation through his dealings with the trading post and had sent him up to see if there was need for another hand. She had also agreed to keep the mare until Jacob came north again, asking him to take the horse south to trade for a good mule. With David's wages from the mine, at least his debt to his father would be paid. Then he could turn his attention to plans with Suzanna.

The cabin beside the shack was now silent. David rolled onto his back, stretched his cramped legs and pumped them in the air to warm his icy feet. He sat up stiffly, beating his arms across his chest to still rippling chills that rattled his teeth and brought goose flesh along his arms and back. As he groped for the stubby candle that sat behind him on a wall joist, the door slammed loudly open and spears of light from an oil lantern stabbed his eyes.

"Whitlock, you look froze stiff." It was Will and he was drunk.

"I am froze," David grumbled. "Keep that lantern here for a while so I can light a fire." He squinted into the glare of the lantern. Will wavered in the doorway grinning widely, a large steaming pitcher clutched in his unsteady hand.

"Better yet, we brought you somethin' to warm your troubled 'art." He set the container heavily on the empty bunk by the door and plopped down beside it. "Hot cider. The lady of the house warmed it up special for you."

David looked at the steaming liquid. "You know I don't drink that stuff. Wait till I get a fire lit and you can take it back in and drink it yourself."

"Nooo. Not a bit," Will said slowly, wagging his large head from side to side. "This is pure and fresh as my own mother's milk, bless her 'art, and fixed up special for you. Missus' orders."

David stepped over to the bunk and sat beside the pitcher, sniffing the acid sweetness of the rising vapor.

"Now, it's spicy, mind you. Cinni-mumun, and maybe a clove or two. But pure as if I'd stomped the fruit with me own two feet. Here." The dwarf waddled over to David's bunk, returned with the clay mug that sat beside the candle and poured it full of hot amber juice.

The mug was warm and comforting in David's hands. He lifted it and drew in a long spicy breath of steam.

"Come on, now then. You'd question your own dear mother, I think. Drink up, and you'll be cozy as a tater in hot coals."

David sipped at the cup. The tart cider nipped at his tongue and throat, glowing warmly as it reached his stomach.

"Too much clove?" Will asked, concerned. David shook his head.

"Feels good. Have some yourself."

Will rose, refusing his offer with an exaggerated wave. "No thank you very much. It's all for you. I have my own special bit of comfort in the house there." He leaned forward and winked slowly, lifted the glass on the lantern and lit David's candle with a lucky swipe, then rolled awkwardly out the door, pulling it noisily behind him.

David sat for nearly an hour in the soft flickering halo of the candle, drinking deeply of the warm cider, refilling his cup and drinking again. The warmth spread into his tired legs and stiffened shoulders, loosening the muscles, taut and cramped from crouching before the coal face. He felt the glow in his lips and nose. Even his hair seemed suddenly warm and he stroked it with his fingers, sending tingling ripples across his scalp.

He leaned loosely against the split log wall, enjoying the warm massage of the liquid. He was tired. Much more tired than he had realized. His arms and shoulders felt the weight of the day's work. Heavy. So tired... pushing him back into the wall and deep into the thinly covered cot.

He filled the cup again and drained half of it with a long draught, thinking of Suzanna. She spoke gently in his ear, whispering of love and longing, and tears welled in his eyes and streamed unrestrained down his face. He pulled the pitcher across the bunk and cradled it, then raised it unsteadily to his lips and poured warm juice into his mouth and across his chin and neck.

Beside him the candle flickered and grew, gradually enveloping him in its sad, melancholy glow. He drank from the pitcher again, sniffling loudly into its open mouth.

"My mother's missing me," he said thoughtfully into the jug. "She is so lonely." Before him in the growing circle of candlelight he saw her sitting, an open hymnal across her lap. David tipped the pitcher again, then lifted his face and voice in sorrowful song.

A poor wayfaring man of grief hath often crossed me on my way. And sue-d so humbly...

Behind him muffled laughter rose again in the cabin. David stood, staggering, and faced the offending wall, waving the pitcher and spraying its dregs around the crude shack.

"Quiet, you...you adulterers!" he shouted. The spreading glow began to shrink about him, closing tighter. With a sudden shattering crash, it went out.

. . .

David's mind awoke before his body, reeling painfully beneath leaden eyelids. It sorted through the jumble of thoughts that raced randomly through it, separating those that seemed most immediate. Dull throbbing ache. Shadowy light beyond his shuttered lids. Daylight. Softness. Thick warm softness. The bed in the back of the trading post. Familiar smells. Sweet – pungent. Sweat and... and rose water.

The heavy lids snapped open and David scanned the ceiling above through bleary eyes. Nothing seemed familiar. His head pounded, begging for his eyes to close again, but he resisted. Low ceiling of heavy planking. Twisting painfully to his right, he studied the lightly curtained window. Beyond, the sun was already above the trees and he wondered vaguely if he had slept for several days. He rolled painfully to his left and his body suddenly snapped to life, joining his racing mind. Arms and legs thrust against the soft mattress in unison, throwing him from the bed onto unsteady feet. On the far side of the bed, stretched languidly above the loose bed covers, lay the smooth brown back and raven tresses of Anna Cochran.

David searched the room frantically for his clothes. Nothing but a sheer pink robe and pink slippers. Snatching the top cover from the bed, he wrapped it about him, lurched into the main room of the cabin and out into the sharp morning air. Will, Frank and Eli sat near the wagon pit watching the doorway, laughing and jabbing at each other as David stumbled into the clearing. Will prodded Frank's hip with a stunted elbow.

"He look any different to you, Frank?"

"Can't really tell with him all wrapped up like that, Will. A little green about the gills, maybe."

David's face burned and he hesitated, glaring at the three through stinging eyes. Then he turned and lurched around the cabin to the empty shed. His clothes lay loosely piled on his wooden bunk, the clay pitcher shattered on the bare floor. His thoughts swirled and acid vomit rose in his throat. Could he have undressed and walked naked through the cold without remembering? And unconscious, how could he have...? He dressed quickly, stuffed his extra clothes into his cloth sack and rolled the star-patterned quilt about the bundle. Cochran would be on the trail by now... probably north of the Hill Spring Road. David left the cabin, skirted it on the side away from the clearing and plunged into the woods, turning west toward the river.

By noon he stood on the low bank that overlooked the pool where he had first seen Suzanna. Spring thaws had been gradual and the river was high and dark, rust colored and heavy with sediment. Stripping away his clothing he hesitated above the pool, then plunged downward into the dark cold water, sinking into its murky depths. The icy river scraped his bare flesh like coarse cloth, stinging his legs, groin and back until they numbed against the pain and cold.

Beneath the surface the water rolled and tumbled, twisting and turning him with crushing arms. Deadened fingers found the stone-paved bottom and he clutched desperately, lungs aching. Slowly he pulled his legs beneath him, felt the pressure of cobbles against his feet and thrust upward, bursting through the surface. He slapped at the water, struggling sluggishly toward the bank. A looped root stopped him from being pulled downstream and he dragged himself from the icy grip of the river, naked and spitting muddy water.

He lay on his stomach on a bed of soft mud, letting the spring sun thaw his limbs and the quiet of the woods salve his mind. As life returned to his body, he crawled upstream to his belongings, unrolled the quilt he had purchased from the fleeing Mormon family for a barrel and a keg, and wrapped it about his shivering shoulders. The Chariton rushed darkly below and he sat as a statue above the pool, gazing downward into its depths as the sun worked westward across the silent forest.

15

SUZANNA

Suzanna liked Ellis Cochran. He was a strong simple man, honest to a fault and eternally good natured. He arrived weekly with a deep wagon load of soft coal drawn by four dun oxen and spent the afternoon and evening shoveling the black, dusty fuel into Jacob Randall's wagons. When he arrived late in the day he spent the night in the small bedroom behind the store and was often dressed, loaded and back on the road before Suzanna arrived at sun-up the next morning.

She came an hour early on this Saturday morning, cooked the miner breakfast while he loaded provisions and sat across from him, trying not to watch too critically as he gulped the eggs, fried salt pork and biscuits.

"The man I sent up to you.... Mr. Whitlock. How is he doing?" Cochran threw back his shaggy head and laughed through his meal, then swilled it down with black coffee.

"So you thought you'd come in and cook me a nice breakfast, did you?" He wiped his mouth with a sooty sleeve. "I think I smell somethin' else cookin'."

Suzanna smiled. "I'm just interested."

"He's a good un," the miner nodded. "Stays pretty much to hisself. But the rest is a shiftless lot and I don't blame him much. Kin I be takin' him a letter for ya?"

She shook her head. "Just tell him I asked about him."

"Won't have no choice," Cochran laughed. "If he's not down in the pit, he'll be askin' bout ya before I git off the wagon. He's smitten, that one is."

"You've never mentioned it before," she said. "He couldn't be asking all that much."

Cochran's ruddy face softened. "I'm not a sharp-witted man, missy...as you well know. But I got a keen feelin' fer things." He lowered his eyes to the table, frowning. "Folks think I don't notice what's going on about me, but I do. The good and the bad. Noticin' I'm good at. Figurin' out what to do... well, not so good." He looked up again, brightening.

"Now you two. Y'er achin' ta know 'bout each other, but don't ask much. Ta me that means there's secrets to be kept and I'm not much of one to meddle in that."

Suzanna reached across the table and squeezed his rough hand. He pushed away from his seat, stuffing the two remaining biscuits into his jacket pocket.

"Best be gettin' on back. Yer friend is the only one who'll be doin' useful work 'til they hear me comin' up the trail."

Suzanna saw Cochran on across the river, then returned to the store to sort and stack a load of pelts that James Dickerson had delivered the afternoon before. Jacob or one of his teamsters would reach the outpost on Monday, pulling two wagons to replace the ones now brimming with coal. With the furs secured under the high box seats, the wagons would turn south again after only an hour's rest.

Suzanna hoped that Jacob would come. If he did, they would spend the hour talking about news from the south and of David Whitlock. Jacob alone seemed to understand. He never mentioned the Mormons, but he and Suzanna now talked without some things needing mention.

Across the room, blocked from her view by shelves of iron kitchen wares and leather work boots, the front door creaked loudly open followed by heavy-booted steps on the plank floor. Ellis had forgotten something. Or Jacob was here early for the coal. Suzanna knotted a final strand of twine about a pile of velvety beaver pelts, stroked the soft, coffee colored fur, and walked around the shelves toward the door.

As she passed the end of the boot rack, iron-clawed fingers bit into her shoulder, dragging her face into a dark tangle of beard. She stood motionless, holding her breath against the stench of the matted hair, choking back the scream that welled in her throat. Gradually the hand eased her away and she gazed into the face of the devil himself, one eye gleaming at her with dark hatred, the other a black shriveled socket.

Suzanna twisted against the tightening grip on her shoulder.

"You're hurting me," she said sharply.

"Where's the little man?" The bearded figure spoke in a low, gravelly whisper.

"Let go of my shoulder," Suzanna snapped. The towering man thrust her roughly back against a wooden shelf, clattering iron pots onto the floor about her.

"Where's the little Mormon lover that was here last time? We got a score to settle."

Suzanna swallowed hard, rubbing her bruised shoulder. "I run this trading post. I don't know who you're talking about."

The man's thick hand shot forward across her cheek, snapping her head back against the emptied shelf.

"Don't lie to me," he rasped. "He lied to me and he'll pay for it. Does he leave a woman here to protect him?" Suzanna blinked back angry tears, licked the salty sting from the inside of her bottom lip, and squared herself again toward the maimed face.

"I told you...." Her voice was low and intense. "I work here by myself." Again the man pinned her roughly against the shelves, clutching the tight material of her bodice and dragging her against his chest. The light cotton ripped in his grasp.

With jaw set tightly and teeth bared, she lashed upward with curled fingers, clawing at his good eye and slammed her knee into the man's exposed groin. He roared in pain, released her dress and doubled forward, retching violently onto her skirt. She spun away, bolting for the open door and lunged into the arms of another man who stepped from outside across the doorway, blocking her escape. She kicked out again, catching him in the thigh, and thrashed at his face with clenched fists. A third pair of arms wrapped around her from behind, pinning her own arms tightly against her sides and forcing her face against the outer wall of the cabin. The man in the rear jerked her right arm sharply up behind her back until she cried out and his bony fingers clutched at her arched neck.

"You move and I rip your throat open," he hissed in her ear. She stopped struggling, stretching to relieve the pain in her tearing shoulder as the two pushed her back into the storeroom.

The scarred demon knelt on the rough floor, staggering painfully to his feet as they forced her before him. Wiping sour spittle from his beard, he slowly drew a long corn knife from a scabbard on his belt and flashed the blade before her face.

"You damned Mormon whore. Don't she look like a Mormon whore?" He straightened as the others grunted acknowledgement. "Your coward husband left you to us, and we won't disappoint him." He scraped the side of the blade roughly across Suzanna's cheek. "You see this scar? I got it from a Mormon whore like you." His voice was low and bitter. "She slashed me with an ice hook. Ripped my eye out with an ice hook. But I've made them pay. A hundred times I've made them pay. And now it's your turn."

Suzanna strained against the arms that bound her, turning her face from the sharp steel of the knife.

"I am not a Mormon," she said coldly, her anger momentarily smothering her fear. "The Mormons have all gone east."

The man sneered. "Not all of them. We caught up with them that your husband said had gone south. They ain't leaving Missouri now."

"He's not my husband," Suzanna said slowly, clipping each word. "I just work for him. And he's not a Mormon either." She prayed silently that someone would come along the trail.

"Mormon. Mormon-lover. All the same to me." The man's lips curled into a smile. "You're like plague rats. Wherever you go, the sickness springs up again."

"If she ain't a Mormon, maybe we better leave her alone," one of the men said nervously. "She must be from around here...."

"I live just up the river," Suzanna said coldly. "With my three brothers."

"She's lying," the leader snapped. "She's that Mormon-lover's woman."

"I haven't ever known one of them to lie about it, Rogers," said the third. "It's sort of a martyr thing with 'em. She's no Mormon and must live up there where she says."

The man named Rogers squeezed Suzanna's face in his broad hand. "That little man lied to us and he's got to pay."

"Let's break the place up then," said the man who held her throat. "But I ain't killin' no regular woman."

Rogers sneered.

"We'll tear the place up. And I don't think we need to kill her. There's other ways." He slipped the knife under the buttons of her dress front and slowly sliced the bodice open.

"Ain't having no part of that neither," said the man and released his grip on her throat and arm. Suzanna stumbled backward, pulling away from the hand that held her face.

"You do what you want," Rogers said. "I'll take care of this myself."

Suzanna again sprang for the open doorway but he caught her flying hair and yanked her backward off her feet, falling upon her with the knife point tightly pressed against her throat. She heard the others retreat out onto the covered porch.

"Struggle, you little bitch." His good eye twitched nervously. "Struggle and I'll hang you inside out for that little Mormon-lover to find when he comes back." He ripped away the top of her dress and tugged clumsily at the lacing of her underclothes. Suzanna lay still, head arched back with the knife beneath her chin, his weight crushing her stomach. Her fingers groped frantically across the floor, feeling the fallen shoes and pans. Her right hand found the handle of an iron skillet. She gripped it firmly, unnoticed by the savage frenzy of her attacker. With a shrill cry, she lashed upward with the edge of the pan, slicing it into his ragged head. The big man bellowed and straightened above her on wavering knees, his black socket filling with blood that streamed down the pale scar into his beard. He shook his head blindly, spraying red drops across her face and naked shoulders. With a choking groan, he raised the gleaming knife, faltered, then crashed the fisted handle down across her temple. The room exploded into whirling, dancing color, then disappeared into total blackness.

. . .

David crossed the river two hundred yards above the trading post, balancing across a fallen tree until able to leap onto the muddy west bank. The plunge into the river had cleared his head and as he warmed on the bank beneath the star-patterned quilt, he felt a sudden passion to tell Suzanna everything, beg her forgiveness and take her to her father to express their desires. Then he would go to Shelbyville until he could buy new mules, bring them back up the Chariton, and take her away from this place.

She might be gone by now. Shadows from the trees west of the wagon trail stretched well into the river and a damp chill signaled approaching evening. If the store was deserted... that would be better. He could spend the night in the back room and wait until she came in the morning. He would have time then to explain – and to soften her disappointment in him. Then, if she still wanted him at all, they could plan what they would say to Thomas Shattuck.

Soft, silvery dusk veiled the building as he rounded the final turn in the river and looked along the stretch of rutted track that led to the main road and the trading post. In the fading light he could see the black square of the open door. She had not gone home. He stopped, straightening his tucked shirt in his trousers, then strode resolutely toward the store.

There were no lights. The door opening gaped dark as the mouth of the Cochran pit and he remembered suddenly his boyhood fear that if he stepped too close to the open cellar, he might tumble in and fall forever.

"Suzanna?" He stood on the porch peering into the darkness. She must be in the kitchen... with the door closed. But there was an oppressive quiet to the building that seeped out across the clearing like a gray winter fog. Nothing stirred in the evening woods. He stepped carefully, feeling with his feet and squinting into the blackness. The sharp sourness of vomit assailed his nostrils and his toe caught a metal object, sending it clattering through the hollow room. David stopped and crouched instinctively, sensing the chaos around him. As his eyes adjusted to the dim light he saw first the jumble of pans and shoes, then pale naked legs protruding from a loose stack of grain sacks.

"*Suzanna?*" His voice choked as he lurched forward, stumbling and crawling to the still body. "Oh, dear God. Please...."

She lay amid shredded clothing, head twisted back and mouth open. David hunched over her, a shuddering sob wrenching his chest, and pressed his ear against her naked, blood-spattered breast. Only the pounding in his own temples broke the silence of the dark room. He groped frantically for her wrist, found it limp and cold beneath his touch and stood whimpering, turning helplessly from side to side.

He knelt again, anxiously pressing his fingers beneath the turn of her jaw. Then more firmly, freezing his own breath and focusing every sense into his probing fingertips. A faint response. Weak. Unsteady. He searched lower on her neck and felt it again. Cradling her head in his hands, he kissed and washed her face with desperate tears, then stumbled through the dark into the bedroom searching for an oil lamp.

Hope failed as the lantern flickered over her stained and swollen face and body. An open gash beside her left eye oozed thickly down across her ear into a blackened tangle of hair. Her right cheek swelled across the bridge of her nose into the purple lump of her eye and her lips, split and swollen, were spotted red and pasty white in the lamp light. Folding tattered strips of dress and petticoat over her, David pressed a square of shredded cloth against her temple, braced her neck and head and lifted the limp body. Hatred burned suddenly in his face and stomach.

"Indians," he murmured, realizing as quickly as the thought came to him that this was not Indian work. It was too senseless. Too savage. Who would have been this brutal?

He laid her gently on the bed, covered her with its single blanket, and went to the kitchen to heat water. Unwashed breakfast dishes filled the dishpan. Someone had been here.

"Cochran!" The thought stunned him – dropped him heavily against the table. He shook his head. The miner could never have done such a thing. Unless.... David
slumped into a chair. Could the man have returned during the night, as David had warned Will that he might? David's affection for Suzanna was no secret in the coal camp, and in a jealous rage....

He started suddenly from his thoughts. Suzanna was still alive. She could tell him. He heaped kindling onto coals that still glowed in the iron stove, boiled water, and carried a steaming crockery bowl back into the bedroom. With soap and towels from the store he began to wash her splattered body, then stopped and stepped away. The blood was not Suzanna's. The stream from her gashed temple ran straight down into her hair, with streaks across her face where her head had been battered back and forth after the initial blow. But the blood on her chest had dripped from above. David bent again and gently touched the towel to her face. Her attacker was also wounded and would not be difficult to identify.

As the night deepened and chilled beyond the walls of the

trading post he sat beside her, wetting her swollen lips with a damp cloth and speaking to her softly. Thoughts tumbled about randomly in his mind. Could Cochran, even if enraged, ravage a woman like this? What had been done to her? Could she hear him? Know that he was with her?

"I'm here, Suzanna," he murmured, pressing his cheek against her face and kissing her swollen eyelids. "I will always take care of you."

A horse whinnied outside the trading post and the outer room danced suddenly with shadows from bright lanterns. David sprang to his feet, searching the tiny bedroom for a weapon. As he turned to bar the door with his fists and body, Samuel Shattuck stepped into the frame, lantern gripped high in one hand, a rifle in the other. He looked coldly at David, then down at the bruised face of his sister. Slowly he raised the rifle to arms-length, its barrel centered on David's forehead.

"Here! In here!" he shouted, eyes riveted on David's face. Footsteps hurried across the outer floor and Thomas and Lyman Shattuck joined Samuel in the doorway. Suzanna's father pushed past his sons and knelt beside the bed, his face ashen. He touched her face, feeling the warmth that was returning to it, and turned to David who stood stiffly gazing down the menacing barrel.

"What happened here?"

David continued to look straight ahead. "I don't know for certain. I found her beaten up on the floor outside."

Thomas looked back at his daughter. "How bad is she?"

When David didn't answer, he glanced up again. "Get that rifle out of his face," he snapped. Samuel slowly lowered the weapon, centering it between David's knees.

"I think she's pretty bad. I found her about dark and she'd been there awhile."

"What was you doing here?" Samuel demanded. David waited for Thomas Shattuck to quiet his son, but the father said nothing.

"I've been working up at Cochran's coal mine. I left this

morning and stopped here on my way south."

"Why didn't you come get one of us?" Samuel's voice was acid.

"And leave her here alone like this? Would you have liked that better?" David's
face and voice reflected his disgust.

"You did the right thing," the old man said. "And we can't take her home when she's like this. You boys go home and bring the wagon down in the morning."

"You need to bring some clothes. A nightgown or something," David said, still watching Samuel Shattuck. Her father looked quickly up at him, then lifted the edge of the blanket. Slowly his head dropped to the cover above her still breast and he held her close.

"Go," he said to his sons. "And bring some clothing."

"What shall we do with him?" Samuel jabbed the rifle at David. Thomas looked up sharply.

"Thank him," he said. Samuel hesitated, then turned and stalked from the room, followed by his brother.

David stood silently beside Suzanna's father.

"Do you have any idea who did this?" Shattuck asked finally.

David shook his head. "Ellis Cochran delivered a load of coal this morning. He's the only one I know has been here."

The old man shook his head. "Ellis could never do a thing like this."

"Whoever it was, Suzanna hurt him. She had blood on her... lots of it... that didn't come from the cut on her head."

"You cleaned her up?" Thomas looked at him with troubled surprise.

David nodded.

"Why were you here?" Shattuck asked. "It wasn't just passing through, was it."

David returned his gaze evenly. "No sir."

"Were you here to see her?"

"Yes, sir."

"You been doing this often?"

"Not for a while. I've been working up for Cochran and didn't get away much."

"But before? You was meeting here before?"

David nodded.

"What was the two of you doing here, when you met?"

"Talking. Nothing more. You know her well enough to know that."

Suzanna's father studied David with a long, searching look, then turned his attention back to the bed. "It wasn't her I was thinking of. You'd best be going wherever it is you're going,"

David hesitated. "You don't need to worry about me either. We met, but we didn't do anything wrong. And I'd like to stay here with her tonight... if I could."

Thomas Shattuck watched his sleeping daughter, his jaw set firmly and his hand resting against her swollen cheek.

"It's too late to travel anyway," he said.

16

DAVID

The spring months had been moody. Mist and wispy fog shrouded the forest at night, lifting during the day into vaporous clouds that hung like dusty curtains over the treetops, too melancholy to burst with rain and too brooding to be pierced by the pale sun. In June the skies cleared and the sun reaped its revenge with baking heat that turned the clay of the Hill Spring Trail into ocher brick. Wheels and hooves of early summer travelers ground the brick into deep, powder-fine dust that plopped heavily underfoot and swirled along the trail in gritty dust devils. In early July the moisture sucked from the ground returned again with humid oppression, smothering the slightest wisp of breeze under its sticky weight.

David slumped back against the porch wall of the trading post in a straight-backed oak chair, his thin shirt clinging in dark patches against his chest and arms. The woods were silent and nothing moved on the trail. At the crossing the Chariton lay flat and motionless, poured thickly between its banks.

He gazed absently across the dusty roadway at the two deep wagon ruts that wound northward along the riverbank into the trees. They had come for Suzanna the morning after her attack, a grim cortege with the men riding solemnly on both sides of the wagon, their wives driving the pair of yellow oxen. The wagon bed was piled high with quilts and blankets and they carried her bruised, sleeping body back through the store, still strewn with signs of struggle, and laid her between the soft layers. The women whispered and peered at David darkly, averting their faces when he turned toward them. They bore her homeward without looking back, the women sitting beside her and Thomas Shattuck driving the team. Four times since Benjamin had been to the trading post. She was conscious, but David knew little else.

"She's doing poorly," her brother said, turning from other questions.

The day after the Shattucks took Suzanna home, Jacob Randall arrived for the coal wagons. He rode north to the Shattuck cabins to ask after her and returned, shaking his head.

"She's bad, David. She's still not come to her senses and needs to take water. Tell me what you know about this."

David shrugged helplessly. "Not much more than I told you. I got here about dark. The door was open and things were scattered about the floor. There'd been some struggle and it looked like she hit whoever attacked her with a skillet. She had blood all over her that wasn't hers and the skillet had blood along one edge." As he talked, Jacob's face clouded.

"I've been thinking this thing over as I rode up to the Shattucks. I'm afraid I know what happened." David looked sharply over at the Englishman.

"Last year, just before I went down for the fall legislative session, three men came by. In fact, it was the night after the Mormon family stopped – the one you traded with for the quilt. The men wanted to know if I'd seen the family. I told them they went south but the men didn't believe me and went east after them." He paused, looking soberly down at his feet, then up at David.

"They told me I'd best not be lying. My guess is they found the family."

"Did you know these men?"

Jacob shook his head. "But I'd know the one again anywhere. A big ragged man
with a huge scar down his face."

"And one eye? His eye was gone?"

Jacob glanced at him in surprise. "You know him?"

David shuddered involuntarily, the muscles in his face tightening. "I've seen him before. The man's a butcher."

"Carries a long cutting knife?"

David nodded. "I saw him use it once to hack a wounded old man to ribbons."

The two moved into the kitchen and sat in the dimly lit room, hunched forward with elbows on the slab table.

"Why did you quit at the mine?" Jacob asked after several minutes. "I thought you planned to stay until you paid off both the mules."

David shrugged absently. "I had some trouble with the other help."

"I have the one mule for you," Jacob said. "That mare brought a good price. If you'd like, you can work here until Suzanna comes back. I'll count your wages toward the second."

"I've almost enough now, with what I made from the coal. I'll give it to you before you leave."

They sat again without talking, each lost in his own thoughts. Finally David stood and walked to the door of the kitchen. "I need to ask you something," he said to the Englishman.

"Must be serious. You usually just ask."

David nodded. "I think you know about my family," he said, turning his head to look at Jacob's face.

Randall nodded. "I've suspected for a long time."

"You're not a believer, are you Jacob," David said.

"You mean a Mormon? Not even close."

"No, I mean in God at all. Do you believe in God?"

Randall leaned back loosely in his chair and looked thoughtfully at this young friend.

"Does that make any difference to you?" he asked.

"I've been trying to understand what happened here," David said. "And what's been happening up here for the last few years. Somehow I have a hard time fitting it into any plan of God's that makes any sense."

"And what makes you think God has some plan?" Randall asked.

"That's what I've been taught," David said, looking through the door out into the shop.

Jacob chuckled cynically. "Most of us are what we've been taught," he muttered.

"And you're not?"

"I'd say I'm more what I've read," Jacob said. "So it's much the same thing."

"And what is that?" David asked.

Jacob put his hand to his chin and stroked it thoughtfully for a long moment. "I now believe that one of four things must be true about God," he said, turning in his chair to face David. "One possibility is that there is no God."

"I think about that sometimes," David admitted.

"It's also possible that there is a creator of some kind who made us all and then left us pretty much to ourselves. There is no right or wrong other than what we create."

"Not much of a God in that," his friend said. "May as well not have one."

"My thoughts exactly," Jacob said, "unless he's watching to see what kind of job we do when left to ourselves."

"It's also possible there is a God who has some set of principles He wants us to live by, but plays games with us. He allows people to try to seek out these principles, come to him in prayer, then gain an absolute conviction that what they believe is right when for most of them it can't be. Otherwise they would all reach the same conclusions. This God is either a jokester or a very cruel God."

"Or maybe He has an adversary who He allows to lead people astray," David interrupted.

"Ah yes. Satan! The devil himself," Jacob chuckled. "He's the reason used by every group that knows it is absolutely right to explain why every other group is absolutely wrong. Very handy, but still cruel on God's part for failing to provide a sure way to know which eternal entity is fooling whom."

David frowned. "So far, I'm not too happy about your choices. So what's your fourth?"

"There could be a God who allows us to approach him in many ways and is acceptant of all of them as long as they encourage goodness toward one another."

David thought about this one and nodded slowly. "And it's also possible, I would suggest, that there is a loving God who cares very much for each human soul."

"That's not much different than my fourth option," Randall said. "I think a God who loves every soul would provide as many ways to approach him as he possibly could. But I base my final choice on the evidence I see. What evidence do you see that God loves and cares for each of us? The purge that's going on with your people? The cholera that took my wife and half our town? The black men who we work like animals and treat even worse or the red men we lock away in camps? One can't help but be overwhelmed by the love...."

David stood in silence for a moment then asked, "So which of these philosophies do you accept?"

"I'm not certain," Jacob said. "I move regularly among the possibilities. But at times like this, I'm not hopeful."

"At times like this," David muttered, looking through the front door of the trading post and on up the river, "I'm not hopeful at all."

Jacob nodded and rose from the table. "A somber note to leave on, but I must be going now. Send word down if there's a change in Suzanna."

The merchant drove the full wagons south down the Chariton, the team pulling the second wagon tethered to the back of the first. David stayed on at the trading post, waiting for news of Suzanna that never came. At night he saw her in his dreams, smiling as she sprang lightly ahead of him onto the small island of her forest sanctuary. Some nights he woke in a chilling sweat as he came again upon her broken body lying in the rubble of the store.

Cochran brought coal to the store and appeared genuinely shaken by news of Suzanna's attack. He was not the culprit.

"I'm a bit surprised you let that randy bunch at the mine get to you," Cochran chided good naturedly.

"There are some things a man shouldn't have to put up with," David said soberly. The big miner nodded. "There's a bit o' truth in that," he said.

As David now sat in the muggy heat of the July morning, he heard again the sound of wagons coming up the trail behind the trading post and rocked forward on the oak chair, pulling the damp shirt from his chest. Jacob Randall steered his teams around the side of the long log building and reined them to a halt. Behind the second wagon stood a strong team of brown draft mules. David stood to meet his friend.

"If those are mine, I owe you another year's work," he said, smiling.

Jacob laughed. "Can't let your father think he isn't getting paid back in full. Your taking care of the place has been such a help that I owe you a little extra. What's the news from up river?"

David shook his head. "No word. Benjamin comes in sometimes but only tells me that she's doing poorly. He doesn't care for me much."

Jacob climbed down from the wagon. "I'm planning on staying overnight to give you time to take these mules up to your father. It wouldn't be proper for you to ride by the Shattuck place without stopping in to see how she's doing. My team is saddle broke. You can ride one, and lead the mules."

David quickly unhitched Jacob's teams, saddled the best trained of the draft horses and spurred the horse upriver, leading the brown team behind. As he neared the Shattuck cabins he slowed the trotting animals to a walk. The oppressiveness of the day settled suddenly on his soaked back and fearful questions flooded his mind, adding to his growing depression.

What if she didn't recognize him? Her head had been battered and he shuddered, picturing her with dull, vacant eyes, huddled in a dark corner of the cabin. And there would be other scars. Deeper scars.

As he worked in the lonely store and struggled to sleep in the closeness of the small bedroom, he often thought about it. Gradually, over time, he decided it didn't matter. She had been unwilling – just as he had at the Cochran pit – and virtue couldn't be stolen. Only given away. She could still be only his, and he hers. If there was a God – the God whom he had come to know before he fled into this wilderness – He knew their hearts and knew what had happened. Suzanna, David knew, might not feel so absolved. Her body might have recovered, leaving a scarred and ashamed soul.

The cabins were still as he approached and his hello went unanswered. He rode toward the houses in the rear, seeing far behind them in the fields the men hoeing knee high spears of green corn. One of the women knelt among squash and bean plants in a small garden beside the north cabin. She looked up, hesitated, then returned resolutely to her weeding as David approached.

"Good morning," he said as cheerfully as he could muster.

She continued to pluck at the invading weeds, nodding without looking up.

"I was riding up to my place and stopped to ask after Suzanna."

"She's not at home," the woman said curtly, eyes to the ground.

A tightening spasm gripped David's chest and stomach. "What's happened to her?"

"I don't know where she is," the woman said. "You'd better stop another time."

Someone called in the distance. David looked across the field of young corn to see Thomas Shattuck striding toward him, beckoning for David to come to him. He turned the mules from the garden and rode to the edge of the plowed ground.

"You're here looking for Suzanna, I suppose," the old man said as he drew close.

"Yes sir. I'd hoped I could see her. I had to come this way to...."

Suzanna's father waved off the explanation. "I expected you before now. She's off in the woods somewhere. She's been going off every morning since the weather warmed up. Don't know where exactly."

"How is she?"

Thomas Shattuck's face furrowed into a tired frown. "She's better, and again she ain't. Her cut's healed up. Left a nasty scar on the side of her head. But she seems to be thinking all right. She's so quiet though. Moody. She wants to be by herself most of the time."

David nodded, relieved and frightened. "Would she see me?"

The old man looked down at his boots, then off toward the trees. "She calls your name in her sleep. I've tried to get her to go down to the trading post but she won't."

"Do you mind if I see her?"

Thomas Shattuck turned grimly back toward him. "That hasn't mattered much before, has it?" He paused, studying the young man on the mule. "I don't much like what's happened, but she needs you now. I think it would do her good."

David turned the mules back toward the river.

"One other thing," Shattuck said. "She doesn't remember anything about the attack."

David turned in the saddle. "Does she remember other things?"

Her father smiled thinly. "She remembers other things."

· · ·

David tethered the animals where the brook tumbled noisily across the wagon trail into the Chariton and walked into the woods along its bank. A hundred paces from the river he crossed the forest trail, remembering his meeting there with the enchanting young woman in the thick shirt, trousers and broad brimmed straw hat. He pushed more quickly along the stream, slowing at the muted splatter of the spring ahead. She did not hear him enter the clearing but sat with her stooped back to him, staring into the white veil of falling water. He stepped quietly onto the soft grass of the islet and knelt behind her.

"Suzanna?" he said softly. She stiffened, sat motionless for a brief moment, then lowered her face into her hands and sobbed. He wrapped his arms about her trembling shoulders and drew her to him, his cheek against her soft hair.

Her shoulders were thin and hard beneath her dress.

"I love you," he said quietly. Suzanna shook her head and shoulders violently, tearing away from his grasp.

"Please go...."

He eased around and knelt facing her, lovingly lifting her chin with the curl of his finger. She covered her left temple with a frail hand, gazing desperately into his eyes.

"Leave me here," she pleaded, tears pooling at the corners of her lips and falling heavily onto her dress. Gently he pulled the struggling hand from her face. A pink scar spread like pale lips from the top of her protruding cheek bone into the hair above her ear. David studied the cut, feeling her anxious eyes, then cupped her face in his hands, turned it slightly and kissed the healing wound.

"You're a beautiful woman, Suzanna," he said, kissing her again. Her eyes brightened and she smiled faintly, sniffling against the tears.

"I've missed you so much," she whispered, her chin trembling in his hand.

"Everything's going to be fine," he said, and she again slumped forward into her hands, weeping bitterly.

"Oh, I wish...I wish that...." She choked back a deep sob, looking up at him again with pleading eyes. "The man.... Whoever hurt me...."

David felt his own eyes well with tears, feeling the pain in her face and body.

"I know. But it doesn't matter. You're the same to me."

"I'm *not* the same!" Her voice bit at him.

"I've thought about it a lot," he said. "And there's something I need to tell you. About me...."

She shook her head slowly, staring at the grass between them. "It's more than that. I...," She choked and slumped even lower onto the grass..."I'm going to have a baby."

David rocked back heavily on his heels, gazing at the thin, pale figure before him.

"*No.*" He shook his head slowly. "That can't be."

She reached for him, begging, and he drew away.

"Please," she whispered. "It's not my fault."

He stood suddenly and she knelt before him, her hair disheveled, cheeks sunken under darkly circled eyes. The pink-white scar throbbed above her pale face and her light gingham dress hung dry and loose in the heavy air. The forest closed in around David. Her whimpering grated at him and the air smothered him. She reached for him again and he let her grasp his leg but didn't touch her.

"Are... are you certain?"

Her sobs racked her frail body and she nodded against his leg.

He closed his eyes, still shaking his head, then pulled slowly away from her. "I need to think...," he said, stepping backward into the stream.

"David.... Please!"

"I need to think," he said again, turning and splashing down the stream toward the river. When he could no longer hear her pleading, he bolted forward, splashing and slipping through the stream into the forest. He ran blindly, scrambling and crashing through the underbrush until he reached the river and the tethered team. Spurring the animals to a gallop, he raced the mile to his parents' cabin, pounding the panic from his body against the broad back of his mount. As the mules entered the clearing he dismounted before they had come to a complete stop and stood panting in front of the house beside the lathered animals.

The doors of both cabin and workshop opened in unison. Lydia Whitlock rushed from the house with arms spread and embraced her son while his father stood silently beside the sod hut. David kissed his mother's cheek and turned to his father.

"Here are your mules," he said.

John Whitlock looked for a moment at his son, then eyed the team critically. "They look like a good pair."

"They're a better pair than you lost. Stronger and better trained."

His father grunted. "Better brush them down... and get yourself something to eat before you come to work. I can use your help."

"I'll be leaving after I eat," David said. "I have work down river."

His father looked at him without answer, then ducked back into the cooper's shop, closing the door after him.

"He's missed you," Lydia said, taking his hand and leading him into the cabin. "Your being gone has had its effect." She cut bread and scooped hot venison stew from a kettle over the fire. As he ate, she sat across from him.

"You've been digging coal, from what I've heard."

David nodded absently.

"That was a selfless thing you did... replacing the mules."

"I said I would." He scoffed. "And I'm hardly selfless."

Lydia sat in silence, watching his face and eyes.

"Something's happened." She placed a hand lightly on his arm and he pulled away.

"I return home after half-a-year away with a new team of mules and I don't get so much as a thank you. And you wonder what's troubling me?"

His mother smiled sadly. "You got a warmer reception than I

think you expected. I can't believe that your father's attitude is bothering you so much. It's something else."

David ate without answering.

"I believe it's probably that lovely girl down at the trading post," Lydia said thoughtfully. "I've met her, you know."

He dropped his spoon into the empty bowl and leaned back loosely. "And you think she's interested in me?"

"I know she is...and you in her. Before you left, I knew there was someone. When I met her I knew instantly who it was."

"Did she say anything?"

Lydia smiled. "Not in words. But she fussed over me like I was Mrs. Van Buren herself. I'm not a fool, you know."

David stared into his empty bowl. "I don't think there is a Mrs. Van Buren," he muttered. "And that must have been a while back."

"Oh, three or four months." She paused, raising a skeptical brow. "And she's lost interest since?"

"She was attacked in the store just after that. Hurt badly."

Lydia moaned softly and pressed his arm. "The poor girl. Is she all right?"

David nodded and lowered his head, the tears streaming down his cheeks. "They raped her," he choked, wiping at the tears with the back of his hand.

His mother pulled her hand away and sat erect, studying his face.

"Ah....And what do you think about that?"

David straightened and wiped again at his face, looked at her across the table. "I've known for a while. And thought about it over and over. I don't think it bothers me."

"But she's too ashamed and doesn't feel like she's worthy of you?"

David shook his head, his eyes again misting. "I saw her this morning... on my way up here. She's... she's going to have a baby."

Lydia was still, then nodded slowly, her eyes still fixed on her son.

"What did you say to her?"

He looked away, wiping his face against his sleeve. "I couldn't say anything." His voice was hoarse. "I ran. I was frightened. I...I felt trapped and suffocated."

"Oh, David...." Lydia pursed her lips and was silent for a moment. "Do you love her?" she asked finally.

David nodded.

"A great deal?"

"I thought so. More than anything. She's all I think about But this changes so much."

"What does it change?"

David looked up angrily. "*What does it change*? How can you ask that? The baby isn't mine. How can I want this baby that isn't mine?"

"It isn't at the moment," she said. "But if you marry Suzanna, it will be your child."

David slammed a fist down on the table top, knocking the bowl and spoon noisily onto the floor.

"You know what I mean. The baby isn't *mine*!"

Lydia was unmoved. "I understand your anger David. But what's done is done. The girl certainly didn't wish this upon herself and it can destroy both of you or neither one of you, as you choose. I've told you before that I believe that sometimes the heart speaks greater truth than the head. My feeling is that you can't walk away from this without it hurting you a great deal."

David sniffed sourly. "I not only walked. I ran. Like a flushed rabbit."

"But you haven't gotten away, have you? There are those things that you just can't hide from. We should know that better than anyone."

David rubbed the sides of the rough table with his fingers. "It hurts me already. She looked so...so...."

Lydia raised a quieting finger.

"Tell me," she said thoughtfully. "Whose child is this? Really, I mean?"

David's face reddened and his lips quivered.

"I don't know. But I have an idea. And if it is, it makes it all the worse. He's a killer. A monster."

"No. You're missing my point. Whose child is this?

David understood but did not answer.

"God's child," she said, pushing away from the table. "Here, let me read you something." She disappeared into the second room and returned with a thin, brown-covered book.

"I was given this by your friend, Mr. Randall. It's the poems of an Englishman. A Mr. Wordsworth. Some of them are wonderfully lovely." She thumbed quickly through the book, finding a passage that she had marked in the margin.

"Listen to this, David. See if this doesn't have a familiar sound to it." She lifted the book in the dim light of the cabin and read in a clear soft voice:

Our birth is but a sleep and a forgetting:
The Soul that rises with us, our life's Star,
Hath had elsewhere its setting, and cometh from afar:
Not in entire forgetfulness,
And not in utter nakedness,
But trailing clouds of glory do we come,
From God, who is our home

Lydia lowered the book, smiling. "God is our home. Yours. Mine. And this baby's. He entrusts his children to us to be cared for. You became mine to the degree that I care for you and love you. It is caring and love that make us parents. Not birth."

David shook his head slowly. "It's a wonderful argument. But by your logic, I have no father. And when this baby comes and its hair is black – not brown. And its eyes dark, will I be able to look at it and think 'you are my child because I care for you'?"

175

Lydia leaned forward intently. "Your father is not a man who knows how to show his caring. He fights it...afraid that it makes him weak and less a man. But he cares for you very much. And he's learned much from your being gone. He's out there now pacing back and forth, wishing he could come in and hug you and tell you that he knows you did your best against the wolves. Better than most men could. That he's proud of what you have done to replace the team. But he's too ungodly stubborn. He'll go to his grave that way." She leaned back again, her voice softening.

"And as for this other matter. Suppose you had married Suzanna and had not been able to have children. What then?"

Her intensity had taken David by surprise and he answered quickly.

"I imagine we would find an unwanted...." He saw the snare and swerved to avoid it. "But this isn't the same. Neither of us would then be the true parent."

"That's a terribly selfish thought, David," she said sharply. "Do you think she wants this? Do you think for even a moment that your agony is the smallest piece of her own?"

David was silent, eyes lowered.

"This baby is innocent," She said, the edge disappearing from her voice. "Suzanna is innocent. I have counseled you in the past but never directed, and I won't now. You do what your heart and soul tell you to do. You certainly are not responsible for this terrible thing and this is no time to be a martyr. Perhaps this tragedy will help you decide how much you really love her."

She stood and busied herself with the dishes as David sat, elbows on the table and forehead cradled in his hands. His mind wandered along wooded paths to the clearing where she knelt forlornly before the tumbling falls, hunched forward in her loose dress. He ached for her and wished he had not run. But could he love this child? This spawn of a man who had murdered David's own people with calculated pleasure? The killer wouldn't know, of course. Nor would the child. Only those who would say nothing.

But could he love this baby? Could he watch her cuddle it to her breast without hating it for what it had done to them?

"One other thought," Lydia said from across the room where she heated water over the fire. "You remember our discussions about true Christianity? I recall you having said once that you believe that true religion is not in acts of obedience, but in the intent and spirit of the acts. You might give some thought to what that means."

David rose from the table and paced across the plank floor. "I've said a lot of things. I seem to be having trouble doing any of them. And I'm starting to believe that if there is a God at all, he leaves us pretty much alone to make our way in the world."

Lydia turned, wiping her hands on her apron. "I know it is hard to believe at a time like this. But suppose you are right. What kind of a world will you be adding to if you can't acknowledge your love for this woman because of something she had no control over? And if you decide there is a God, does belief have any value without trying to fulfill its spirit and intent in practice?"

David chuckled cynically. "I was a child when we talked about those things. Life has taught me some hard lessons since. Don't condemn me by my old words."

"They don't condemn," she said. "But they may help at a time like this. I have a belief," she said, thrusting her hands into the pockets of her apron, "that there are two rivers of life that run through us all. One of light, and one of shadow. The decisions we make basically determine which of those streams will guide our lives. I think today you are standing between those two rivers."

David turned stiffly and walked from the cabin into the sweltering afternoon. The door of the workshop was still closed and he heard behind it the faint sound of plane against wood. His father loved him, she said. He snorted, thinking of Thomas Shattuck. Now there was a father who loved. The old man had said nothing to David the night they sat together with Suzanna in the bedroom of the trading post; just quietly held her hand. Yet he had allowed David to share his time with her, sensing that she would want it that way. And now that she was in trouble and a father's love was not sufficient, he was willing to yield to the love of another – someone he viewed with disapproval but who could take away her shame and heal her heart.

David's chest heaved suddenly with a shuddering cry and tears streamed unrestrained down his cheeks. He turned toward the house. His mother stood in the doorway, her face soft with compassion.

"I need her," he choked, hearing the workshop door open behind him. Lydia nodded silently. Without looking back, he walked quickly to the path that cut through the woods to the stream. As he entered the forest he broke into a trot, then ran frantically along the path, dodging and ducking until he reached the brook. Thrashing westward along the stream, he burst breathlessly into the clearing below the spring. Suzanna was gone, the grass where she had been still crushed in an uneven circle. For a moment he panicked, turning wildly on the grassy island as if expecting to see her lying lifeless a few feet into the trees. Had she gone to the river? Deeper into the woods? He leapt the stream and plunged again along the path laid by Suzanna's frequent visits to the spring, running until he reached the Shattuck clearing.

Suzanna's brothers still worked the field of corn far to his right. David paused, struggling for breath, and searched for a white head among the men. Thomas Shattuck was not with them. He stumbled forward again past the empty garden of beans and squash and around the side of the front cabin. Her father stood in the open doorway, arms folded tightly across his chest, his leather face chiseled.

"Is she here?" David asked, gasping for air. Shattuck did not move.

"I...I know I hurt her. I was surprised. Frightened. I needed time to sort things through."

The old man remained silent.

"I love her," David said simply, meeting his cold gaze squarely. "I want her... and the baby."

Thomas Shattuck's face began to thaw.

"When I sent you to see her, I expected some help from you. Not more trouble."

"But you didn't tell me.... I wasn't expecting...."

"It wasn't my place to tell you. She's the one had to do it. And it sounds like you weren't man enough to hear it."

David pulled in a long breath and stood erect. "I told you. It scared me. Like suddenly being told by somebody you love that they're about to die and not knowing what to do."

The old man's face flushed beneath his weathered skin and his eyes became distant. He stood looking through David at some moment in his past, then unfolded his arms and stepped from the doorway.

"She's inside. I don't know what happened, but it can't happen again. If you go in now, it's got to be because you know what you're doing." David nodded and stepped past him into the cabin.

"She's in the loft."

He climbed the sloping ladder to the plank platform, seeing her slight figure curled tightly on a bed against the back wall. Crawling onto the rough floor he rose to a crouch beneath the low roof and moved slowly toward her. In the dim, deeply shadowed light from the door below, he could see her back rise and fall unevenly in fitful sleep and knelt beside her, gently touching her shoulder.

"Suzanna?" She stirred, breath quickening.

"Suzanna?"

Her breathing stopped as her eyes opened, looking into the wall, listening for what she feared had been only part of her dream. He bent over her, kissing her ear and she began to weep softly.

"Why have you come back," she whispered.

"I've come to take you with me."

She closed her eyes again, remaining on her side.

"I can't bear any more. Please leave me alone. You have no obligation to me."

David slipped an arm beneath her and turned her gently toward him.

"You're wrong," he said, drawing her close without resistance. "I love you, Suzanna. Very much. And there's obligation in that. To you. To me... and to the baby."

Slowly she wrapped her arms about his shoulders, her slim body shuddering as she wept. He rocked her on the low cot until she ran out of tears.

"You're all I've wanted for so long," she said. "How could this happen to us?"

He pressed his cheek against her hair, speaking softly into her ear. "Not so long ago you asked for an answer to our problems. My mother now knows about you. Your father about me. And both seem happy to have us together. What more can we ask?"

Suzanna nuzzled against him, kissing his neck. "I didn't want this kind of answer. I'm so sorry...."

He silenced her with a finger across her lips. "I don't want to hear that. Ever again. We can't always pick the answers we get. Today we start over."

He sat as she packed her belongings into a rough wooden trunk and carried it for her down the loft ladder. Her father stood in front of the cabin with his oxen yoked to the wagon, three large sacks of provisions already in the wagon bed.

"Bring the team back soon," he said as David lifted the trunk in beside the sacks. "I don't want you gone too long." He wrapped his daughter in his arms, her face against his worn cheek, then turned her firmly back to David.

"Take good care of her, son," he said.

Suzanna stepped to the wagon, then turned suddenly to her father. "What about the others? Samuel? Lyman...?" The old man shook his head and lifted her up onto the high seat.

"Not now. Maybe later."

David snapped the reins across the backs of the team and turned them toward the Chariton trail. Suzanna waved until the cabin was out of sight behind them, then grasped his arm tightly and rested her head on his shoulder.

"We'll stay with Jacob at the trading post tonight," David said. "I'll ask him to return your father's team and get the horse I left at my parents' cabin. He can break the news to them. I want us to keep going tomorrow until we find the first clergyman. By tomorrow evening... well, who knows, Mrs. Whitlock...."

17

SUZANNA

James Keyte's store in Brunswick needed the same woman's touch that had transformed the trading post on the Chariton River. Within twenty minutes of her introduction to Reverend Keyte, Suzanna had convinced the man that she was the person who could do it. She met with him at the store the morning after the Whitlock wagon creaked noisily into the small town of twenty homes at the confluence of the Missouri and Grand Rivers and stopped at the shop, asking if its proprietor knew of any cabins to let. Mrs. Keyte was tending the shop and suggested they go to a yellow frame home across the dusty road.

"Taylor and Frances Wisdom still have their cabin out on the edge of town and I don't believe anyone is in it," she said.

"Could you use any help in the store?" Suzanna asked as Mrs. Keyte walked them to the door.

"Oh, Lord be praised!" the woman said, taking Suzanna's arm. "Do you know how to keep shop? We've been needing someone since the baby came. I just can't seem to manage everything!"

"I was shopkeeper for a store up on the Hill Spring Trail," Suzanna said confidently. "Ran it mostly by myself."

"Be here in the morning at 9:00 to meet with the Reverend," Mrs. Keyte said. "And thank you Lord!"

When Suzanna met the Reverend in the wood framed shop that stood a hundred yards up the main street from the river dock, Mr. Keyte was alone in the store. Suzanna told the minister about the changes she had made at the trading post and walked him through the shop, suggesting additions that could be made to dry goods, clothing items and confections. Before they returned to the front counter, the Reverend offered her the position and asked her to stay to finish the day.

"You've made my life much simpler," he said with a smile, "and much more peaceful."

"You've made mine much less stressful," she said with a laugh, then added, "...and I understand you also have a saw mill. Could you use an able hand who is also a skilled cooper?"

The Reverend chuckled. "Is he as capable as you?"

"Oh, much more so," she said.

"Send him to the mill tomorrow," Keyte said. "It's on the road west of town. I could use another good man."

"He's gone there this morning," Suzanna smiled. "If you're going there now, you'll probably find him looking for work."

As Suzanna arranged the new women's hats that had arrived that morning by river from St. Louis, she thought about how much her life had changed in a month's time. She and David had reached Jacob's trading post late on their first evening together, finding the Englishman gone and the thick plank door locked with the heavy iron padlock. Suzanna retrieved the spare key from under the step ledge and David dug candles from one of the boxes of provisions to light their way into the dark interior.

They had eaten a meal of brown bread and cheese as they traveled south but Suzanna started a fire in the iron stove to make tea.

"You can sleep in the back room," David said as he stoked the flames with coal from a bucket beside the round iron stove. "I'll lay out some blankets on the floor here and wake you when I get the team harnessed in the morning."

"I would be willing to share the bed," she said shyly, holding his hand against her cheek. "You could just hold me close...and I know we can wait until...."

He turned the hand to cup her face. "Maybe you can," he smiled. "But I'll be safer with a door between us. We'll start at first light. When I took a load of barrels to Hannibal a few months back I went south down the river and passed through a settlement called Bloomington. It's about half a day south of here and they were putting up a little church. We should get there by early afternoon and can find a minister."

She didn't argue with him about sharing the bed, knowing he was right. She yearned for him so badly her body ached and she curled around her pillow on the soft mattress in Jacob's back room imagining the next day, wondering if she would ever be able to sleep. The next thing she remembered was David shaking her gently to tell her it was morning and the wagon was ready.

At the tiny settlement of Bloomington, a cluster of eight log cabins that huddled beside the Great Trail as a spur wound west from Hannibal, they stopped at a home beside a log building with a roughly hewn cross fitted to its ridgepole. Suzanna stayed on the wagon seat surveying the row of cabins while David walked to the plank door. Though the day was warm, no one moved along the road and there was no activity around the cabins.

"I wonder if anyone is living here now?" she said to David and in answer, the door swung open and a small, jovial man stepped into the afternoon sunshine and squinted at the couple.

"Afternoon," he said pleasantly.

"Afternoon," David said, shuffling awkwardly and offering the man his hand. "We're looking for someone to marry us...."

"Rather marry you to each other," the man said, grinning broadly and pausing until he realized neither had caught his attempt at humor. "Joseph Owenby. Where you folks from?"

"Upriver from here about half a day," Suzanna said. "No ministers up our way and you are the closest one."

"Must be the season," Owenby smiled. "You're the third couple this month. Didn't realize there was so many folk scattered about in this part of the state and all wantin' to git married.

Anyone with you?"

"Just the two of us," she said.

"That's all we need. 'Cept a couple o' witnesses." He turned back and called into the house. "Kate, got another weddin'. Can you go for someone to be a witness?"

Suzanna glanced again at the quiet row of cabins. "Where are the other people?" she asked.

Owenby looked down the road as if the question puzzled him, then brightened. "Our fields are back through the woods along the river. There was a place there where we didn't have to clear too much timber. Everyone will be there workin' on the crops. I'm just gettin' a sermon ready for Sunday."

"So you're a minister and can marry us legal?" David asked, looking from the cabin to the log building with its makeshift cross.

"Been called directly by the Word o' God," Owenby said, "and ordained by the Holy Spirit hisself. And anyhow, Macon was just made a county and this here's the County Seat. I'm also a county judge and justice of the peace. Gotcha covered either way, if you got a dollar."

"I've got a dollar," David said, reaching for the leather pouch in his pocket as Owenby's wife Kate emerged from the cabin wiping her hands on her apron, nodded pleasantly at the couple and hurried toward one of the other homes that formed the small settlement.

"Save it til we git to the signin,'" Owenby said, helping Suzanna from the wagon seat and ushering them toward the log church. "Come on in and we'll git you two hitched up."

The interior was dim and musty and smelled of mice and damp wood. Twenty wooden chairs stood in four neat rows facing a rough wooden lectern and Owenby walked them to the front, pushed the first row of chairs to the side and opened shutters on two side windows. The stream of sunlight fell squarely on the lectern and brightened dust particles that hovered in the air like a thousand tiny jewels, giving Suzanna the first sense that she was in a sanctuary. Owenby returned to the lectern and picked up a slate and short nub of soapstone.

"What would the names be?" he asked, and wrote them as David gave him their names and birthdates. Kate Owenby entered the church bringing a tall, angular woman with her. "This is Julia Hutchison," she said. "She'll be bein' our other witness."

The Reverend Owenby, Justice of the Peace, clustered them all in front of the lectern with Kate and Julia standing at either side. He smiled brightly at the couple and Suzanna felt suddenly very alone. She had dreamed of this day all her life, imagining that she was standing before an alter in a new store-bought dress with a garland of spring flowers woven into her hair. Maggie and Judith were at her side and her family and all the settlers from along the Chariton were gathered behind her. But here she was in a musty log room with two strangers, wearing the plain cotton dress she had had on for two days . She pressed closer to David and blinked back tears that she wasn't sure came from her consuming love for this man or from her fear that he was all she had left in the world.

Joseph Owenby cleared his throat, interrupting her thoughts.

"David Whitlock, do you take Suzanna Shattuck to be yer lawful wedded wife?"

David looked at the little man in surprise, seeming to have expected some other preliminaries to the ceremony.

"Whatdaya say?" Owenby prompted.

David nodded. "I do."

"And do you..." he glanced at the slate, "...Suzanna Shattuck, take David Whitlock to be yer lawful wedded husband?"

Suzanna pressed against David's shoulder, forgetting the garland of flowers and knowing that the tears were because she loved this man so much.

"I do," she said.

"Y'er now man and wife," Owenby said. "You can kiss the bride."

"That's it?" David said, giving Suzanna a puzzled glance.

"All it takes," Owenby said. "No sense keeping you two single any longer than need be. Ya got a place to stay tonight? Hutchison's got a nice little barn you kin stay in."

David turned Suzanna to him and kissed her softly, then pulled her tight against his body. She felt the aching grow and wrapped her arms around him, tears streaming down her face.

"We're headed down to Brunswick," David said. "We'll sleep under the wagon tonight."

"Suit yerself," Owenby said. "You need to stop by the court house – that's the second cabin down the road on yer right – and sign the book. You can give me yer dollar then."

As they drove south along the rough track that led toward Brunswick, Suzanna couldn't get close enough to David. She pressed against him, nuzzled her head against his shoulder and finally pulled one of his hands away from the reins and looped his arm about her shoulders. Neither spoke for a long while, each lost in thoughts about what it now meant to be married.

"Not much of a wedding," David muttered finally. "I'm sorry."

"Not much of a minister," Suzanna laughed. "Do you think we're really married?"

"Better be," he said. "I'm planning on it."

They rode another mile without speaking. "Maybe we should find a place to stop before too late," she said finally. "I don't see any reason to keep going 'til dark."

"Do you think anyone else is going to be coming this way?" he asked.

"I don't think there's anyone but us between here and Brunswick," she smiled.

"Start looking for a good place to stop," he said.

They pulled the wagon into a small clearing beside a shallow creek, unharnessed and watered the team, then hobbled them in the meadow.

"Would you like me to start some dinner?" she said, poking nervously into one of the boxes of provisions.

"All I want is you," he said, wrapping her from behind and pulling her onto the grass.

"Let me get some blankets," she said, feeling her heart quicken and a warm flush run through her body. "Shall we get under the wagon?"

He lifted her back to her feet and they pulled blankets and the star-patterned quilt from the wagon seat and David spread them out in the clearing. "You said there was no one between here and Brunswick. Who do you think will see us?"

"This just seems so... open," she said, looking around them.

"It's a beautiful day. Let's enjoy being out in the air," he said. "I'll go feed the mules and you can get ready and between the blankets."

Suzanna paused and looked away from him, the flush burning in her face. She also had often thought of this moment as she curled in the loft of her father's house. What she knew about the physical part of love between a man and a woman came from living with animals all her life and from her sisters-in-law – and that was scarce little. From the livestock she knew how things worked. From her sisters-in-law she learned that it generally wasn't a shared partnership. When the subject came up as they sat together sewing, Judith seemed embarrassed and ashamed to talk about it at all and usually just said, "Men have their needs and women have their duties." But Mary was more open and had once turned to Judith and said, "Women have their needs too, but men just don't want to take the time to care about them. I've started telling Benjamin when he comes back from his days on the road that he can't just get off one mare and climb on this one. Gotta rub this one down a little first."

Judith had blushed bright red and muttered, "Oh, Mary, you sound like some kind of a harlot...," but Mary only laughed.

"Maybe they know some secrets we don't," she said, and turned to Suzanna who had wanted to ask Mary what it meant to be rubbed down, but then thought it might be better to just imagine.

"And, Suzanna, when your time comes, make him be patient. You've got something he wants worse'n a bear wants honey, so he's going to do whatever you tell him. So tell him he needs to take time for both of you... right from the start."

As she stood in the meadow on the warm afternoon of her wedding day Suzanna wasn't entirely sure what it was that needed time for both of them. In her day dreams she had been in a fancy hotel room in Quincy or St. Louis, had just taken a warm bath and was standing beside a wide soft bed with a thick eiderdown. She had dabbed rosewater beneath her ears and between her breasts and the room held the faint smell of roses. But as she looked across the meadow thick with summer grasses and bright with wild daisies and black-eyed Susan, she decided this might be even better. A light breeze rustled her hair and the late afternoon sun was warm against her face.

"I'm a little frightened about this, David," she said softly.

He took her hand and looked down at it as he spoke. "I guess I am too. And I know you've got to be thinking about the trouble you had...."

She shook her head firmly and squeezed his hand. "Oh no! It's not that at all. I don't even remember anything about that. I just don't really know...what to do." She paused, then said quietly, "Have you been here before?"

His face reddened and he swallowed hard. "You're the only woman I've ever wanted to be with," he said.

They stood in awkward silence with the meadow humming about them until Suzanna decided David was waiting for her to take the next step.

"Go take care of the mules," she said finally. "We have the rest of the night to figure this out."

"Maybe we *should* get beneath the wagon," he gulped. "I'll go around to the other side and you can get covered and I'll come under with you."

She smiled and nodded at the quilt on the grass. "This will be perfect as it is," she said.

It had been perfect and Suzanna finally knew what it meant to love someone with every fiber of her body, heart, and soul. As twilight fell, they stretched side-by-side with their hands playing over each other as the sky darkened, sparkling from horizon to horizon with a brilliance Suzanna never remembered seeing before. A three-quarter moon crested the horizon, bathing the meadow in a soft golden glow, and they walked together to the stream and slipped into a shallow pool, wrapping around each other as if their skin and muscle and bone kept them from being close enough. When dawn broke she found them lying beside the wagon still wrapped together in the starred quilt, neither wanting to let go for fear of losing something that had been so indescribably wonderful that it might never happen again. But it had happened again, over and over, and each morning she awoke not wanting to let go but knowing that even when she did, one was now part of the other in a way that could never be separated.

As Suzanna arranged the hats in James Keyte's shop on the dusty main street of Brunswick, she hummed to herself as she basked in the warmth of those moments. She knew that she was fortunate that Sheck Rogers had knocked her unconscious before he assaulted her. She had no memory of that night after the men came into the trading post and to her, David's consuming love was all she knew of close physical contact with a man. She wished she could sit again with Mary and Judith and tell them that there was so much more than just being rubbed down or doing one's duty.

The bell tinkled over the door and Suzanna turned from her display.

"Well, aren't you a picture," he said, smiling broadly and opening his arms to her.

"Jacob!" she exclaimed and rushed to him, hugging the little

Englishman until he gasped for breath.

"It's good to be welcome!" he laughed. "I'm on my way to the capital and knew from your letters that David was working at the mill and you at this shop. So I took the long way round and came by to see the married couple. Didn't see the mill as I came into town so I stopped here first...."

"Can you stay for dinner? We've talked every day about when you might be coming. David will be so happy to see you."

"I will indeed," he said brightly. "And I'll stay here in the inn this evening. I have something I'd like to talk to both of you about."

"How mysterious," she said. "Can you tell me now?"

"I need to talk to you both and we can at dinner. But I'm gone too much from Shelbyville now. I can't keep up with my own enterprises. I'd like you and David to come manage them for me. I could pay you a decent wage and would be willing to give you half of any new profits above what they currently make...and you could develop your own to add to them. It's turning into a very good place to do business. Plus, I could see you much more often."

"Well, my!" Suzanna arched an interested brow. "You'll have to talk to David, of course, but it does sound enticing. You should stop at the mill. It's just along the road on the other end of town."

"I'll drop my things at the inn and go see him now," Jacob said. "I would like very much to know what you both think of the idea before I leave tomorrow." He gave her a lighter hug and she followed him out onto the porch.

"Join us for dinner at 7:00," she said. "David can tell you how to find our home. It's very simple, but always open to you. So good to see you, Jacob."

She stood on the porch and watched him lead his horse up the street toward the new inn that stood at the intersection with the wagon road to Jefferson City. David wasn't content at the mill. There was so much more he wanted to do. But Reverend Keyte had been good to them both and she didn't care for the thought of leaving the shop after only a few months. The young wife of Hyrum Morris had spoken to her about working at the store and seemed to have a knack for figures and for knowing what would sell. Perhaps she could offer to school the girl for a few weeks....

18

JACOB

The activities of Sheck Rogers had become a matter of special interest to Jacob Randall. As accounts of the atrocities committed by the one-eyed killer filtered south to Jefferson City, he was viewed by some as a vigilante – a folk hero reaping vengeful justice upon the few remaining Mormons in Missouri. To most, Randall included, he was a cold blooded murderer.

During the summer of 1840 the Mormons, now settling in growing numbers in Illinois, petitioned the Congress of the United States for redress for losses suffered in Missouri. Rogers responded with a series of brutal attacks in the northeast. Reports reached the capital that he and a small band of armed henchmen had crossed the Mississippi into Hancock County, Illinois, set upon four Mormon men on the road north of Quincy, and dragged the captives back across the river to the settlement of Tully. There the victims were stripped naked, hanged until unconscious, then revived and beaten with gads until the flesh of their backs hung in shreds. The men, barely living, were locked in a smokehouse and left for dead, saved only by a passing farmer who heard moaning cries from the isolated shed.

Through a network of sympathetic north woods informants – Indians, trappers and settlers – Jacob traced Rogers' bloody trail through 1841 and '42. In the late summer of the first year, a family traveling north along the Smith's Trail toward Nauvoo was massacred beneath their wagon as they slept. Roger's signature was on the work. Both the man and woman had been savagely butchered after the murder.

The following spring as ice cleared on the Mississippi the

riverboat *Memphis Star*, plying upriver from the Ohio with a load of Mormon converts, mysteriously burst into flame above Hannibal. A lone survivor, dragged burned and in shock from the freezing water, babbled about river pirates and their giant one-eyed leader. The band had boarded from small boats, doused the decks with fuel oil, then retreated to their skiffs where they hurled torches onto the deck and sniped at terrified passengers who plunged from the inferno into the icy river.

News of the riverboat disaster reached the state capital from the east, brought by boatmen on the Missouri and passed to the unfinished senate chambers of the new capitol building through an intricate grapevine that connected the waterway with the seat of government. The session had just adjourned for the day following uninspired debate on the issue of compensation for runaway slaves. Jacob Randall slumped back in his chair, exhausted at having accomplished so little. Like the session, the chamber in which he sat was incomplete, still without plaster on the walls after six years of construction. So many things seemed incomplete at the moment and he was anxious to get away from the building, the issues, and the people around him. As he gathered his papers together Austin Noland approached through the labyrinth of polished desks. A sardonic smile creased his smooth, flawless face.

"You heard, I assume, about your boatload of Mormon friends."

Jacob looked up at him, expressionless. "Since I don't know what you mean, I assume I have not."

"Burned on the Mississippi and sank to the bottom near Hannibal. Everyone lost, I'm told."

"That's tragic," Jacob said, turning back to his scattered papers. "I'm surprised you seem to take such satisfaction in the report."

"They're massing again in Illinois, Randall. Thousands of them like locusts to ripening grain. It won't be long, I guarantee it, before they swarm across the river to reclaim their Zion."

Jacob pushed the papers together into a neat stack and tucked them into his leather grip.

"My guess is that they've had quite enough of us for some years to come," he said coolly.

Noland laughed. "They have short memories. Perhaps we should lend this fellow Rogers to Illinois and let them turn him loose on the fanatics before they come back. From what I hear of this boat incident, it was his work."

Jacob looked up sharply. "Sheck Rogers? What did you hear about him?"

Noland shrugged. "Apparently they dragged a man half frozen from the river. Before he died he talked about a one-eyed man who had boarded the boat and doused it with fuel. Couldn't be anyone else." The senator from Jackson County paused, obviously amused by Jacob's sudden display of interest and distaste. "You're not too keen on this Rogers, are you Randall?"

Jacob snorted. "He's a madman. A murderer with no regard for life nor law. As one who is entrusted with making the law and one for whom life holds a certain sacredness, I can't very well condone his behavior."

"There are some situations," Noland said blandly, "for which the law makes no acceptable provision. What does one do in a democracy, for example, where free voice and practice are held at such a premium, when one voice develops in the body politic that is so cancerous that it begins to destroy the life of the system? The body can't destroy it. By doing so it would carve at its own strength; free expression. Instead, it must find a surgeon; someone who cuts away at the disease without directly feeling the pain."

"A fascinating metaphor, Mr. Noland," Jacob said evenly, "and one that displays your usual lack of compassion. I prefer to think of those voices of dissent as conscience rather than cancer. And when we or anyone else quiet them, we become not healthy, but unconscionable."

"Ever the crusader," Noland chuckled. "And what of action? Do we allow any action to be similarly unrestrained?"

Jacob fixed Noland's pale gaze firmly with his own. "That

seems to depend," he said, "on whether the actions are merely a desperate attempt to protect the voice or a vicious effort to silence it."

As the two stood eyeing each other with open contempt the high carved doors of the chamber pushed open and a breathless page hurried onto the floor, surveying the remaining senators with a sufficient sense of importance that all eyes turned to him.

"More news," he announced. "Bad news. Former Governor Boggs has been shot by an assassin at his home in Independence."

An uneasy murmur rippled through the assembled lawmakers. Jacob frowned, struggling to keep the impressions that surfaced in his mind from becoming thought. He despised Boggs as a man but he had just spoken of the sanctity of life... and he should not now choose to be discriminating. Plus, this would be fuel to the fire.

"I have some details," the page called above the growing din of excited voices, waving a crumpled paper. "It was a blast of heavy shot from close range. Through a closed window as he read."

"Is he dead?" a voice asked from the back of the chamber.

"Not at this report." The page reviewed his message. "Four balls entered his neck and head, but he was alive when the messenger left Independence. A large German holster pistol was found below the window – stolen recently from a shop in the area."

The Chamber hummed again with conversation.

"An interesting coincidence don't you think, Mr. Randall?" Noland frowned. "A boatload of Mormons sinks and burns on the Mississippi, and their archenemy is mysteriously shot by assassins."

"Particularly coincidental since the incidents must have occurred on opposite sides of the state, over two hundred miles apart, at approximately the same time. Hardly related, I should think," Jacob said dryly.

"They had a hand in this attempt on Boggs," the Jackson County Senator said. "Mark my words. And there will be hell to pay."

"I suspect," Jacob said, picking up his case and pushing past

Noland toward the door, "that they will have had a hand in it, whether any of them are in the state or not. Things seem to work out that way."

Noland remained in Jacob's way, forcing him to squeeze past with awkward difficulty.

"This is all going to catch up with you one of these days, Randall."

The Shelbyville merchant did not reply, but circled the cluster of legislators who had gathered around the senate page and exited the chamber. The capitol rotunda echoed hollowly, his leather heels clicking under the raw brick arch of the dome. He suspected that Noland was right. In fact, it was catching up with him already. He found it harder and harder to sit through the sessions listening to men wrangle over trivialities or defend legal injustices while he sat by, impotent from lack of wit or support to bolster his cause. North of the state in the Iowa Territories the last gasping remnants of the proud Sac and Fox were corralled by treaty and distrust in a disease ridden, starving camp at Ottumwa. In slave camps not a hundred miles from where he walked, black men, women and children labored and lived like cattle, though often beaten beyond the point that a man would punish good stock. And there was this Mormon problem. If only Smith and his Mormons had picked some other place to build their Zion. There couldn't be many left in Missouri but as long as one remained – and he knew one did – someone like Sheck Rogers would be hunting him. In fact, this one worked for him, managing his mercantile enterprises. Since their conversation about his faith at the Chariton trading post he had never spoken to David about it and since coming to Shelbyville, David had shown little interest in religion at all. But his family still lived up along the Chariton.

Jacob walked out onto the broad north steps of the capitol, pausing to clear his lungs of the cigar-laden air of the chamber. Below the hill the brown Missouri River swept beneath the domed capitol, bringing dark news from east and west. Elections were

197

coming up in the fall. He was glad that he had decided not to run.

19

THOMAS

Thomas Shattuck came to Shelbyville only once, almost five years to the day after David and Suzanna left the cabins on the Chariton. He arrived just before noon and stood on the wide railed porch rapping so lightly on the door that he would have gone unnoticed had Suzanna not seen his silhouette against the window. When she opened the door he smiled nervously and looked about as if fearful that someone had seen him arrive.

"Hello, Suzanna. I just came to see how you were getting on."

She wanted to throw herself into his arms but sensed his embarrassment and led him instead into the sitting room where she hugged him tightly and kissed his rough cheek.

"I'm so glad you came. Each time David has gone north to the Chariton store I've wanted to go with him, but your letters tell me it isn't the right time yet. Will there ever be a right time, do you think?"

He held her stiffly, a man grown unaccustomed to displays of affection.

"The time will have to come. Samuel will either have to change his views or find another place to be when you visit. We can't have family who isn't welcome at our home."

He sat awkwardly in a deep overstuffed chair and looked around the tastefully furnished room.

"Towns just don't set right with me anymore, I guess. As soon as I got in among all these houses, I started feeling closed in. Like someone was watching everything I was doin'. And after all these years in a cabin, I just don't know what to do with myself in a house as fine as this. Seems like I shouldn't touch or sit on anything."

Suzanna sat across from him on the settee feeling an embarrassed uneasiness of her own and struggling to help them both. He looked no older to her, but there was a meekness about him that was unnerving.

"It really isn't that fancy. And you can't do anything to it that the children haven't done. They tear through here like a couple of the Martin's hogs broke loose."

"Ah, the children...." He spoke as if testing the sound of the words. "I still can't get used to you having little ones. My own little girl...."

"And another on the way." She patted her stomach lightly. "Sometime in December. Johnny and Elizabeth have gone around to the store to get David but should be back in a moment."

"Tell me about them," he said. "You talk about them in your letters, but there's so much letters can't say."

With a smile Suzanna remembered again the long ago walks with her father beside the river, and quiet nights in the cabin when her brothers were off at Gallatin. They had always started the same with him asking exactly what he wanted to know or telling her just what he had on his mind. There was nothing veiled about him at all and she loved him for it.

"They're as different as night and day. I think sometimes that Johnny doesn't have a still bone in his body and won't live to see another birthday. He climbs and jumps and bangs into things. And David is no help. He encourages him. But Elizabeth is just the opposite. You wouldn't know that she was her mother's girl, the way she likes to dress up and stay so neat and proper."

Thomas Shattuck began to relax back into the chair. "She's her grandma's girl...after her namesake. Your mother was as proper a lady as I ever met. And even when we didn't have much for her to fix herself up with, she always looked like a picture." His eyes wandered off for a moment, then returned to Suzanna. "And what about David? Has he taken to the boy all right? I've worried that...."

She pushed the thought away with a wave of her hand.

"We never even think about it. Johnny doesn't know, of course, and I don't think either of us has ever felt he wasn't just ours."

The brown in Thomas' rough face deepened. "I shouldn't have said a thing about it. It's just crossed my mind at times."

"No, I'm pleased you did. I've needed to talk to someone about it from time to time and there's no one around that knows but David and Mr. Randall. It doesn't seem right to talk to either of them about it."

"What's there to talk about, if everything is going as it should?"

"Oh, it's nothing in particular – but feelings about things in general. About how things seem to happen that bring everything to where it should be."

Her father nodded without speaking.

"Like with Johnny's birth. He picked a time to come when the midwife was with two other women up at Bethel. And I was having so much trouble that David couldn't go for anyone else. The baby was turned and came backward and had gotten himself all tangled up. I was beyond being able to help much but David pulled and turned and unwrapped Johnny as well as any midwife could. And cleaned out his mouth and spanked him to life. He gave birth to the boy as much as I did. I think sometimes that it was meant to be that way; so that the life could be David's. Elizabeth's birth was easy as you please."

"I don't pretend to understand such things, but they seem to happen that way," Thomas mused. "David's been good for you, hasn't he."

"If we were only able to see you more often... and David's parents... our lives would be perfect."

At the rear of the house a door slammed noisily and children's feet chased across the wooden floor of the kitchen. Johnny stopped abruptly in the sitting room doorway and studied the man in the chair with bright, curious eyes. The blond head of his sister peered shyly beneath his arm. Suzanna stood and beckoned the children to her, tousling her son's dark curls and pulling Elizabeth out of the folds of her skirt.

"Children, this is your grandfather. My father. He has come to visit us and meet you two."

Johnny stepped forward but stopped short of the chair as his grandfather rose. "You live up on the Chariton, don't you," he said, matter-of-factly. "My father takes letters up to you sometimes and brings yours back."

"Yes he does." Thomas Shattuck squatted in front of the boy and smiled at the open, questioning face. "Are you able to read yet? I think your mother was reading when she was about your age."

"I can read my name. And write it too. But Elizabeth can't. She's too little."

Again the door banged in the rear and Suzanna called into the kitchen. "In here, David. We have a guest."

He came to the door wiping his hands on a towel, his face clouding as he saw Thomas Shattuck. "Nothing's wrong, I hope."

The old man stepped toward him and extended his hand. "Nothing that a trip down here to see my family hasn't set right. I should have been here long ago."

David took the hand and Thomas pulled him forward, slapping his broad back. "You've done what you said you would and I thank you for it. This is a right nice family."

"We'll have to all come north the next time I visit the Chariton post," David said, a note of embarrassed emotion in his voice. "I imagine the children have some cousins they'd like to play with."

"I'm afraid we're not quite to that point," the older man said, stepping back toward the chair. "I've come a long way since you two left the river but there's some that hasn't moved a bit. One of them, it hurts me to say, is Suzanna's brother. Samuel's a strong-headed man and sometimes it keeps him from seeing beyond his own stubbornness."

"I wouldn't think there was much left for him to worry about, with the Mormons all in Illinois," David said.

"There's still your family up river and I'm afraid he holds to the idea of 'one rotten apple spoils the barrel.' He hasn't done anything, but he frets about it a lot."

"My parents haven't caused any trouble, have they? My father can be difficult if he decides to be."

"None at all. I haven't even seen them, aside from them passing on the wagon when they go to the store. They don't need to cause trouble to upset Samuel.... In fact, I think he still likes to think that you were responsible for Suzanna's troubles at the trading post. He knows better, but it gives him a bit of something to support his feelings. I keep thinking that one of these days something will come along to show him what a fool he is, but it's escaped him so far."

Suzanna stepped between the men and took them each by the arm. "Let's have some lunch and we can tell you what we've been doing since we saw you last. It might help Samuel to know what respectable people we've become."

David scooped Elizabeth up with his other arm and Thomas Shattuck reached for the hand of his grandson who grasped him firmly and led the family into the kitchen. As they sat at the table the boy knelt up on his chair and leaned forward toward his grandfather.

"Did you ever get the wolf, Grandpa? The big gray one that can eat up a whole calf?"

Thomas laughed and looked questioningly from David to Suzanna.

"David tells the children stories every night," she said, "and Johnny's favorites are about the big gray wolf. You are always the great hunter."

The old man leaned back loosely in his chair and scratched at his white beard. "Yup, he's a big one," he said, squinting down his nose at Johnny who gazed seriously up at the man. "Haven't seen him for a while and he's too smart to bother my animals. But he's still around. Some folks tell me that they see him now and then. Mostly by hisself."

"Will you get him some day, Grandpa? Father says you've almost got him lots of times."

"Almost have. But he gets away every time. I'm beginning to think he's supposed to be there, just to torment me."

"Could you tell me a story about him after lunch? Tell me about when you chased him up to the dens."

"I have a better idea," Thomas said. "Why don't you and your father come up when you get a little bigger and we'll go after him together."

The boy knelt straight up in his chair, his eyes widening. "I could get him. Can we go, Father?"

"I'd like to do that," David said. "When grandpa tells us it's time, we'll go up."

Thomas reached across the table and patted the boy's hand. "I think you're just about big enough," he said.

20

DAVID

As David turned his mule team past the old Upton house and squinted through the first light of morning at the gutted stone walls of the ruined building, he was thinking about Johnny, Thomas Shattuck and the gray wolf. The chance to hunt the animal had not come soon, and it was now almost a year since the conversation. But memories of the wolf, almost forgotten in the bustle of keeping the Shelbyville businesses and family matters in order, had been rekindled the morning before... at the Chariton trading post.

"I heard the big gray wolf last night," an old farmer related as David showed him a new self-scouring plow that had been developed by a fellow over in Illinois. "I thought maybe we were rid of him. Hadn't heard that howl for... oh, near six months now." The farmer laughed to himself, leaning against the porch post.

"I remember the first time I ran into him. I was carrying this young spiked yearling home across my shoulders. Then there he was blocking my path as big as a bull calf. He smiled that smile of his, all crooked because of his teared-up face. Fangs dripping like a dog with the distemper. Why, I dropped that buck right where I stood and scrambled up the nearest tree, watching while he and his pack ate the whole thing, bones crunching and snapping like kindling wood. He didn't leave no more than the head and hoofs to take home for my day's work."

"He's always by hisself now," the farmer's son said. "I seen him three times last fall before the snow came and alone each time. He's got too mean to hunt with a pack. He took down one of Starner's heifers right in the corral and by the time old Everett grabbed his rifle and got out to her, the wolf had ripped her open and run. There's the devil in that one."

"How about you, Whitlock?" the farmer asked. "Did you ever see the gray one when you was living upriver?" David nodded and smiled thinly, remembering the morning that had turned his steps toward that moment at the trading post.

"I was working a mule team in deep snow north of here. Logging...back during the winter of thirty-nine. You remember that one?"

The two men nodded soberly.

"I started the team back through the woods pulling a white oak log and there he was, set like a steel trap across our path. He wasn't alone then but was running with a small pack. I got most of them from a tree, but this black bitch and the gray, they got the team...." He paused, drifting into thought, while the men muttered and nodded with understanding.

"A born killer, that one," the farmer said.

There was an irony in it all, David mused. In some ways, the wolves were responsible for his being here. For his having Suzanna, and the store. But they seemed to resent his security and were still after him.

In front of him the emptiness and decay of the Upton house only added to the sense of gloom that had hovered over him during the night. He had been on the road since noon of the previous day, making the return trip from the post to Shelbyville without stopping. It was May 24th, Elizabeth's third birthday, and a promise was a promise.

He had started the trip back in good spirits, anxious to see if the workmen had finished the new addition to the house and to discuss with Suzanna the possibility of asking his father to come south to manage the Shelbyville Cask Company. But as the day wore on, thoughts of the house addition and the barrel shop led his mind into paths that it had been taking more and more often of late, especially when he was alone. He had usually managed to divert his thoughts, sensing where the path led. But during this past night he had let them go and they had taken him where he feared.

For the past seven years – in fact ten, if he counted the three on the Chariton – David felt that he had been stumbling backward through his life. Retreating. It wasn't that things hadn't gone well since he and Suzanna came to Shelbyville. In many ways, they couldn't have gone much better. But they seemed in the main to be beyond David's control – reactions to others rather than planned decisions of his own.

As he thought back on it now he imagined that it was the visit with his mother the day before that had again twisted the clamp that seemed to grip his chest and trigger the thoughts. She had come to the trading post, knowing from his letter that he would be there. They met with a long, silent embrace, then she held him away.

"You look good David. It's been nearly two years. You need to come up more often."

"Our life seems to get busier all the time; with the three children and the store."

His mother paused, watching him carefully. "Your father would like to see you. He asked if you could come up."

David eased away from her and looked out the window at the two farmers inspecting the plow in front of the post.

"Why the change all of a sudden? He hasn't wanted to have anything to do with me since I left."

"It isn't a change. He's just finally beginning to admit what he has really wanted for all these years. He misses you...and he's getting older. That begins to soften all of us."

David frowned. "I wasn't expecting this and it couldn't have come at a worse time. I need to be leaving within the hour. Tomorrow's Elizabeth's birthday and I promised to be back by morning. He couldn't come down?"

"He doesn't like to come down. You know that. But I'm sure he'll understand. He knows about the birthday. In fact, he reads all of your letters over and over."

Lydia hesitated, laying her hand on his arm. "There's been more talk about the church. The settlement at Nauvoo has become very large and people fear they'll come back to Missouri. Samuel Shattuck's one of the most outspoken and John is afraid he'll ignore his father and bring trouble to us."

"Thomas said Samuel was bitter," David said, looking again out the window and up the trail toward the Shattuck homestead. "Suzanna's wanted to come back to visit, but her father says the time isn't right. When he came down last spring he said Samuel still seems to think I had something to do with Suzanna's attack. It's hard on the old man."

"I never see them," Lydia said. "It's a shame... with us living so close and being family. I think Thomas still stays away from us to protect us."

They stood together for a moment without talking, then David turned again from the window with a wry smile. "You can tell father that he was right. That might make up for my not getting up to see him."

"Right? In what way?"

"I've become a cooper. At least in a sense."

Lydia raised an amused eyebrow.

"It really happened by chance," David said. "I was standing in the store one afternoon when this fellow walked in and asked where he could get a regular supply of oak kegs. The ones that you send down barely meet my current demand, so I decided to go into the business myself. We're doing quite well with it."

"You're right. That will amuse your father," Lydia laughed. "And please him. What does this gentleman do with all these kegs you make?"

"Oh, you'd find him quite the character. His name is Wilhelm Keil. *Brother* Wilhelm Keil, I should say. He's a self-styled minister of Methodist origins, I believe, who's set up a community above us on the North River where all things are shared in common. 'For every man according to his capacity: To every man according to his needs'. That's their motto. The first time I met him he informed me that they were 'many with one aim' and that part of that aim was to make fine whiskey. We furnish the barrels. I've trained three apprentices and they're busy full-time."

As he spoke, his mother continued to smile but her eyes clouded. "You're settling in very well, it seems," she said.

"Things are going well for us."

She reached over and again took his arm. "And what about you and your belief, David?"

He felt that she had been waiting to ask, anxious that he not get away without her knowing.

He shrugged with resignation. "We read the Bible every night and try to live as we should. Suzanna is stronger in her faith than I am." He looked at her sadly. "It seems as though I have two fathers I need to come to terms with."

"I don't know how it can happen... with this isolation...." Her thoughts wandered, and he brought her back with a hug.

"I'll have to get the children up to see you. That will cheer you up. They're growing so fast. Johnny is going to be taller than I am, and twice as broad."

They spent the hour talking about the children and carefully avoiding thoughts of religion and isolation. He loaded for the return trip as they visited, then helped her to the seat of the old family wagon. As he rounded the corner of the trading post heading south, he turned to wave. His mother sat erect behind the two brown mules. She looked so much older. He needed to bring the children soon.

As evening came he thought again of their conversation. She was right about the church. Sometimes that terrible day at Haun's Mill seemed so far away. So distant. In the quiet moments of early morning when he awoke before the family and sat in the dark of the parlor, it crept into his thoughts. He wasn't that person anymore but he hadn't yet decided who he had become. He spoke only to Suzanna about it and she listened sympathetically and with growing understanding.

"If this troubles you that much, David, we need to be doing something about it," she said. "If you decide you want to go to Illinois, I'll go with you."

"I don't feel like that's where I belong anymore," he would say, but the conversation never went much further.

The other thoughts that had occupied his seventeen hours on the road were of Jacob Randall. Though he knew he admired the little Englishman more than any other man, he was finding it more and more difficult to be in Shelbyville with him. To the people of the growing community, Jacob was the well spring of the town's success. He was a pillar in the strongest sense; a man of unwavering principle, unbridled imagination, and boundless energy. He was all that David felt he was not. The villagers knew of their friendship and enjoyed talking to David about him. And the more David learned, the more he respected Jacob and the harder it was to be with him.

They told David about the beginnings of Shelbyville; about how William Broughton first began to sell equipment and supplies from the front room of his home at Oak Dale in the fall of 1833. He had boasted at the time that he could name every homesteader between the south fork of the Fabius River and the middle fork of the Salt. A year later when he moved his Mercantile Store and Post Office to the south side of Shelbyville's newly formed town square, the region had either changed or as some were inclined to suggest, Broughton had been exaggerating in the first place. Hundreds of new settlers fleeing the cholera epidemic in Palmyra had moved into the upper reaches of the Salt drainage and in St. Louis talk of a soon-to-be-formed Shelby County drew speculators into the area anticipating rising land prices. On the day of its opening, Broughton's post office roster displayed more unfamiliar names than it did those he knew.

When the merchant died of the flux in the summer of 1835 it

was one of these newcomers, a small sandy-haired Englishman named Jacob Randall, who purchased the store from the Widow Broughton.

"He was a dandy one, right from the beginning," one of Shelbyville's aging founders told David as he sat with two of them one late winter afternoon around the iron stove in the store. "Never said as much, but you could tell as soon as he got this place that he planned to change things around here. Stop all the barter and haggling that had been going on twixt the rest of us and make us civilized folk. Wanted to bring a bit of law and order to us at the same time."

The second old man had leaned back contentedly in his chair and chuckled. "As I remember it, Jacob did better at bringing commerce than law and order."

Randall's business had indeed grown and expanded with amazing speed, taking the town with it. In November of '38 the entire community gathered to dedicate a new courthouse in the center of the square, a solid red brick structure with an impressive white bell tower and white-pillared front that looked directly south across Main Street at Jacob's store. The merchant had played a prominent role in laying out the town into blocks around the new brick edifice, with numbered streets running east-west beginning at First Street on the north edge of Shelbyville. The north-south streets, like Jefferson City's, bore the names of early American patriots; Adams, Jefferson, Madison, and on the west side of town, Lafayette.

By the summer of 1839 when Randall hired the young couple from up near his trading post on the Chariton to manage the Shelbyville Mercantile, commerce was firmly established in the community. It had arrived, however, before civility.

On the sultry night that David and Suzanna Whitlock arrived in the prospering Shelby County village, John Faber shot and killed John Bishop in the brick tavern that sat diagonally across the square from Jacob's new bank. Suzanna Whitlock found the entire incident barbaric.

When chinch bugs destroyed the wheat crop in '42, the Whitlock's handling of the crisis as proprietors of the store simply served as greater confirmation to those in Shelby County of Jacob Randall's business sense. Rather than raise prices to take advantage of the shortage, David reduced them to his own costs to keep the farmers and the community that supported them from going under. A hundred pounds of flour fell to $2.50 in gold, $3.00 in city money. Potatoes and corn were priced at 18 cents a bushel, a hundred weight of pork at $1.50 and beef at $1.00.

The efforts of the Mercantile to stabilize the economic crisis did not eliminate stresses among the farmers whose crops were devastated by the plague and that winter brought even greater violence. One late November evening Stephen Franks discovered his neighbor, Willard Evans, filling a sack from the Franks' corn crib and shot him dead on the spot. Franks claimed that in the failing light of dusk he had not recognized the culprit and residents let the incident pass without undue alarm.

The shooting of Daniel Thomas on Christmas Day was a different matter. It was true that young Thomas had been sharing very freely his opinions that Mary Upton had been unchaste with at least three men, including himself. But most agreed that Thomas was being kind to the promiscuous Mary by suggesting only three paramours. When the girl's father entered the boarding house on Second Street and shot Thomas in the head as he sat at Christmas dinner, the residents of Shelbyville decided they had seen enough. Upton had prepared his family for escape before the shooting and by the time a posse was formed had fled into the woods without trace. Rumor reached Shelbyville the following May that Upton had gone to Putnam County and had himself been shot by a son-in-law named Cain while chopping a hog trough from a section of maple.

As David now looked at the shell of the Upton house, he remembered Daniel Thomas's death as a turning point for the community and as a final confirmation of Jacob's role in Shelbyville. Though young Thomas had wandered into town only three months before the shooting and was known as something of a scoundrel, the small cemetery on the hill northwest of the village overflowed at his burial. The service was less sad than grim and as the townspeople turned from the graveside, Jonathan March stepped onto a stump beside the graveyard's iron gate and called for the selection of a constable and judge. The meeting was brief and without discussion. March was chosen as constable and Jacob Randall agreed to serve as judge. In the four years since, Shelbyville had been both thriving and peaceful.

Directly in front of him along the road to the east, the sun burst suddenly above the horizon and David stretched on the wagon seat, shaking off a desire to pull the mules to the side of the trail and sleep. In many ways his feelings about Jacob were of greater concern than was his spiritual ambivalence. They seemed more immediate. Each month he felt that he became more and more a part of Jacob Randall's success – and less and less certain of his own.

Traffic along the Hill Spring Trail was growing steadily and new homesteads now spread east and west of the crossing and southward down the river. Grist and saw mills on Locust Creek supplied flour and lumber to a small settlement of log and clapboard houses that nestled contentedly around Hill Spring. The demand for goods and supplies was growing by the month. David had opened another outpost for Jacob thirty miles east along the trail with Willard Davis as shopkeeper. The man's arm had been taken in a milling accident, but his manner and disposition attracted the settlers of Scotland and Knox Counties to his company. The two northern stores were now the hub of social activity in the region with men stopping to trade, have equipment repaired, and swap yarns while women sorted through new bolts of cloth and talked of building a school house. Life was changing in north Missouri. There was something in all of this settling that added to David's unease.

21

DAVID

"Father's home! I told you he'd be here early!"

Johnny jumped from the porch and dashed across the yard to meet David. Behind him Elizabeth stepped carefully down from the porch in a new pink frock and hurried to the gate. Suzanna appeared in the doorway, smiling at the excited children and cuddling a sleeping baby to her breast.

"I didn't expect you for several hours but Johnny said you'd be here at sunup. The children have been up and dressed since five."

David bent from the wagon seat and lifted the boy up beside him, tousling his dark curls with a tired hand. Seeing the children had immediately brightened his spirits and reminded him of his reason for returning home without rest.

"It's a special day. I couldn't disappoint you two now, could I?" Elizabeth stood by the wagon wheel, reaching up to be lifted.

"And here's the birthday girl." He swung from the wagon and swept her up beside her brother. "Johnny, do you think you can drive the mules around back?"

The boy smiled proudly and lifted the reins. David patted the rump of the nearest animal and the team plodded slowly forward, guided by habit and hunger around the corner of the house to the stable.

"David, I wish you wouldn't do that. If the team bolted for some reason...."

David pushed through the gate and joined Suzanna on the porch, wrapping her and the baby in a gentle squeeze. "They're so tired they couldn't run if the devil himself were after them. And how's my littlest one doing?"

She gently lifted the sleeping baby toward him and they looked down together at the round contented face.

"...to be so at peace with the world," David said, kissing the baby's soft forehead, and again squeezing his wife. "And you? Did I leave you too much to worry about? I see they finished the new room." She was more beautiful than ever, he decided. Still slim and strong, but with a healthy fullness that had come from bearing children.

"Just yesterday," she said. "I rushed them to have it ready when you came home. Did you see your mother?"

He nodded. "Believe it or not, my father wanted to see me. But I didn't have a chance to go up there with the rush to get back. It would have added another six hours. But things must be improving."

"Did she say anything about my family? Had she seen them?"

David shook his head. "Samuel hasn't changed. Mother thinks we should come up and stay with them. Maybe if you were nearby again...."

"He's a stubborn man, Samuel is. I doubt he'll ever change, even if he finds out how wrong he is."

David's face clouded and she looked up at him.

"You've been brooding again, haven't you? I knew if you spent the night on the trail, you'd get to thinking."

"It's worse than ever," he said. "I need to figure out what to do about it."

At the east end of the quiet street a lone horseman appeared among the sleeping houses, the hooves of his dappled mount echoing noisily against the hard-packed clay of the road. David and Suzanna stepped to the edge of the porch, watching his approach. The rump of his horse was piled high with tightly bound pelts and a long Kentucky rifle lay loosely across his saddle.

"This should take your mind off things," Suzanna laughed. "That looks like Jess McAllister and I suspect we'll have to do a bit of business before the birthday party."

David chuckled. "And spend an hour or two visiting. I think old Jess saves up all his talking until he gets here. And his bathing, too."

Suzanna jabbed him with her free elbow. "Now be kind. He's a lonely man and we're about the only people he has to call friends. He spends so much time up there along Fox Creek that I don't think he sees another soul for weeks on end." She waved at the approaching trapper who smiled broadly and returned her greeting. As he neared the fence, he laughed aloud through sparse, tobacco stained teeth.

"Didn't really expect no welcomin' committee. Thought I'd have to camp here on the grass for an hour or two 'fore you folks rolled out."

Suzanna stepped from the porch to greet him. "David just got back this morning from the Chariton trading post. It's Elizabeth's birthday and the children wanted to be up when he got home."

The old trapper swung from his horse as the two children trotted around the corner of the house. "Well, how 'bout that! And how old are you then, Miss Lizbeth?"

The girl rushed to her mother who now stood beside the gate, wrapped herself in the long skirt and thrust three chubby fingers toward the trapper.

Jess laughed again and reached into his saddle bag. "Almost old as me. Bet I've got somethin' here for ye." He pulled a small, intricately carved wooden doll from the leather pouch, squatted beside his horse and extended it to the girl. Elizabeth hesitated and Suzanna urged her forward. She walked cautiously to the shaggy trapper, quickly snatched the doll and hurried back to the security of her mother's dress. Suzanna took the carved figurine and examined it carefully.

"Why, Jess. This is beautiful. Did you do this yourself?"

The trapper reddened beneath his salty beard. "Not much else to do in the evenin's. And here, Master John. I believe I have one for you too." He fished again and found a small wooden horse, caught by his skilled knife in mid-gallop, mane and tail flying. The boy, less bashful, took the carving and looked up with admiring eyes at the grizzled old man who turned to speak to his father.

"If you been up on the Chariton you probably heard about all the goin's on up north."

David nodded. "Lots of new settlements. It won't be long before there are towns like this all through the woods up there. That won't be good for trapping, I'm afraid."

Jess shook his head. "No, that too. But I was meanin' the Mormons. I was in Palmyra a few days back and heard they was movin' again. Been chased from Illinois, I guess. They're headed 'cross Iowa by the thousands. Those folks don't seem to be able to find a place where they can get along with nobody."

David glanced quickly at Suzanna who stood beside the gate without expression. "What's caused the trouble for them this time, Jess?"

The trapper shrugged. "Don't know much about them at all. Never met one myself. I was over on the Grand River in Thirty-seven when all the fightin' was going on, but I stayed out of the way." He paused, chuckling through his beard. "Got stopped on the Great Trail one day by a band that was hunting 'em. Had to swear on the Holy Book that I weren't one. From what I hear, they're a secretive group. Believe in visits from angels and think the Injins is God's special people."

Suzanna pulled Elizabeth in tightly against her leg. "Where are they going, Jess?"

"West is all I know. That's why I asked about 'em. There's supposed to be a big camp of 'em up on the headwaters of the Chariton. More have moved on to the Grand and set up a camp there."

Suzanna shook her head slowly. "I hope they find a place where people will leave them alone."

Jess McAllister nodded. "I'll go round and unload these furs at the store. You folks got some celebratin' to do." He grasped the reins of his horse and walked her back toward the stable with Johnny running beside him, galloping his wooden stallion through the air.

David placed an arm around Suzanna's shoulders. "It sounds to me like they may never be left in peace."

"I'd think by now they might be willing to be a little less outspoken about what they believe."

David looked down at her seriously. "If we can't be outspoken about what we believe in this country, we've reached a sorry state. No matter what we believe."

She thought for a moment. "You're right," she said. "We should know better than anyone that when you force people to be quiet because you disagree, everyone loses."

"There's no freedom in having to live in secret and alone," he said grimly. "I don't know how long mother can survive...."

Johnny Whitlock led the trapper back to the yard gate. "Can Jess come to Elizabeth's party? He brought her a present."

Suzanna smiled. "'Mr. McAllister', Johnny. And I think we'll fix him some breakfast first." She waved the children into the house and David leaned against the gate post, scratching the stubble that sanded his chin after a night on the road.

"I thought we'd seen the last of the Mormon problems here. Maybe folks will let them go west without trouble."

Jess cut a thick plug of tobacco with the knife on his belt and thrust it into his cheek. "Not everyone. I ran across this feller in Palmyra who's still huntin' em. Big ugly sort. He was boastin' he's learned the whereabouts of two Mormon families that's still in Missouri. One down near Hannibal and another up where you've just came from. North of the Hill Spring Trail on the Chariton. He was drummin' up help to go burn 'em out."

As the man spoke, David straightened against the post, his heart quickening and stomach tight.

219

"When was this?"

The trapper looked at him curiously. "Three days ago. The man and a band of six or seven left for Hannibal about the same time I started down here."

David stepped quickly toward the house then paused, remembering his guest. "Excuse me, Jess, but we're going to have to postpone the party. I'll have Suzanna come over to the store and give you your supplies." The trapper chewed silently at his plug, spitting into the gray dust of the street.

"I'm sorry, Jess. I think I know the people up on the Chariton. They're decent folk and I can't let them get attacked without warning."

Jess nodded. "I'd get moving if I was you. You're late as it is."

Suzanna was in the kitchen fixing breakfast and looked up brightly as he came into the room, the smile fading under his dark expression.

"I'm going to have to go back up to the trading post," he said. "Jess says the man that's been hunting down Mormons in the state has learned about my family. He might be on his way up there now."

Suzanna paled and stood silently for a moment searching his face, then wiped her hands and untied her apron. "We're going with you then. You've been gone too much without us."

David shook his head. "I need to go quickly. And it may be dangerous."

"That's why we're going. I don't want you to ride up there and not know what's happened to you. You said it was time for decisions and this might be one of them. We're going together."

He held her by the shoulders at arm's length. "This is our private battle. The Whitlocks'. And a wagon will slow me down. I may be too late already."

"I remember you taking great pride in making me a Whitlock," she said firmly. "And you know that this has been my battle for a long time now too. In a number of ways. If you're too late already, it won't matter when we get there. If we're not, I doubt this killer will travel at night. We can be there by morning."

David looked at her soberly, then lifted Johnny from his chair at the table and patted the boy's bottom. "Run over to Mr. Randall's house and see if he's up. Ask him to come over if he can. Quickly!"

While Suzanna packed clothes and food into two wooden boxes, David harnessed fresh mules to the store's smallest wagon. When he returned to the house, Jacob Randall stood in the living room with Suzanna.

"I understand Mr. Rogers is active again," he said.

David nodded grimly. "I don't know how he learned about these families. The man seems to be able to sniff them out."

Jacob frowned. "There are few secrets in this world. You never told me... in as many words. But I knew for a long time before we discussed it. And I suspect there have been Mormon deserters over time. One of them may know about families who settled elsewhere."

"Some did. But I can't believe they'd tell that devil."

"He can be persuasive." The Englishman stepped toward the door. "Give me a few minutes and I'll ride up with you."

David caught his arm. "Thank you Jacob, but this is our affair. And there's the store to take care of and the other businesses. I appreciate it but we could be gone for some time. I'd feel much better knowing you were here...."

As David loaded the wagon and Suzanna gathered the children, Jacob went to the store with Jess McAllister, returning with a new percussion rifle and four small boxes of cartridges and caps.

"Don't worry about being back until you know everything is straightened out," he said.

David climbed into the wagon bed with the children and Suzanna took the reins and turned the mules toward the road that her husband had traveled only an hour earlier.

．　．　．

They reached the river by early afternoon and turned north, Suzanna pressing the team to a brisk walk throughout the morning while David slept in the wagon. As the day lengthened, high gray clouds blocked the sun and a light soaking rain started in showers, then fell steadily. She halted at evening twenty miles south of the Hill Spring trading post to cover the children with heavy canvas and feed the exhausted mules.

David stretched and stepped over into the seat box.

"We're making good time. Better than I thought we could. We should be there by early morning if the mules hold up." He took the reins and forced the team northward into the rain with Suzanna huddled beside him beneath a square of brown tarpaulin.

"Are you rested?" she asked.

He smiled and pulled her closer. "I feel good. Better than I've felt for a long time. It's too bad this is what's bringing us back, but we needed to do it anyway. I'm glad you insisted on coming."

"You want those men to come, don't you?"

"Yes. I want them to come," he said.

In the early hours of morning they passed the silent trading post and a half an hour later the Shattuck homestead. He shook her gently awake as they passed and she gazed longingly at the cabins.

"Seven years," she said. "It doesn't seem possible that it's been so long."

David looked at the dark shadows of the three huddled cabins. "Nothing's changed much. It's like no time has passed."

"Some things have changed. Father seemed so...so quiet when he came to Shelbyville last autumn. He's tired, I think. Tired of everything that's happening about him that he can't control. And Samuel's little one must be four by now. I wish we could stop. Just for a moment."

David kissed her cheek. "As soon as we know everything's all right, we'll come back."

"They won't see me. It would be worse than not stopping."

"Things can change. I think it's time they did."

They clung together silently as the homestead disappeared behind them into the rainy night.

As they passed through the small brook that ran across the wagon track and tumbled into the Chariton, Suzanna straightened on the seat. "Who would have guessed when we first met just over there in the woods that we would be coming back like this."

David pulled the wrap more tightly about them. "And who knows what's ahead now. You may wish you'd stayed at home."

She snuggled against him. "Home is with you," she murmured. They rode the remaining mile without speaking, pressed close together on the wagon.

22

REUNION

The Whitlock cabin stood black and silent against the forest as David reined up the team in the middle of the clearing. The rain had stopped and the clouds scattered, leaving the air heavy and cold and smelling of dark earth and wet leaves. Johnny stirred and sat upright in the wagon bed, peering about with startled curiosity.

"Be still," David whispered, gesturing for Suzanna to stay on the wagon seat. He climbed to the ground and walked cautiously to the cabin, trying the door without knocking. It was tightly barred and he rapped gently, stepping away to examine the shuttered window.

"Who's there?" John Whitlock's voice rolled deeply through the heavy plank door.

"It's David. Open the door." There was a long pause. The door opened slowly and the cooper stepped in his nightshirt out onto the damp grass looking first at his son, then at the woman on the wagon seat. His hair and beard were streaked with salty gray, his face more deeply creased than David remembered.

"There's trouble coming," David said simply. "We've come to help."

"Who is it, John?" Lydia Whitlock appeared in the doorway, squinting into the dim light. Her face was thin and pale and her eyes widened in fright as she saw her son.

"What's happened? Is everyone all right?"

David put an arm around her shoulders and led her to the wagon. "We're all safe. But trouble might be on the way. If it isn't here yet, we should be fine till morning. But here are the children I promised you. Earlier than expected."

"Oh, they're beautiful!" She looked into the wagon, covering her mouth with a thin trembling hand, then lifted the baby from Suzanna's arms and cuddled him against her. "I've so wished that I could come and see you. But I didn't know if...." She bent her head to the baby's, then looked up again to the wagon seat.

"This is Thomas?" she asked.

Suzanna nodded. "And this is Elizabeth." She reached behind her and lifted her daughter onto the seat. The girl blinked sleepily and snuggled against her mother. Suzanna pulled her older son to her and looked at John Whitlock who still stood silently beside the cabin door.

"And this is John. Johnny, this is your grandfather. You were named after him."

The boy scrambled over the seat and down to the ground, running to clutch his father's leg. John Whitlock watched the boy silently, then stooped and extended a huge hand.

"I thought I was the last John Whitlock in all the world. I'm glad to learn there's another." The boy reached for him and the cooper lifted him lightly. "We'd best be getting inside," he said. "What's this about trouble?"

As his mother and Suzanna carried the children into the cabin, David beckoned his father away from the door.

"You've been discovered somehow. A band of men may be heading up this way." John Whitlock considered the news unmoved, then turned and walked through the dark to the workshop with David following. He struck a light then leaned back against the heavy work table with arms folded tightly across his chest.

"How do you know this?"

"A trapper came to the store yesterday from Palmyra. He overheard a man plotting to burn out two Mormon families; one near Hannibal and the other north of the Chariton trading post."

"You don't know for certain that they meant us then."

"Who else could they mean? You know everyone up here. It has to be you."

The big man frowned. "I've been worried about trouble. People are getting nervous about all the Mormons over in Illinois. Is it that man Samuel?"

"No, another who's much worse. It's an obsession with him. His name is Sheck Rogers and he's been murdering families across the state for the past ten years. He won't stop until we're all gone."

"And you came up from Shelbyville to tell us this?"

"We left yesterday morning. I was afraid they might get here before us."

His father began to speak then stopped, looking down silently at the packed clay floor.

"We may not have much time," David said.

The cooper nodded and pushed away from the table. "You shouldn't have brought your family. If these men come, this will be no place for them."

David smiled grimly. "There's more to all of this than you can imagine. Suzanna's not the kind of person who stays behind."

John Whitlock grunted, glancing about the small workshop. "We'll put them all in here. Your mother's too old for this sort of thing. She can watch the little ones behind a barred door and a yard of the good earth. Your Suzanna can help us inside with the rifles."

The two men hoisted and dragged the table, lathe and shaving bench to one side of the room, clearing an open space near the fireplace, then returned to the cabin. Lydia and Suzanna stood beside the doorway to the inner room talking in hushed tones and turned as the men entered.

David took Suzanna's arm. "We're moving the children to the workshop. Mother can care for them there and the rest of us will stay in the house." Suzanna looked uncertainly at the tall thin woman beside her.

"Should we all be out there?" Lydia asked. "Those walls are like a fortress."

David shook his head. "We can't just give them the house. If there aren't too many, we can hold our own."

They gathered armloads of blankets, quilts and tick padding from the beds and carried them to the shed, adding the boxes of food and clothing from the wagon. The children had again fallen asleep, exhausted from the long jarring ride in the wagon bed. As David bent to pick up his oldest son, a rough hand grasped his arm.

"I can carry the boy." John Whitlock gathered the child into his burly arms and nestled the dark head beneath his white-streaked beard. Johnny stirred, snuggling comfortably into the man's reassuring arms, and slipped again into secure slumber.

As David unharnessed the team and corralled them with his father's mules he noticed the sharpening edges of trunks in the circle of forest that surrounded the clearing. Dawn was gradually stripping away the protective curtain of night. He looked westward into the shadowy woods, remembering the circle of wolves, the scream of the mules, and the chilling snarl of the gray killer. The wolves were returning. He lifted the rifle and cartridge boxes from the wagon bed and walked quickly to the workshop. This time he would not drop the caps.

"We need to get ready," he said. "The night is over."

23

SUZANNA

Morning awakened soft and pink through thinning clouds beyond the river. A doe drank undisturbed in the shallow ford between the cabin and the east bank and in the rain-soaked forest behind the house, birds trilled and squirrels chattered and chased in tandem through the lacy cover of freshly leafing oaks. Suzanna had missed the woods. In the quiet dark of her bed beneath the gables of the home in Shelbyville she often strained to hear the night songs of the forest; hooting owls and the coo of roosting doves, the rustle of possums and raccoons across the leafy woodland floor. But rows of frame houses and spreading fields of timothy, grain and hemp caught and absorbed the forest songs before they reached her.

As she sat now at the open window of the cabin watching the doe drink, she listened again to the music of the woods. David had removed the swirled panes of window glass from their frames and the fresh, loamy scent of damp earth filled her nostrils. She felt secure and at home, the purpose of their journey fading into thoughts of probable misunderstanding. Jess McAllister had not heard clearly – or the marauding band had given up their chase.

To her left along the base of the embankment the sod hut was quiet and asleep. They had decided not to light a fire in the workshop. Nothing to notify intruders that the shop was any more than an empty storage hut or smokehouse. The children must be stirring by now, she thought, becoming suddenly aware of the aching fullness in her breasts and the need to feed the baby. Once awake, the tiny boy's cries would penetrate even the thick walls of the workshop until his belly was satisfied.

David slumbered fitfully on the floor in front of the fireplace, his father sitting silently at the lone south window, gazing into the stretch of trees that separated the cabin from the Shattuck homestead down river.

"It's going to be a beautiful morning," she said.

The figure at the window nodded, then turned.

"I'm glad you came... even if it had to be with bad news. It's been too long."

Suzanna leaned against the window sill.

"Yes. It has been too long. I've missed my family and David has missed you."

John Whitlock continued to watch her but was silent for a minute. When he spoke he had turned again to gaze out the window.

"We should have come to see you. Lydia wanted to, but I thought David should come back first. That was wrong, wasn't it."

"It's been wrong for all of us to stay away," she said.

"Lydia tells me that you're in the coopering business. David's a good cooper. Good as any I've seen."

Suzanna looked toward the fireplace at her husband, hoping that he was awake and had overheard, but he did not stir.

"I think he would like to hear you say that," she said, but again there was no answer. She rose quickly and walked to the door. "I need to feed the baby. Do you think it's safe to go out?"

He studied her question as if his mind were elsewhere, then looked back at the quiet forest and nodded.

"Move quickly to the shed and call to Lydia when you reach the door."

Suzanna opened the door, glanced again at the deer by the river, then swiftly crossed the forty paces to the sod shed. The doe looked up curiously, then lowered her head again to the water. Suzanna rapped sharply on the heavy planks.

"Lydia, it's me."

Heavy objects scraped across the packed earth floor and the door opened narrowly, allowing her to slip in. The room was musty and dimly lit and smelled of acrid smoke from the oil lamp. Johnny and Elizabeth sat contentedly on their bedding eating bread and white cheese and Lydia held the fussing baby. Suzanna unfastened her dress and sat beside the children, cuddling the baby to her breast.

"This is an adventure, Mama." Johnny looked up at her with bright enthusiasm. "Grandmother says we're on an adventure."

"We are indeed," she said, smiling at the other woman with grateful admiration. She loved her instinctively, sensing her caring heart and quiet intelligence.

"You're lucky to be able to have this adventure with Grandmother. I want you to do exactly what she tells you to do."

"Can we go outside? I want to play outside."

"Inside for now." She patted the curly head. "Perhaps later."

Lydia smoothed her wrinkled dress and stretched.

"The night was quiet. I thought they might come during the night – if they are coming."

Suzanna nodded. "I'm hoping we were wrong. David gets so alarmed about these things. Unnecessarily sometimes."

"I don't think he ever liked the idea of our coming up here," Lydia said, sitting beside her on the blankets. "He thought it cowardly."

"For my sake, I'm glad you did," Suzanna smiled. "But it hasn't exactly kept you out of trouble."

"Nor you, for that matter," Lydia said. The two women sat silently while Suzanna nursed, watching her dark-haired son who now played contentedly in the corner with scraps of wood from the workbench. Suzanna's attack at the trading post now seemed so distant. She thought of it rarely and still remembered little about the day. And Johnny – he was their son; hers and David's.

The baby dozed into satisfied sleep and she rose stiffly, passing him back to Lydia.

"I'd better get back to the house. I'll come back at noon and relieve you for a while. I think it might be a long lonely day in here." She gave the woman's arm a gentle squeeze, kissed the children and eased through the narrow door opening, walking briskly toward the house.

As she reached the center of the opening between buildings she stopped in mid-step, her heart leaping. The woods were silent; as still as the disquieting hush before the first crash of thunder rips an April sky. She glanced at the treetops where birds and squirrels now hunched noiselessly against the branches. The surface of the river was motionless, without leaf or twig floating on its lifeless face. As she searched the bank for signs of the drinking doe, two riders moved out of the woods onto the small flat across the Chariton. Then two more...and another two, until eight men sat grim and silent, watching her across the hundred yards that separated them.

Suzanna was barely aware of the seven. Her eyes were riveted on their leader, a tall rough-bearded man with a single angry eye that glared from beneath a flat, broad-brimmed hat. Her racing mind robbed her body of motion and she stood as if rooted to the dew-covered grass, groping into darkened corners of her memory. She knew the face. She could smell it breathing down on her with its dark socket and twisted scar. Slowly the protective veil slipped away and she saw him crouching over her, groping, gnashing; remembering him rear back in rage as the skillet sliced into his temple. She saw the huge fist rise, clutching the long blade that still hung from his belt, and from deep within Suzanna's soul a bitter, raging cry swelled and shattered the oppressive silence of the woods. Instinctively her body tensed, coiling like a cornered panther and she glanced backward at her children's hiding place, then to the cabin door to her husband and the rifles.

The cry jolted the horsemen to action and with shrill whoops and shrieks, they spurred their mounts into a foaming gallop through the shallows of the river. Suzanna wanted suddenly to stand and fight and searched about for a weapon. A flat bladed spade leaned beside the cabin door and she sprang for it, reaching for the thick hickory handle. The door burst open and John Whitlock wrapped her with a burly arm and dragged her into the room. From the window, a rifle cracked and as the door closed behind her, Suzanna saw the rider beside her attacker rise in the saddle, mouth agape, and tumble onto the near bank.

The fatal shot startled and confused the riders who had expected to take the homestead by surprise. They wheeled to left and right, retreating in a dash of spray across the river where they huddled together on prancing horses beyond the screen of trees.

David pulled Suzanna to the window.

"You almost got yourself killed! What in creation were you thinking about?" His eyes flashed more with fear than anger.

"He's there!" Suzanna peered breathlessly around the edge of the empty window frame. "The big one with the scar. He's the one who came to the trading post."

David looked narrowly across the river at the band of men as his father joined them at the window.

"Jacob and I guessed as much. He was one of the men who roughed him up at the store a few months before they found you there."

The cooper adjusted the copper cap on the nipple of Jacob Randall's percussion rifle.

"I think they weren't expecting us to be ready for them. They don't have torches. They were expecting to force their way in and murder an old couple in their beds, then burn the cabin from our own fireplace."

"There's one less to do it now," David said grimly. "I suspect they will divide up and not come straight across at us again... unless it's to draw our fire."

"Maybe they will leave," Suzanna ventured. "Now that they know we're ready for them."

"Not him," David said. "He's waited a long time to...."

Across the river the band separated and splashed again into the ford; two riders galloping north around the high bank and five south into the trees, led by Sheck Rogers.

John Whitlock returned to the south-facing window and the three stood tensely at their posts.

The woods south of the cabin erupted suddenly with shouts and gunfire as the five broke from the trees, rifles leveled at the window where the cooper stood. Balls thudded against the log wall and shattered the half-closed shutter beside John Whitlock's face. He fired at the crouching riders, kneeling to reload as David rushed to replace him at the window. The attackers charged, circled back to the woods to reload, then charged again.

The men at the window worked in rotation, firing, kneeling, loading and firing again. The old Hall's that had once dropped four wolves in a clearing west of the cabin spewed gas and smoky flame from the seam in front of the breach, blackening David's face and singeing his hair. Suzanna stood against the east wall watching the river through the front window, expecting the other two riders to round the bluff at any moment and rush the cabin door.

A resounding crash from the direction of the workshop spun her across the open window frame to where she could see the front of the sod hut. One of the attackers crouched above it on the bank, rifle in hand, while the other heaved heavily against the door, forcing it gradually open with each thrust.

"David!"

Her scream brought him leaping across the room, forcing a paper cartridge into the extended breach. His shot caught the man at the door squarely between the shoulders. He staggered backward, clutching at the air as if grasping for some invisible support, then tumbled sideways onto the rain-soaked grass. A ball smashed into the window frame and David dropped to one knee, pushing the hooked lever to spring the breach upward. When he stood, reloaded, the man at the top of the bank had scrambled back into the woods. On the south edge of the clearing the riders had also retreated, circling back across the Chariton and into the shielding forest. From the window that faced the river Suzanna could see them faintly, their crazed leader snarling and gesturing at his confederates.

She looked again at the workshop, gasping in horror as a slim, dark figure appeared in the shadows of the partially opened door, then bolted into the clearing. Suzanna smothered the cry in her throat, realizing that her alarm would draw the attention of the killers.

The men across the river also saw the movement in the clearing. One rose in his saddle, pointing frantically toward the cabin. The leader wheeled his horse and with an animal cry that froze the trembling boy in his tracks, drew the murderous knife from his belt and spurred his horse into the river at full gallop.

Suzanna sprang for the door. The men reached for her, clutching at air as she threw the bolt and dashed into the open clearing. Her hand found the handle of the spade as she passed and she swung it across her chest, running like an infantryman with loaded weapon.

The killer bent low over his horse's neck, his single eye fixed on the quailing boy, unaware of the fury that rushed toward his sightless side. As he neared the lad, he rose slightly, lifting the long knife for a slashing blow.

"Mormon bastard!" he snarled, leaning again toward the boy.

Like a forest cat Suzanna sprang, eyes narrow and teeth bared. Raising the spade high above her shoulder with both hands, she threw her body forward with the snapping release of a bent sapling. Her hatred for this man fused with desperate love and fear for her son, bursting from her in a rising cry that echoed in the circle of forest and jolted the attacker upright in his saddle. The sharp edge of the flat blade sliced sideways through cloth, ribs and cartilage into his exposed side. His horse reared violently, pawing the air with flailing hooves. A foreleg struck Suzanna in the chest, bowling her backward onto the ground, and an iron shod hoof cut into her thigh as the horse bolted for the safety of the river. Its rider slumped forward, bouncing loosely on the frightened animal's back. As the horse reached the Chariton and splashed into the ford, Sheck Rogers rolled slowly sideways and dropped into the water. He tried to rise, stumbled, then pitched forward, disappearing beneath the rain-swollen surface.

Suzanna pushed up onto her knees, the injured leg buckling beneath her. Across the river the five remaining riders leveled their weapons on the mother and son in the clearing and spurred into the crossing.

"Run, Johnny!" Suzanna screamed, reaching for the boy who had collapsed, sobbing, onto the grass. "Run for the house!"

Instead he turned and crawled toward her on hands and knees, whimpering softly. A ball thudded into the grass beside Suzanna's shoulder and she rolled toward her son. As the boy reached her, powerful arms circled their waists and Suzanna was lifted upright like a small child. She threw her arm across the shoulders of John Whitlock and hobbled beside him toward the cabin, her son holding tightly to the man's thick neck.

The distance she had crossed in seconds, dashing to protect Johnny, now seemed endless. She heard the dull thud of another shot as it hit the big man's side, felt him shudder and heard his muffled groan. He hesitated, gasping, then continued toward the cabin.

David filled the doorway, exchanging fire with the horseman as rapidly as he could load and prime the percussion rifle. Another rider pitched into the river but the others, seeing their prey crippled and exposed, urged their horses up the near bank, shrieking wildly. Suzanna measured the distance that separated them from the door and from the charging gunmen and knew they would not reach the cabin.

"Take Johnny," she whispered, pushing the man and boy on in front of her.

John Whitlock tightened his hold on her waist and struggled forward. She looked across his heaving shoulder at the riders, seeing three of them raise their weapons in unison, aimed at the stumbling trio. The cooper swung around suddenly with his back to the horsemen and pulled Suzanna in against his broad chest, tucking his grandson in beside her. The rifles discharged and he slumped forward, dragging them under his falling body.

Suzanna pulled her son closer beneath the still weight of John Whitlock and heard David's rifle thunder above her, aware that he now stood over them facing the charge. She struggled to free herself, to stand beside him, but could move his father only enough to twist toward the four remaining riders. She felt no fear. Only an overwhelming sadness that the new happiness in her life was ending so senselessly. She was with people who had come here to be left alone but she had not been able to do it. She had loved them instead, and now she would die with them.

A single shot, distinct by its direction, echoed suddenly through the clearing and one of the riders lurched forward in the saddle, his face contorted with pain and surprise and he pitched in front of the galloping horse. From beyond the shielding point of forest that ran to the river on the south, Thomas Shattuck rode with eyes and rifle ablaze. At his side galloped the Englishman, Jacob Randall, and behind them the Shattuck sons on black, lather-soaked horses.

Like a highland battle cry, the Durham brogue of the Shelbyville merchant rose above the din of battle, stopping and scattering the charge of the three remaining gunmen.

"Damn your murderous souls to burning hell!" he shouted as another rider reeled and pitched to the earth. The others spun in panic toward the ford, splashing into the river with David's rifle cracking behind them and Suzanna's brothers twenty yards in pursuit.

Thomas Shattuck and Jacob swung to the ground beside the group in the clearing, gently lifting the fallen cooper from Suzanna and stretching him on his back on the damp grass. John's eyes opened slowly, focusing on the white bearded face that bent over him, a faint smile flickering over his stained lips.

"Thank you, neighbor," he said weakly. "I thought we were done."

David knelt beside his father, holding the man's limp arm.

"We need to get him inside. He's taken three or four balls."

The big man shook his head slightly, licking at his dry lips.

"I'm not going anywhere. This is as good a place as any. Get your mother."

As he spoke, the door of the workshop scraped open and Lydia, pale and trembling, stepped out with the younger children. She paused, picking through the clustered group with her eyes to see who had fallen, then with a gasping cry rushed to her husband's side.

"Oh please, dear Lord. It's all my fault. The boy slipped past me and was gone before I could stop him."

The cooper's bearded face furrowed in a scolding frown.

"It's no one's fault, Lydia. We all did what we could do. Don't let me hear that talk." He licked again at his lips and smiled up at her.

"Do you think your Mormon God will have me, Mother?"

"You'll not find out for a good long while," she pleaded. "I need you here with me."

He wrapped a giant paw around her fragile hand.

"I can feel it going, Lydia. Where's David? I need to talk to David."

"I'm here." David leaned forward, taking his father's other hand.

The cooper pulled him closer, straining his head upward.

"Another circle of wolves...And I was here to help you this time." He paused, swallowing, his voice fading to a whisper. "You have good children. I want you to love them always – as much as I've always loved my boy. But show them a little better than I did. Do you hear me David?"

His son bent forward, wrapping the big man in his arms, tears streaming from his face onto his father's paling cheek.

"I hear you," he said quietly.

"I can't see you, Son. I can't see...." His eyes became distant and his face relaxed into a soft smile. "Oh. Now I can," and his eyes closed.

24

SUZANNA

Suzanna sat cross-legged on the verdant carpet of her forest hideaway and watched her children play in the cascading waters of the spring. Beside her the baby cooed and kicked happily at bright flowers and the sky arched blue and clear above the circle of oak and hickory.

"I found this place the first summer we lived here," she said, smiling at David who stretched beside her opposite the baby, hands behind his head. "I was eleven. It has always reminded me of my mother... though I don't really remember her much. Just softness and sweet smells and warmth. I wanted the children to come here before we left."

"Do you know what it reminds me of?" David asked.

She shook her head.

"It reminds me of the loveliest woman I ever saw. She was standing right on this spot dressed in blue gingham and twisting a flower into her hair...."

Suzanna laughed lightly and stretched out beside him. "As I recall, you'd seen her in several states of dress before that. And you almost left her here once." Her eyes misted at the memory.

"Not really. I just found her again... and myself too."

"Sorry?"

"About what?"

"About how things have changed since we first met here?"

He shook his head slowly. "It's you I've wondered about. I knew it would be hard for me. You got a bit more than you bargained for."

Suzanna turned toward him. "You never get more than you bargain for. Nor less for that matter, I think. You get what you get, that's all."

David propped himself up on an elbow. "You mean you think you *deserved* some of the things that have happened to you?"

"It has nothing to do with deserved. It's more like 'couldn't prevent.'"

David stretched out again, his brow furrowed in thought. "You're starting to sound like Jacob. I don't think life just rolls along and sweeps us with it. We make choices, and they have their consequences. It isn't just fate."

"No. I didn't mean that we had no control over it," Suzanna mused. "I just meant that when we make a choice... like mine to look for you in the woods or to accept Jacob's offer to tend the trading post, we can't know what will follow. Once we make the choice, we also accept what lies along that path."

David sat up and plucked at the long grass between his legs. "And this latest choice. Are you sorry we're leaving?"

Suzanna also sat again and stroked the baby's back. "About some things. My father. Our home in Shelbyville. This place. There are good memories here."

"And bad ones...."

"Yes, bad ones too. And I won't miss the Cask Company. It was taking too much of your time and I don't think you enjoyed it. Jacob was good to buy it from us so quickly and help us sell the house." She looked off distantly into the surrounding trees. "But I'm frightened a bit, not knowing where we're going or what will be along this new path."

David grunted in agreement and they sat quietly, watching their youngest child play.

"I was thinking a new store and a cask company might be part of our new life," he said. "I didn't realize you were opposed to it and it's something we know well and can make a success."

"Maybe so," she said. "And I do think it's the right choice to move on, if that's what you mean. It seems so sudden sometimes...as if perhaps we haven't thought it all through. Rogers is gone and no one else would bother your mother if she were to stay...." Her voice faded off as she realized that it had been said before and had not been true.

"It's more than Rogers," he said. "I believe I've been thinking it through all the time we've been in Shelbyville. I haven't been fair to you in some ways, not sharing it with you until lately."

"The need to start somewhere on our own, you mean?"

David nodded

"I knew long before that," she said. "I've known for months that you needed to get away from Jacob. And I know you've become uncertain about your faith and that you've felt guilty about it. We need to find a place where we can start over completely."

David looked over at her with mild surprise. "You've never said anything about it."

"And you've never said anything to me about what happened at the trading post. Some things are too deep to come up easily. But yours has been rising and needs to be dealt with."

"It's not exactly the same kind of situation."

Suzanna arched her forehead. "Guilt is guilt. Neither of us could really do much about what happened, but we both have felt blame I think. In a way I've taken care of mine. Now you need to take care of yours."

"It may not be the right thing. I don't know which of Jacob's Gods I'm likely to find."

"And you think there hasn't been uncertainty here?" she smiled. "Certainty can't be our reason for what we do or don't do, or we'll never decide anything. We need to do what we think is best for us and for the children."

The baby rolled over between them and grasped his mother's fingers. Suzanna picked him up and squeezed him close. "And I think I've learned that what is best is a new place for us. This place brought us together – but also with Jacob and the Cochrans and with that devil, Rogers. What happened here was a result of all of us coming together here. In a new place we'll come together with new people, and new things will happen. We can't know for certain, but I believe they will be good things."

David looked over at her curiously. "You're sounding more like Jacob all the time. Like everything happens for a reason."

"Maybe not for a reason," she said. "But it happens. Some of it we can do something about. Some we can't. But then we are left to decide what to do about it."

David rose and pulled her up into his arms. "I remember being with you here once before when neither of us had any idea what to do," he said.

"We didn't really have each other then," she said softly. "And I think maybe that was the day we began to figure it all out."

They stood between the arms of the spring, holding each other and weeping silently.

"Shall we ever come back? To the woods and the river ...and this spot?" she whispered.

"I don't know. I think we've a long way to go before then."

She released him and lifted the baby between them.

"I love this place. It always makes me feel so safe...."

"I know. But I think we should go," he said softly. "We have a lot to do before evening." He lifted her and Thomas, twirling them in a tight embrace. "You can still feel safe. I've taken good care of you so far, haven't I?"

"I prefer to think that we've taken good care of each other," she said. They gathered the children; Suzanna carrying the baby and David with Elizabeth sitting astride his shoulders, a bouquet of black-eyed Susan clutched in her chubby hand. Johnny ran ahead down the stream until he found the faint overgrown trail, then led the family north toward the Whitlock cabin.

Where the rough wooden wagon had creaked into the clearing ten years before with little more than light bundles of clothing, a cooper's shaving bench and a sack of onions and potatoes, a new wagon now stood heavily loaded with sacks of beans and flour, barrels of dried venison and vegetables and the contents of the Whitlock households. The brown draft mules were harnessed and impatient, ready to begin their journey. Lydia stood beside the wagon clutching an intricately carved picture frame against her breast, gazing wistfully at the empty cabin.

"Do you think Jacob will find someone suitable for it?" she asked as they entered the clearing.

David lowered his daughter to the grass and placed a gentle arm about his mother's shoulders. "Jacob will find someone. He told me of a man from Columbia who's been looking for a place up here. A man with a family. They sounded like good people."

"Will they care for the grave, do you think?"

"Jacob said they are good Christian people. He mentioned the grave to them."

They turned to the wagon and David lifted his mother to the seat, cushioned with a brightly patterned quilt; red octagons with white star points at each side, radiating across a field of blue. Suzanna was already in the wagon box and he lifted the children to her, seating them in front of the pile of tarpaulin-covered furniture and provisions. As the mules pulled forward without encouragement, he reined them to a stop between the cabin and the stooped sod workshop. They sat silently, tears welling in the eyes of Lydia Whitlock.

"Grandmother?" Elizabeth pulled herself up with her mother's arm and offered the bright bouquet of black and yellow flowers. David climbed again from the wagon and lifted his mother and daughter to the ground. Lydia took the girl's hand and together they carried the flowers into a small fenced plot on the west side of the workshop. Elizabeth watched her grandmother, kneeling with her as she knelt beside the grave and hand-in-hand they laid the spring bouquet beside the already graying oak marker.

"We'll miss Grandfather, won't we," Elizabeth said quietly and they cried together for a moment, then rose and walked resolutely to the wagon.

David snapped the reins to the mules' backs and turned them toward the river, then northward up the grassy wagon track that bordered the west bank of the Chariton. As they reached the trees a lone rider appeared on the trail behind them, trotting his black mount until he rode silently beside the wagon. A mile north of the clearing he signaled the wagon to halt, turned his horse and reached to grasp his daughter's hand, his white bearded face red and moist.

"I love you, Suzanna," he said, his voice husky and wavering.

She pulled his hand to her cheek and pressed it tightly. "We'll be back, Father...when we've settled somewhere."

The horse shuffled sideways and she released him.

"God be with you, Mrs. Whitlock," he said, then saluted David and spurred the prancing horse, galloping back down the Chariton without looking back.

Ahead of the wagon, the trail grew faint, winding over low hills and disappearing into the thick forest.

.   .   .

Thomas Shattuck reined in his horse at the edge of the Whitlock clearing and leaned forward onto his saddle. The Mormons were gone and with them his Suzanna. He would not have wished it this way. But there were few things that had gone exactly as he'd wished. David was a good man and he and Suzanna were happy.

A flash of color caught the old man's eye; the yellow of breeze-rustled flowers beside the oak grave marker. He had watched John Whitlock die in his son's arms, had helped David build a plain wooden coffin using the cooper's own tools, and with the help of the little Englishman from the trading post, had lowered him into the ground. He should have gotten to know the man. They had lived only a few miles apart and John Whitlock had died without them ever sharing an evening... without talking about their children who now were leaving them both behind. It was a mad world. Neighbors shunning neighbors. Bands of men hunting other men because of their beliefs. He didn't understand the Mormons but he should not have left them alone. If he'd gotten to know them...been friends...this cabin might still bustle with life and his daughter and grandchildren still be here near him.

Across the clearing a gray form moved in the shadows and stepped into the sunlight of the meadow. Thomas Shattuck tensed, reaching slowly for the rifle that hung beside his knee. The battered gray wolf looked at him with dull, icy eyes and lowered his muzzle with curled black lips. The old man had not seen him for over two years and leaned toward him, squinting to be sure. The wolf's coat was thin and ragged, torn along both sides, and as he moved slowly along the edge of the clearing, he dragged a forepaw. But the marks were there on the face. It was the gray wolf of the bramble-covered wash.

Thomas raised the rifle and the wolf stopped, his growl low and yapping. Ribs protruded from his gnarled sides and his tail curled beneath thin haunches. The man sighted at the bony side just behind the animals limping shoulder, then slowly lowered the rifle. The old wolf was weak and beaten. His howl wouldn't raise a sleeping doe from the thicket. To kill him now would be to shoot out of hate and vengeance. Thomas Shattuck was tired of hate and vengeance. He fired at a thick trunk behind the animal's cringing back and the wolf yelped, then limped sullenly into the trees.

Thomas dismounted and walked to the grave, kneeling beside the thick roughly carved marker. "May the good Lord receive you with his blessings, John Whitlock," he murmured. "And look after both of our families, wherever they are."

25

DAVID

David halted the team at the brow of a gentle grassy knoll. Below them Shoal Creek meandered across an expanse of open Iowa grassland, its banks lined east and west with cottonwood, sycamore and rings of white-capped wagons. The family had traveled since before dawn, leaving the forests of Missouri two hours behind and expecting with each hill to see the Mormon camp below. As they were beginning to fear that the wagons had moved on from the Chariton headwaters, they topped the rise and looked down onto the sprawling camp. Suzanna sat beside David on the patterned quilt, gazing at the circled wagons in quiet awe.

"There must be a hundred of them," she said as Lydia knelt in the wagon bed to look between them. "I'd expected something... smaller."

"I feared most of them had been killed by now," Lydia said. "But look at this...." Her voice trailed into thought.

Johnny pushed past his grandmother and climbed onto the seat between his parents. "Is this it, Mother? Is this where we're going to stay?"

"Not here," David answered for her. "But we'll be stopping for a while."

As they surveyed the scene below a single rider separated from the circle of wagons nearest the hill and galloped toward them, slowing to an easy canter as he approached the wagon.

"Hello, friends," he said amiably. "Can I give you folks directions?"

"We've come to find your camp," David said.

"Up from the south?"

"Missouri," David answered. The man leaned slowly forward and studied the group in the wagon. "We're not just a regular wagon train...."

"We know who you are," David said.

"Not many of us left down in Missouri."

"Fewer now. In fact, we're the last we know of."

The man leaned over and extended his hand to David. "Joseph Wright," he said. David took the man's hand and introduced his family.

"Wanting to join our train?" Joseph Wright asked.

"My mother would like to join if there's some way a single woman can become part of the camp. We have provisions for her."

Wright looked thoughtfully at Lydia Whitlock. "I'm sorry to say, but we have quite a number of widows in our group. Two of our wagons are just women. I think we can find a place for you. And the rest of you aren't coming?"

"We'll travel with you for a few weeks if we may," David said. "Iowa's petitioned for statehood and we're planning to set up a trading post along the Missouri, south of the Council Bluffs along the trail that runs down to Independence. We hear there's some good stands of white oak down along the Nodoway River. We'll homestead somewhere along there and set up our shop."

Wright sat upright again, gazing back at the circled wagons.

"You may be the wise ones. We think we're getting away from trouble but it will come with us." He turned toward Lydia. "Are you ready for that?"

She smiled thinly. "I'm not looking to run away anymore," she said.

"We're forming up a new company of ten right now," Wright said. "I think they're a wagon short."

They followed him down the hill and through the clustered

rings, turning up the western fork of the creek until they reached the far end of the encampment where nine wagons stood end-to-end in an open loop. As the Whitlocks stopped beside the circle, campers rose to meet them, lifting the children from the wagon and helping the tired women to the ground.

"Lydia! Lydia, is it you?" From one of the groups they had passed as they moved through the camp, a woman hurried toward them with fringed bonnet waving loosely behind tightly knotted hair. Lydia Whitlock watched her approach, her eyes suddenly brightening with recognition and she rushed to embrace the woman.

"Elsie! Oh...thank God, you're alive! Since the Mill I've thought of you so often...." The company closed around them, carrying the children and guiding Suzanna to the cook fire between the wagons. David watched them from the seat; his mother clutched in the embrace of a friend and Suzanna and the children surrounded by caring families. Johnny raced away from the group with four other boys, leaping across a fallen log and dashing toward a long rope that dangled from a cottonwood branch over the banks of Shoal Creek.

"There's a spot for you here," Joseph Wright said, pointing to a gap in the wagons. David stood and looked backward across the white expanse of wagon canopies at the distant forest that stretched southward along the Chariton River, then turned and gazed across the deeply rutted grasslands to the west.

"When do we break camp?" he asked.

"For your group, tomorrow," Wright answered.

David flicked the reins gently and guided the team forward into the ring, completing the circle.

Author's Notes

I have made every effort to bring as much historical accuracy as possible to this novel while still exercising the creative license that makes the book a novel. The principal characters are my creations – David, Suzanna and their families, Jacob Randall and Sheck Rogers. And although the Great and Smith's Trails crossed the state as described, The Hill Spring Trail was also my creation since I needed a reasonable way to get a family up into the northeast woods to hide. So the journal entries and letters describing the Hill Spring Trail in the first section are fictitious. Virtually all of the episodes concerning conflict with the Mormons, the attack at Haun's Mill, the development of government buildings in Jefferson City, cholera in Palmyra, the shooting of Governor Boggs, etc. are historically accurate and the newspaper accounts of the Mormon Wars and letters from citizens and military officials are quoted from the historical record. My intent has been to describe the period and the conflicts that plagued the state much as they occurred.

I have also tried to depict the small settlements that developed north of the Missouri River as they were at the time; Bloomington, Shelbyville and Brunswick for example. Many of these communities either boomed or disappeared between 1840 and 1860 with the major migrations west. Bloomington was replaced by Macon as the county seat of Macon County during this period. Should you discover errors in the historical record, I would appreciate learning about them. One of the values of online publication is that I can continuously update the version available for Kindle. Plus, I would enjoy hearing from you!

Visit http://allenkentbooks.com

OTHER NOVELS BY ALLEN KENT

The Whitlock Trilogy (Historical Fiction)

River of Light and Shadow

Wild Whistling Blackbirds

Suzanna's Song

Unit 1 Novels (International Thrillers)

The Shield of Darius

The Weavers of Meanchey

The Wager

The Marburg Mutation

Straits of the Between

Ring of Thorns

Mysteries

Guardians of the Second Son

The Colby Tate Mysteries

Murder One

Eye for an Eye

Young Adult Adventure

Switch

www.ingramcontent.com/pod-product-compliance
Lightning Source LLC
Chambersburg PA
CBHW070556130626
46556CB00001B/185